NEVADA BARR

FIRESTORM

AVON BOOKS, INC.
1350 Avenue of the Americas
New York, New York 10019

Inside cover author photo by T. Bennett Photography
Published by arrangement with G.P. Putnam's Sons
Visit our website at **www.AvonBooks.com/Twilight**
Library of Congress Catalog Card Number: 95-38311
ISBN: 0-380-72582-7

First Avon Books Printing: May 1997

Printed in the U.S.A.

WCD 10 9 8 7 6

FIRESTORM

"COMPELLING . . . EXCELLENT . . .
NEVADA BARR IS ONE OF THE BEST."

Boston Globe

"A FAST-PACED AND SUSPENSEFUL WHODUNIT . . .
Barr is a splendid storyteller . . .
She describes a terrifying blaze sweeping across a section
of Northern California with such authenticity
and in such chilling detail
that you can smell the smoke and taste the ashes."

Los Angeles Times Book Review

"A STELLAR PERFORMANCE ON EVERY COUNT.
NO MATTER WHAT YOU READ MYSTERIES FOR,
IT'S IN HERE . . .
Anna, surrounded by an exceptionally well-developed cast,
shines as ranger, detective, and heroine—
truly a woman for all seasons . . .
A superior puzzle wrapped in her most
exciting adventure yet."

Kirkus Reviews

"A GREAT READ . . .
Some of Barr's most vivid writing . . .
Ranger Anna is a delightfully complex character."

Florida Times-Union

"A CHILLING TALE . . .
Nevada Barr has hit her writing stride . . .
Her Anna Pigeon has been a pleasure from the first,
but in *FIRESTORM*, the author seems to find
not just her voice, but perfect pitch.
It is the best of the series."

Washington Times

"GRIPPING . . . BARR IS AS PRECISE
A CRAFTSWOMAN AS AGATHA CHRISTIE . . .
SHE'S MADE THE GENRE HER OWN."

San Jose Mercury-News

"THRILLING . . .
Barr writes with a cool, steady hand
about the violence of nature and the cruelty of man."

The New York Times Book Review

"HARROWING . . .
EMOTIONALLY CHARGED AND
INTRICATELY PLOTTED.
Barr brings the forest to life and
replaces firefighting's glamour with
the grim reality on the line."

BookPage

"OUTSTANDING . . .
Neatly turning this Northern California dilemma
into a classic locked-room mystery,
Barr skillfully creates a murder story that seems
to have no solution. *FIRESTORM* is the
most fully developed of her mysteries . . .
Anna Pigeon is smart, determined and able enough
to compete with anyone in the mystery business."

Dallas Morning News

"A REAL PAGE-TURNER . . .
dished up with plenty of Barr's acidic humor."

Grand Rapids Press

"TOP FLIGHT ENTERTAINMENT . . .
Anna Pigeon is a delight."

Booklist

"A BRILLIANTLY EXECUTED MYSTERY . . .
A HARROWING TALE OF ENVIRONMENTAL CRIMES
AND DEADLY DIVIDED LOYALTIES."

Washington Post Book World

"FRIGHTENING . . . INTENSE . . .
No one delivers the thrill better than Nevada Barr . . .
You don't need to be a mystery buff to appreciate
this finely written tale of fire and murder . . .
It's much more than a well-crafted mystery . . .
You can almost smell the smoke and feel the misery . . .
For those who read mysteries to figure out whodunit
before the end, be warned:
Barr will stump you almost every time."

Colorado Springs Gazette Telegraph

"ONE OF THE YEAR'S BEST . . .
A creative tour de force . . .
Everything about this book is top notch:
pace, setting, characterization, plot,
mystery elements and style."

Deadly Pleasures

"ANNA IS WONDERFUL."

Winston-Salem Journal

"SPINE-TINGLING ADVENTURE . . .
The tension approaches unbearable . . .
While Anna, with her compassion, toughness
and abundant one-liners,
calls Kinsey Milhone to mind,
Barr's character is a true original.
And for excitement, her line of work can't be beat."

Publishers Weekly

Also by Nevada Barr

Anna Pigeon Mysteries

ENDANGERED SPECIES
ILL WIND
A SUPERIOR DEATH
TRACK OF THE CAT

and

BITTERSWEET

Coming Soon

BLIND DESCENT

For Brodie,
in gratitude for
his unfailing kindness and patience,
virtues I may not possess but deeply admire

ACKNOWLEDGMENTS

Special thanks to Dave Langley,
Rick Gale and Steve Zachary

1

If she'd had a foot fetish Anna would have been an extremely happy woman. Cradled in her lap was a prime example of *pedis giganticus* belonging to one Howard Black Elk. More mole foam than flesh was visible.

"Fighting on slopes keeps tearing 'em off," Mr. Black Elk told her between gulps of Mountain Dew. "Anybody but you does 'em they're gone by lunch. You got the touch."

Absurd as it was, Anna took great pride in the durability of her blister dressings. Caesar's army may have moved on its stomach, but firefighters moved on their feet. After ten days of skirmishes, the army battling California's Jackknife Fire was proceeding a bit gingerly. The line queued up outside the medical unit tent was Anna's barometer, and the pressure was rising. Sho-Rap, the Shoshone and Arapaho firefighting crew out of Montana, seemed to suffer more than most. Maybe because they were big men. Even with the protective fire boots they were required to wear, gravity hit them harder.

Anna eased the ruined dressings off Mr. Black Elk's foot and examined the carnage. Black Elk was an Arapaho Indian but he wasn't with the Sho-Raps. He was a member of the San Juan crew from the southwest. "You busted open the blisters," she accused.

"Got to let 'em drain."

"No you don't. They'll get infected." She looked into the man's face to see if she was getting through to him. "Are you going to quit that?"

"You betcha."

Anna didn't believe him. She cleaned the ball of his foot and his heel with hydrogen peroxide. When he winced at the sting she said, "Serves you right."

A heady sense of Normandy, Tripoli, John Wayne and *Twelve O'Clock High* reverberated through fire camps. Like everyone else, Anna reveled in it. A soldier's life—particularly in a war where death was highly unlikely and the battle soon over—was a life enhanced with an illusion of importance untrammeled by responsibility. Orders were simple: climb, stop and dig. Hard physical labor and the ability to sleep on rough ground were all that was asked. Anna found peace in the freedom from choices.

With great care, she began reconstructing the protective barriers of foam, Second-Skin and bandages on Mr. Black Elk's foot. The rest of the San Juan Plateau crew began drifting over from the chow line to swell the ranks waiting for medical attention.

The San Juans were an interagency crew with firefighters from the Forest Service, the Bureau of Land Management and the National Park Service. Three of the firefighters were from Mesa Verde National Park, Anna's duty station. Anna had arrived independently when the call went out for more emergency medical technicians to man the medical units.

These units provided care to the firefighters in the spike camps. As the Jackknife cut a black swath through the Caribou Wilderness and Lassen Volcanic National Park in northern California, Incident Base—the main camp housing supplies and command headquarters—needed units closer to the fireline. Small camps, called "spikes" by firefighters though officialdom no longer used the term, were springing up like fire moss.

"You guys with blisters go ahead and take the dressings off and clean your feet with peroxide," Anna said to those waiting. "I think Stephen's got a spare bottle."

"Go easy with the stuff," Stephen Lindstrom, the other EMT, said. "We won't have any more till tomorrow afternoon."

Lindstrom was with the Forest Service out of Reno, Nevada. When Anna and three crews had been spiked out nineteen miles from base camp, she'd begged for and gotten him. Efficient and gentle, he was one of the better EMTs she'd worked with.

"How 'bout I get you some dinner before them hogs swill it all down?"

Anna looked in the direction of the familiar Memphis drawl. Jennifer Short, a seasonal law enforcement ranger from Mesa Verde, leaned against a sugar pine near the outdoor examination room Anna and Stephen had pieced together from a ground cloth and twelve folding chairs.

Jennifer had been on the Jackknife fire for seven days, one day less than Anna, and she was still wearing makeup. Anna couldn't help but admire her. Anybody who stuck to their beliefs under duress deserved respect. The sooty fingerprints around her nose and the trails of sweat running through her dust-coated rouge only added to the effect: bloody but unbowed.

"Thanks," Anna said. "Stephen, want some supper?" Belatedly she asked Jennifer, "Would you mind?"

"Why I'd just lie down and die if he said no," Jennifer said, and winked.

Dividing her time between bites and blisters, Anna managed to finish her supper and thirteen feet in the next hour. Kneeling at the fourteenth and last, she began unlacing a well-worn, custom-made White's fire boot. "Helps if you remove your boots for me," she said mildly.

"My feet's not what hurt."

Anna rocked back on her heels and took in the face attached to the expensive boots. "San Juan crew, crew boss, right?"

"John LeFleur." The firefighter stuck out a hand with spatulate fingers reminiscent of the toes of Amazon rain forest frogs Anna'd seen hopping through various PBS specials. She forced herself up from her knees. Cold, fatigue and hard beds were taking their toll. Getting old, she chided herself. Once hard work had made her tougher; now it only made her tired. She stuck out her hand and, trying for a pressure that was manly without being macho, took LeFleur's.

His bottom lip was swollen and bruised. Dried blood caked where the skin had split. "Does your face hurt?" she asked. The third-grade insult, "Because it's sure killing me," flickered nonsensically through her mind, but John LeFleur certainly wasn't hard to look at. Anna had him pegged for forty-five or so—his hair was still there and still brown. The nasolabial folds chopped like hatchet marks in his weathered face; heavy brows protected blue eyes.

"Walked into a door," he said, fingering the injury. "All I need's a cold pack."

When Anna returned from the tent with the desired item, the man was lighting an unfiltered Pall Mall.

"Can't get enough smoke on the fireline?" Anna crushed the cold pack to mix the chemicals that provided the cooling effect.

"I'm an old fire horse," LeFleur admitted. "One sniff of smoke and I start to snort and stamp. This is my thirty-seventh project fire. My eighth in California."

Anna was impressed. What she said was: "My, but you must be old."

"I can still work most into the ground." The crew boss took the cold pack and pressed it against his lip.

"You'd have to look a long ways to find a door up here," Anna commented.

Sudden anger flared in his voice and his eyes. "If I run into it again, I'm going to bust the son of a bitch up for kindling."

Anna let the remark pass without comment. Spike camp was too small a world to make enemies. As far as she was concerned sleeping dogs could lie or take the first ride down the mountain.

Since no new pilgrims had arrived at her canvas Lourdes, Anna sat down next to LeFleur while he enjoyed his cigarette. From inside the shadowed tent she could hear Stephen busy with the inevitable litter left at day's end. In a minute she'd go help him. At the moment it felt too good just to sit.

Light was draining from the sky, taking the day's heat with it. Anna rolled down her sleeves and hugged herself. The camp was situated on the back of a mountain ridge amidst a landscape of mountains cresting like waves in every direction. To the west and southwest the trees breathed up black smoke. As the day faded, pinpricks of orange blossomed.

A garish blood-red sunset fired the sky, the last rays bending through smoke so thick the neck bones of Lassen Peak were obscured. Near the horizon the smoky pall blotted out the sun. Higher up, smoke sucked fire from the sun and burned in the heavens as the Jackknife burned on earth.

Anna shoved her hands in her pockets to retain their warmth. "The end of the world looks pretty doggone festive, if you ask me," she said.

LeFleur stubbed the cigarette out on the sole of his boot then shredded the paper and scattered the tobacco. "That's where we were today." He pointed across a narrow valley to a burning hillside. "We cut line to that outcrop of boulders and tied into the dozer line."

The area he pointed to was on a steep forty-percent slope and choked with dog-hair thickets.

"Bitch of a climb," Anna said.

"Try it with a chainsaw on your shoulder." LeFleur lit a second Pall Mall and contemplated his day's work. "I'm going to be out of the game soon if I can't move into management. Time to leave the backbreakers to the kids."

Since he didn't seem to be talking to her as much as to himself, Anna felt justified in changing the subject. "Speaking of kids, how did Jennifer do?" The Jackknife was Jennifer's first fire. Her red card and fire boots were both so new they squeaked. After working with Short in Mesa Verde, Anna had developed a reluctant fondness for the southern belle.

"Fireline's no place for a woman."

"Did she screw up?"

"No."

"What then?"

The crew boss laughed. "You're not going to drag me into that. You know what I mean."

Anna did and quelled an urge to bite the man. Anna had served her time on firelines and knew quarter was given to no one. On her last three project fires she'd gone out as a medic or security or, as in the case of the Jackknife, both. The work was less backbreaking and more challenging, if not physically, then cerebrally.

"Jennifer kept up," LeFleur said finally.

"Don't dress it up on my account," Anna said dryly.

LeFleur laughed. "She's okay. Works right along. She's got blisters on both her hands but never complains about anything but how big her butt looks in NoMex," he said, referring to the baggy, fire retardant wool pants all firefighters were required to wear.

"A wolf in femme fatale's clothing," Anna said with satisfaction. Abruptly, she asked: "Are you married?"

"Are you offering?"

Anna squirmed figuratively, if not literally. She was tempted to tell him the information wasn't for her but knew whatever she said at this point was bound to sound lame. "Just making conversation." Letting it go at that, she watched the reds deepening into night. Darkness was brought on early by smoke. Sparks of orange, just hinting at the vastness of the burn before sundown, pricked the sides of mountains in three directions.

The coming of night had hushed the constant growl of retardant aircraft and the helicopters that chopped into the heli-spot below camp. The small sounds of raccoon, deer, owl, coyote and cougar had been silenced for eight days. In its infancy, the Jackknife had made a name for itself by taking two newsworthy sacrifices: a young man camped out near Pinson Lake and his dog. Tabloids had made hay with photos of the charred remains of the pooch while thousands of wild things lost went unmourned.

Anna didn't mourn them now. Tiny corpses left behind by fires—squirrel, fawn, bunny—didn't sadden her as they once might have. Wildland fire returned many needed things to the earth.

An icy breeze was sucked down through the trees. Fire raged over thirty thousand acres of prime timberland. Creeks boiled dry, birds fled, fledglings died in the nest, smoke hung in the valleys for a hundred miles, and still Anna could not get warm. She buttoned the top button of her shirt and turned the collar up. Soon she would have to go in and get her coat but she was not yet ready to move. The folding chair and ground cloth felt like home. Marooned as it was, an island of life in a sea of black and flame, the tent village seemed cozy.

Three twenty-by-fifteen-foot tents, their white canvas reflecting the evening light, were clustered around a central clearing. Time Keeping operations were housed in one of the big tents. It was there hazard pay, overtime and wages were recorded. The LeFleurs of the world might fight fire for the love of it, but for most it was a living, a way of making ends meet.

The San Juans were housed in the second tent and Anna and Stephen shared the last with medical supplies and emergency gear. East of the main tents—and hopefully downwind—was a slum of blue Porta-Johns. The honey-pot industry was one place

Anna was against unisex application. Privately she believed the Shoshone lost to invading armies because they had such lousy aim.

Between the tents and the toilets was the mess area; twice a day meals were trucked in from base camp. A long table lined with basins and soap for washing was just beyond. Cubies—square, plastic five-gallon containers for water—were stacked in a translucent wall on the far side of the table. Basins and table alike were smudged with the ubiquitous soot that tinged hair, nails, skin and clothes of everyone in spike camp.

Down at Incident Base, showers housed in semi-truck trailers with their own generators for hot water provided the crews with some relief from the endless grime. In spike camp dirt not removable with basin and towel remained for the duration. Long-haired firefighters—and at this camp they were in the majority, with twenty men from Sho-Rap and four women including Anna—kept it braided back. After an hour on the fireline, hair took on the consistency of cotton candy.

LeFleur finished his second Pall Mall. Night was upon them. He handed Anna back the spent cold pack. "Bedtime for this boy."

"Watch out for doors," Anna said as he left.

Laughter from the medical tent lured her from the night. Jennifer and Stephen were wrestling with an uncooperative Coleman lantern. Providing more laughs than light, they argued about the perfect number of pumps required to create the ideal pressure in the lamp's fuel chamber.

As Anna came in the Coleman roared to life and the peace of the evening was pushed aside. Obnoxious though it was, the harsh light was necessary. For the next couple of hours Anna and Stephen bandaged cuts, handed out analgesics, mole foam, nasal spray, hand lotion and, when called for, sympathy.

Near midnight they crawled into their sleeping bags, laid out on the unheard-of luxury of army cots. In less than five hours they'd be back at it, packaging feet for another day on the line.

In soft beds and climate-controlled bedrooms Anna had trouble sleeping. At fire camps the nightmares left her alone. Exhaustion claimed mind and body during the brief respites allowed.

From the modest confines of her yellow fire-issue sleeping bag, she squirmed out of her underwear: plain, white cotton; underpants that wouldn't melt at high temperatures and adhere to the flesh. The western forests might burn but Anna's underwear shouldn't ignite.

"Got the scoop on John LeFleur's lip," Stephen said as Anna dropped the maidenly garment to the floor. Lindstrom loved to gossip. One of his endearing qualities, as far as Anna was concerned.

"Do tell."

"Wellllll," he said, drawing out the word in exaggerated confidence, making her laugh. "Jennifer said—"

"Wait," Anna interrupted. "In my exalted capacity as spike camp security officer-cum-medic, am I going to have to take any action on this tidbit? Because if I am don't tell me."

"Jennifer *said*," Stephen pressed on, "that John got into an altercation that led to fisticuffs. Wish I'd been there," he sighed dramatically. "I do so love violence. That other BLM guy, Leonard Nims, took a swing at John. Connected on the second try."

Anna vaguely remembered Nims. He was a GS-7 supervisor from the Bureau of Land Management in

Farmington, New Mexico. Prematurely white hair and a black mustache gave him striking looks and the hard muscled body of an athlete belied his age—late forties, she guessed. Nims would have been handsome if he could have dropped his Napoleon complex. At five-foot-eight or -nine he hadn't earned it. The chip on his shoulder reduced his stature.

"Jennifer said Joseph broke it up," Stephen went on. Joseph Hayhurst was a Mescalero Apache born and raised in the foothills of California, educated at Berkeley, a latecomer to his Indian heritage. The juxtaposition of cultures had created a fascinating mix of New Age artist and Indian rights fundamentalist. He wore his hair long and tied back, as did most of the Shoshone and Arapahos, but it was cut short in front and curled around his face. A fashion a multitude of white artists strove for in closet trysts with their girlfriends' curling irons.

"Jennifer said he threatened to spank the both of them if it happened again because darned—'darned,' don't you just love it? 'Dagnabbit, you motherfuckers, now quit that . . .' "

"Anyway . . ." Anna was too tired to enjoy a ramble, however entertaining.

"Anyway, *darned* if he was going to get sent off the fire before he'd paid for last winter's vacation."

Joseph was a squad boss for the San Juans. A crew consisted of twenty firefighters divided into two squads. The crew boss was responsible for all twenty, the squad bosses for eight to ten firefighters each. If anyone got into trouble, the troublemaker wasn't the only one sent home. All twenty were demobilized.

"What was the fight about?" Anna asked.

"Back in Farmington John works for Nims. Now he's Nims's boss and Nims is working for him. I guess it wasn't sitting too well. Jennifer says they haven't got on from the git-go. Nims is the crew boss trainee, so LeFleur is training his own replacement, so to speak. The Bureau of Land Management is grooming Nims for better things. In lieu of LeFleur, is my guess. By the by, was you and LeFleur a-sparkin' out there in the gloaming?"

Anna whistled a few bars of "Matchmaker" from "Fiddler on the Roof." "Firefighters hate sparks."

"Do you know why Smokey the Bear never had children?" Stephen asked.

"Because every time his wife got hot he hit her with a shovel."

"Old joke," he apologized.

"Old jokes are the best."

"Goodnight."

"About damn time."

"Darn time, please."

Headlights raked across the canvas wall, chased by the growl of a diesel engine.

"Oops," Stephen said.

"I'll get it." Anna sounded as if it were a doorbell ringing at an inappropriate time.

The truck driver, Polly or Sally—Anna floundered for the name—was one of the many local people hired to assist in the logistics of feeding, cleaning and fueling a city of a thousand souls appearing suddenly in the wilderness. The girl always seemed to avoid Anna. Whether the avoidance was personal or coincidental, she had no idea.

"It's late, I'll have to stay over," the driver said defensively as she bounced her plump little body out of the vehicle. Four of the six nights spike camp had been in existence she'd found some way to have to stay over. Anna suspected she had a sweetheart.

"Makes sense," Anna said amiably, and waited to

see what reason would be given for the long trip up the mountain this time.

"I got a thing here for you or John what's-his-name, the crew boss guy." As she leaned into the cab the girl's head vanished behind a curtain of lush brown hair, clean and worn loose. After a moment's rustling she emerged with a folded sheet of paper. She handed it over, and Anna was aware of a cheap but enticing perfume.

"Thanks . . . Sally." She hazarded a guess at the name.

"Paula."

Anna'd lost a round. "Paula. Sure. Sorry. Breathing too much smoke."

Paula seemed anxious to get away so Anna quit muttering apologies. "If you want you can pitch your tent behind the medical unit," she offered. "There's a flat spot there."

"No. I got a place all staked out." The woman bunched a tent into her arms and started toward the trees behind the Porta-Johns where the Sho-Raps were camped.

Anna unfolded the note and read it by the light of her flashlight. "The body of the man found burned near Pinson Lake just outside Lassen Volcanic National Park has been identified as Joshua Short, brother of seasonal park ranger Jennifer Short, out of Mesa Verde, Colorado, now serving on the San Juan Plateau crew."

"Jesus." Anna turned the page over in hopes of finding more information but it was as blank as it had been two seconds previously. Jennifer's brother. Anna thought of her own sister, Molly, how lonely she would be were she to lose her, and tremendous sadness swept over her. Carefully she refolded the note and tucked it in her shirt pocket. This was not a bit of paper to be passed carelessly from hand to hand. That it had arrived so publicly bespoke a crassness or negligence Anna had trouble crediting the information officer with. On a hunch she shined her flashlight into Paula's truck. On the second sweep she found it: a blue For Your Eyes Only envelope with her and LeFleur's names on it had been torn open and hastily discarded. The spike camp's inamorata was a nosy little beast.

Clicking off the light, Anna stood for a moment in the silence and breathed the pleasant odor of pine smoke. The death note in her pocket was heavy as a brick. Moving slowly to put off the inevitable, she wandered in darkness toward the San Juan crew tent.

One end of the tent was tied open for fresh air. The other closed off in complete darkness. In September, in the Cascades, nights were cold, and frost was on the ground most mornings. Anna looked down the row of inert forms. Several world-class snorers sawed at the air but no one was awake. Between the sleeping bags was a tangle of yellow fire packs. The packs were a nightmare of webbing and plastic buckles designed to hook together all the necessary components needed on the line: fire shelter, water, fusees, gloves, helmet, goggles, brush jacket and earplugs.

Near the open end of the tent LeFleur lay on his back, one arm thrown over his eyes. Joseph Hayhurst was curled next to him, his hands tucked under his cheek like an innocent. Anna spotted Nims by the white hair. His face was to the back of the tent. Jennifer was lost in the darkness somewhere between the sleeping men.

After a moment, Anna turned and crept away. Tomorrow would be soon enough to tell Jennifer. This might be the last good night's sleep she would enjoy in a while.

2

"It's time."

The voice came through warm thick darkness and was most unwelcome. Anna retreated, curling deeper into oblivion.

"We miss your bright eyes and sweet smile." The same voice, sugary this time, but still odious.

"Bugger off," Anna grumbled.

"Oooh, now there's a thought . . ." A rough shake loosed Anna entirely from the comforting embrace of sleep. Stephen, sitting on the army cot laid head to head with hers, was lacing up his boots.

"It's still dark," Anna complained.

"And cold. The glamour never stops. You've got ten seconds to do girl things, then I'm lighting the Coleman and to hell with your modesty."

"I would have had a son about your age if I hadn't drowned him at birth."

The EMT laughed. Anna could hear him groping for the lantern as she dragged on her underpants. Drafts, sharp as knives with the early frost, stabbed into the warm sanctity of her sleeping bag as she performed her morning contortions.

Finally decent in a yellow NoMex fire shirt, she unzipped the bag. The new day hit her thighs like ice water. By the glare of a flashlight she watched Lindstrom battling the Coleman. Twenty-six or -seven, six-foot-two, strong, even-featured, with sandy hair so thick it stood out like fur, he reminded Anna of the boys who'd ignored her in high school. His hands betrayed his bulk with their long sensitive fingers. The hands of a flutist. Or a gynecologist. Once or twice Anna'd glimpsed a mean streak but it only served to make him more interesting.

He looked at her with narrowed eyes. "Anna?"

"I'm awake. Don't push me." She dragged on the olive drab trousers one leg at a time like the rest of the world.

The only people up earlier than the medical unit were the food servers and Anna blessed them in the name of Pele the fire goddess and half a dozen lesser gods as she poured her first cup of coffee. About halfway through the stumbling dark, back toward the medical tent, caffeine burned the remaining fog from her brain and she remembered her chores. Jennifer Short's brother was dead.

Remembering the dead, a fading image of Zachary wavered behind her eyes: a slender dark man, forever twenty-nine, brown eyes glowing across an electric candle in a Brew and Burger in Manhattan. "If you asked me to marry you, I'd say yes," Anna had said. And he had asked.

Zach had been dead for so many years she should have quit counting. There had been other men since, men to spend the days with, men to pass the nights, but none to soften the loneliness. One, maybe, she amended: Frederick Stanton, an offbeat FBI agent she'd worked with on two homicides, once when she was a ranger on Isle Royale in Lake Superior and again several months ago in Mesa Verde National Park. Dinner, a hike through Indian ruins, a kiss that reminded her the animals went two by two, then he was on a plane back to Chicago.

Just as she'd been metaphorically dusting off her hands and consigning her emotions to a well-stocked Ships Passing in the Night file, a letter had come. Not a love letter, that would have set off alarms. Men who fell in love with women they didn't know were prone to other easily abandoned fantasies. Frederick's letter was funny. Laughter, like touch, was a form of pure communication, the funny bone an underappreciated erogenous zone.

Anna touched her shirt pocket as if she carried Stanton's letter over her heart. The death memo was still there, one of the perks of never changing clothes. The feel of the slick paper jarred her into the present and she cleared her mental decks for what lay ahead.

Spike camp had awakened. Muttering firefighters, subdued from too little sleep, boiled out of tents like yellow jackets from a disturbed hive. Flashlights sparked off lemon-colored NoMex and the tramp of heavy boots scuffed the worn earth.

A small woman, surrounded by three men so big that, in her white tee shirt, she resembled an egret among cows, chattered out of the dark woods beyond the Porta-Johns. Paula. One of the men was Howard Black Elk. The other two were strangers to Anna.

"Wait up," Anna shouted. The girl looked alarmed, her three bodyguards undecided, the desire to defend Paula against some imagined attack and the urge to flee battling in their brains. Flight won and the girl was alone when Anna reached her.

There were those rare creatures who suffered from a phobic reaction to authority but finding four of them together was unlikely. Anna made a mental note to pry into Paula's affairs when she didn't have more pressing matters to attend to.

"Hold off going down the mountain," Anna said. "I may have a passenger for you."

Paula looked relieved and again Anna felt a flash of suspicion, an occupational hazard. Sometimes she had the sense of being a cat in a world of birds, some bigger and meaner than she. Small furtive movements set off her alarms but she was never sure whether she was predator or prey. "I'll get back with you in thirty minutes or so."

Jennifer Short was in the breakfast line. In the name of nutrition, Anna put off telling her for another quarter of an hour. Then, having exhausted all delay tactics, she took Jennifer and her crew boss, LeFleur, behind the medical tent under one of the great old Jeffrey pines that shaded the camp.

To the east the sun was consuming the glitter of hot spots with its own superior fire. Lurid red light, filtered through smoke, bathed the camp.

"I have bad news," Anna said, and she handed the younger woman the note. As if in slow motion, Jennifer's face crumpled. Her mouth opened slightly as she read, her lips and eyes took on the soft quiver of a child's, tears ran down her cheeks. Once she looked to Anna as if for a reprieve but there was none.

"Her brother died," Anna explained to LeFleur. One of the crew boss's callused hands reached out but stopped before it reached Jennifer. He shot Anna a look of such anger for a second she thought he might try and kill the messenger.

After a moment he said to the air between Jennifer and Anna: "You'll want to demob. Get home. Anna will work it out." With the air of a man escaping, he walked away.

Jennifer stopped him: "I won't go."

LeFleur looked back without turning.

"He died in this fire, in the Jackknife, that's what it says. I need to stay, fight this fire." Jennifer pushed her face back in shape and mopped her tears with her sleeve.

"That's not the way it works," LeFleur said. "We can't use you if your mind's on something else. Go home."

He was right, but still Anna wanted to smack him.

"There's nothing wrong with my mind," Jennifer snapped. For an instant anger banished grief and Anna took back her slap. LeFleur's unorthodox therapy seemed to give at least short-term relief.

The crew boss stared at Jennifer and she glared back. Tears poured down her face, but the softness, the quiver had gone.

LeFleur lit a Pall Mall and flicked the match toward the barren earth around the medical tent. Crew bosses had close to absolute power over the twenty firefighters under their care. On a fireline, as in battle, somebody had to be in charge. After a lengthy weighing of Lord knew what factors he said: "If Anna can square it with the brass you can stay with the San Juan."

"Go on out with the crew today," Anna said. "I'll catch a ride down the mountain and see what I can do."

Jennifer nodded curtly. "Excuse me," she whispered, and left Anna and LeFleur under the pine.

They watched her walk away, spine straight, shoulders back.

"Women on the fireline," LeFleur said disgustedly, stubbed his cigarette out on the sole of his boot, shredded the paper and let the tobacco scatter.

"Dead brothers aren't exactly a gender-based liability," Anna said mildly. LeFleur chose not to answer.

"Time to rally the troops," he said.

Anna returned to the medical unit to help Lindstrom finish the morning calls.

The line outside the tent had lengthened each day they'd been spiked out. Bodies, nerves, psyches were being worn down by work and hard living. Accidents were becoming more common; cuts, bruises and colds epidemic.

Lindstrom looked up with relief as Anna pushed into the tent. "Sure been lonely around here without you," he said pointedly. "Howard Black Elk's pining away. Says nobody does his feet like you. My, my, I do believe it's love."

"I'll do him," Anna said. A long folding table took up the center of the tent. Two shallow boxes covered the surface. Carefully arranged in each were the tools of their trade: scissors, gauze, compresses, blister dressings, splints, salves, triangular bandages, tweezers, antihistamines. The paraphernalia of Mom's medicine cabinet on an industrial scale. Backboards, leg splints and cervical collars were stored beneath.

Anna picked through the boxes plucking out the Rx for Black Elk's feet.

"What was all the cloaking and daggering this morning?" Lindstrom asked. "Much hush-hush cloistering and whispering. Don't tell me my beloved Jennifer is going to have that barbarian LeFleur's baby. I couldn't bear it."

Anna laughed. It felt good. "Nope. Real bad news. Remember that burned corpse they found near Pinson Lake?"

"The dog guy?"

"Yeah. They identified the body."

"Schnauzer? Shiat zhu?"

"It was Jennifer's brother. She took it hard. I didn't even know she had a brother but then I haven't known her all that long. As to what a boy from Memphis was doing in the mountains of California, your guess is as good as mine."

"Joshua lives here. Lived here, I guess I should say now, shouldn't I?"

Anna looked up not only because of the unexpected answer but the wooden monotone that had crushed Stephen's usual vibrance.

"You knew him."

"Knew him." Lindstrom nodded. "He did some freelance work for the Forest Service in Reno setting up our new computer system. We—"

"Cut the sewing bee short." A slightly nasal voice with a raw-edged twang sliced between Anna and Lindstrom. From the corner of her eye Anna could see Leonard Nims planted just outside the tent flaps, the only agitation between two lines of patient firefighters. With impatient taps he forced a filtered cigarette from a box marked Harley Davidson.

She ignored him. "Good friend?" she asked Stephen.

"Good friend."

"Fucking women," Nims hissed just loud enough Anna would hear. "Next thing they'll be hiring faggots. Don't ask, don't tell, give me a fucking break. If you ladies will excuse me." He pushed into the tent and began rummaging through the items on the table. "It'd be nice to get some attention before a man bleeds to death."

Neither heat nor light had yet penetrated the tent's interior, but by the harsh glow of the Coleman, Anna noted two scratches running from Nims's temple to the middle of his cheek where a tree or something had scraped his face. The deeper of the two oozed beads of blood into the black stubble of beard.

Lindstrom laid a hand on Nims's wrist, stopping the pillage of their supplies. The shorter man's face grew mottled red and his eyes bulged slightly.

Good candidate for a stroke, Anna thought hopefully.

"This'll do for you," Lindstrom said evenly, and he handed Nims a small tube of Neosporin.

Wordlessly, Anna took the ointment from Nims's fingers and replaced it with an alcohol pad and a vial of iodine.

"The ointment would've worked," Lindstrom said as Nims left.

"Iodine will hurt more."

Stephen laughed. "I want to be just like you when I grow up, Anna."

She waited a second to see if he needed to talk about Joshua Short. He didn't and there wasn't time. Gratefully, Anna turned back to her work.

By the time the last firefighter was cared for, the sun had crept clear of the heaviest smoke and poured into the compound burning off the morning's chill. Anna tipped her face to the light and felt renewed. "I'm going down the hill," she said as she heard Stephen clearing up rubbish from the shift. "Make a list of what we need. I'll come back by after I've made sure of my ride."

"Riding down with Polly Wolly doodle all the day?"

"If she hasn't lit out on me."

"She may have. I've noticed when the men leave camp it loses much of its allure for our heroine."

"I'll pick you up some cream," Anna said.

Stephen meowed unrepentantly.

A heavyset man around thirty with a belly that hung over his belt and the thinning hair of a much older man was pulling cold lunch boxes from inside a truck and setting them on the tailgate where the crews could help themselves. Neil Page: Anna dredged the name up from some list she'd seen. Page was in charge of spike camp supplies. A local himself, he'd recommended the local hires and supervised the handful of drivers who trucked food up from Incident Base.

Anna leaned on the truck's bumper and waited till he grunted back, another box in his arms. "Seen Paula?" she asked.

"Probably rifling wallets in the tents." He puffed and loosed a brown stream of tobacco juice over the tailgate. "Greedy little bitch."

Anna waited.

"Last I saw her she was squabbling with—" A pile of lunches slithered from Page's arms and scattered across the packed dirt. To show what a great gal she was, Anna gathered them up for him.

"With who?"

"Hell if I know," he growled, as if Anna'd gotten personal. "They were over by that truck of hers. You can do your own snooping."

"Thanks," Anna said dryly.

"Anytime."

Anna found Paula stretched out on a folding lounge chair in her truck bed, her pants legs rolled as high as they would go and her shirt tied up baring her midriff. It was too early in the day to hope for any tanning action but Anna doubted that was the focus of this particular exercise. Slanting morning sun the color of molten lava lighted the girl most flatteringly, much to the enjoyment of columns of firefighters headed for the line.

"Sorry to make you wait." Anna leaned against the truck and watched the display sputter to life.

"Yeah. Well." Paula slapped her trouser legs down and fumbled at the knot in her shirtfront. "I got a lot of stuff I gotta get done today."

"Me too. I'll need a ride down the hill as soon as I get a list from Stephen. I shouldn't be more than five minutes." Anna left Paula to finish dressing.

Anna hadn't been out of spike camp since she'd been detailed there the week before. This outing felt like a holiday. She liked watching the world go by the window: the endless trees, the sameness of the evergreen color, the red of manzanita and the gold of the soil, sun-dappling the lichen and pine needles in intricate mosaics. All overlaid by strange smoke-filtered light, as if seen through tinted glass or the dire prophecies of some ancient soothsayer.

And she was going to get a hot shower. As the miles bumped by and the plume of dust they laid grew longer, she could almost feel the water combing through the muck of dirt and ash in her hair, scratching her itchy scalp, sloughing off the grime of camp.

Even Paula's chattering as they jolted down the rough logging roads didn't take the edge off. Once

Paula Boggins found out Anna wasn't going to bite her she never stopped talking. For a while Anna listened, learning more than she ever wanted to about all the things Paula needed to buy during her short stay on Planet Earth, then she tuned the girl out. Fortunately Miss Boggins wasn't the type to require answering and Anna let the words flow over her with the engine noise.

In contrast to the small and isolated spike camp, Incident Base, with its one thousand souls and all the supporting staff and machinery for the campaign, bustled like the big city: parking lots, tents by the score, buzzing phones and faxes, hot and cold running personnel. Anna took in the sights. She bought fresh underwear at a commissary that had sprung out of the back of a semi-truck trailer to offer life's necessities: fire boots, chewing tobacco, candy and Tampax. She stood in the shower, an eight-by-eight metal room in the back of another trailer, with a central column surrounded by showerheads to accommodate six women at a time, until long after guilt should have forced her to stop wasting water. She dried herself on the gigantic paper towels trucked in for that purpose. She braided her hair and studied her face in the polished aluminum that passed for mirrors over the line of washstands outside the canvas dressing room. The gray tracing age through her braids was taking over the brown but the soft reflection of the metal was kind to the lines and wrinkles carved in her forehead and around her eyes. She visited a "Women Only" Porta-John the women in the Communications and Information tents had taken over in what was being termed the Honey Pot Uprising.

After a full sit-down meal in a mess tent with shade and netting to keep the flies and yellow jackets at bay, Anna felt ready to face the brass.

Logistics sent her over to Time Keeping and Time Keeping to the Command tent. Wherever there were two government employees to rub together, a bureaucracy flared up. Anna was beginning to remember the isolation of spike camp almost nostalgically when she finally cornered the Operations section chief and got her questions answered.

Short's staying or going was a moot point. Spike camp was due to be demobed. Two of the three crews were coming out tonight and the San Juans would head out the following day.

The fire was gearing down. They estimated containment soon. The National Weather Service predicted a cold front due in twenty-four hours with a seventy percent chance of rain below forty-one-hundred feet and snow at the higher elevations.

The Jackknife was about to fold.

Anna would stay on at Base as an EMT until the fire was completely controlled but even she and Stephen would probably be demobed by the end of the week. Good news, Anna guessed. She'd miss the money—overtime jacked her paycheck up enough the IRS took notice—and the boot-camp simplicity would be replaced by grown-up worries. But home meant comfort and her cat and clean clothes.

She arranged a lift back to spike with the helicopter taking up hot suppers and bringing down the two women in charge of Time Keeping. With an hour to kill till her ride left, she scored a Pepsi from one of the ubiquitous coolers of soda, candy and fruit that littered every fire camp she'd ever been in, and wandered down the dusty road from the Command area tents.

Constant traffic had pulverized the soil to a fine gray powder that flowed over the toes of her boots like fog. Pines, their lower branches made ghostly by dust, leaned close, breathing out a faint scent of resin. The helicopters had momentarily abandoned their constant water brigade to and from area lakes to dip their buckets.

In that odd pocket of silence, it occurred to Anna the forest would heave a great sigh of relief to be rid of this shantytown with its garbage and buzz of engines and saws. Wildfires were business as usual. They'd burned since the first tree had been struck by the first bolt of lightning. Forests had survived, evolved, grown stronger. But man, hacking firelines with Mcleod and dozer, shovel and pulaski, took some assimilating. Sometimes the fighting left more lasting scars than the fire.

Where the dirt road turned clear of the trees and into the main body of the camp, under the shade of a ponderosa, two security guards in Forest Service green sat at a folding table looking bored. One, ankles crossed on the back of an empty metal chair, read a dog-eared copy of *Praetorian*. The other appeared to be amusing himself by interrupting. Both were relieved when Anna meandered up.

Looking out of place, a phone sat on the corner of the table, its wires vanishing into a shallow covered trench leading beneath the roadway.

"You can use it," the nonreader offered. "Anybody can. Five minutes free anywhere in the country."

"No kidding?"

"Swear to God." He crossed his heart and looked so solemn Anna laughed. Like a majority of firefighters he couldn't have been more than twenty-one. His boyish good looks probably got him carded in every bar he walked into.

"Anywhere? Free?"

"Yup. You should see the line at night when the crews come down. Sixty to a hundred guys waiting to make their call. It's empty now," he said invitingly.

The plain black plastic did look seductive, with its promise of access to another world, one presumably where people were just dying to hear from you.

Anna wished she had someone to call.

"Come on, when was the last time Uncle Sam gave you a freebie?" the young man cajoled.

Anna thought of calling her sister Molly but a glance at her watch told her it was three-ten New York time. Molly would be with a client.

"Go on. Reach out and touch somebody."

"Do you sell used cars in the off season?" Anna teased.

"Car stereos."

"What the hell." She picked up the receiver. Cradling it to her ear, she dug her wallet out of her hip pocket. Crunched between her Visa and her library card was a gold-embossed business card. On one side, scrawled in letters as gangling as their creator, were the words: "Call me if you need anything." Anna flipped it over. "Frederick Stanton, Special Agent, FBI" was printed in black, along with the number.

An onslaught of butterflies the size of pterodactyls flapped through Anna's innards as she dialed the number. "Frederick Stanton, please."

She made it by the secretary. The young security guard nodded encouragingly.

"This is Agent Stanton."

Anna's mind froze. Her tongue clove to the roof

of her mouth—at least that's what it felt like. Quietly she hung up. "Busy," she said.

"Try again."

Anna shook her head. "Got to get back to spike."

So much for her sojourn in the fast lane.

3

By noon the next day spike camp was all but gone. The medical tent and the supply tent were in the final stages of disassembly. Wearing shorts and a tee shirt, Paula stood by watching as Anna and Stephen loaded the canvas into the back of her truck. Neil Page, a chaw of tobacco distending his lower lip, rested his belly on the truck's radiator, staring glumly at the engine. An oily red rag protruded from his hip pocket, flagging exposed derriere decolletage. A screwdriver and crescent wrench, the only tools he was conversant with, were balanced on the fender.

"I'm not hanging around up here all day waiting for you to get that damn thing up and going." Paula sucked on an orange Gatorade. The colored drink painted a Kool-Aid smile on her round face.

"Like you got a choice," Neil muttered.

Tossing her hair, Paula pouted at Stephen. "When they coming to get you? There room for me? I'll sit on somebody's lap if I got to."

"Yeah. And talk about the first thing that comes

up," issued from under the truck's hood along with a stream of brown tobacco juice.

"Fuck off, Neil. Can I?"

Stephen pushed the roll of canvas farther up on the bed. "No problem, little lady," he mimicked John Wayne's classic cadence.

If she got the joke, Paula didn't let on. "When ya goin'?"

"Tonight with the bus that comes for the last of the San Juans."

Paula turned her back. "That's later'n us even. That don't do me no good."

"No lap for you," Anna said as she and Lindstrom went back for the tent poles, pulled up and piled neatly beneath their sheltering tree. Nearby were the jump kit and emergency gear that would remain until the last of the crew rode down in the evening.

"A fella'd want to wear rubber gloves just to hold hands with that little number. I don't know where she's been but I bet it wasn't clean enough to eat off of." Stephen tossed his head in a good imitation of Paula Boggins. "A boy's got his reputation to consider."

In mutual and unspoken accord, he and Anna flopped into the shade where their medical unit had been. Lindstrom propped his head against his hard hat and folded his arms across his chest. "Old firefighting maxim," he said. "If there's time to stand, there's time to sit. If you can sit, you can lie down. If you can lie down, you can lie down in the shade."

Anna folded herself up tailor fashion, one foot on the opposite thigh in a half lotus. She'd never managed a full lotus, though there'd been a time she thought it worth pursuing. The difference between a half and full seemed the difference between complacency and spiritual awakening. The first was comfortable. The second made one's bones ache.

The wind had shifted, blowing in from the northwest ahead of the storm. Smoke veiled the sun until it was a blood-red ball. Anything obscuring the sun made Anna uneasy. Had she been an aboriginal she had little doubt that at the first signs of an eclipse she would have been in the vanguard sacrificing virgins to appease the gods.

To the west she could see the barren domes of Chaos Crags and the ragged thrust of Lassen Peak. Drought had plagued California for three years without reprieve and no snow clung to the volcano's flanks. Pines draping her sides showed a hint of rust: drought stress. Dry as tinder.

Beyond the peak was a wall of dirty white. The front pouring in across the Cascades. The blessing of rain, but most assuredly in disguise. Thunderstorms, spawned along the leading edge, were lit from within by lightning. "It better be a wet one," she remarked. "Or it'll light more fires than it puts out."

Stephen opened one hazel eye. His lashes, like his hair, were short and very thick. It gave him a dreamy look Anna was a sucker for. "Cloud to cloud. Stuff's not reaching the ground."

Anna studied the oncoming clouds. "It's moving right along though."

In unexpected ratification, her radio began issuing a warning to expect gusting winds. All morning voices had scratched over the airwaves. Crew bosses talking to squad bosses, and air to ground communications. Everything winding down. Anna'd pretty much quit listening. Now she turned it up.

"Maybe LeFleur'll pull the squad," Stephen said. "We can get off this mountain a couple hours early. I could stand that."

"Spike medical unit, this is the San Juan."

"John must have heard you." Anna pulled her radio off her belt. "I bet he's ordering a bus."

"Spike medical," she answered.

"We've got an injury. A log rolled down on Newt Hamlin. Looks like a busted knee. Closed but bad. He's hurting. We're going to need you, Lindstrom and the litter to carry him out."

"Affirmative." Anna got an exact location from him and signed off.

"Looks like we've got to work for our suppers today," Stephen said.

"Who's Hamlin?"

"A swamper with the Forest Service out of Durango, Colorado."

"Brown hair, buzz cut, looks fresh off the farm?" Anna asked cautiously.

"That's right. The *big* guy. The really, really big guy. Monstrous. An ox."

"Any place to land a helicopter below the line?" Anna radioed.

"Too rugged," LeFleur replied.

Anna made two more radio calls requesting a chopper at the heli-spot near spike. "Looks like we haul him up the hill," she said.

Lindstrom groaned. "We should've gone into pediatrics."

Spike camp was located on a ridge that ran north and south. To the east the slope was relatively gentle and the vegetation thinned from an old burn. Partway down a heli-spot had been cleared on a natural shoulder in the hillside. A wide sandy creek bottom, dry this time of year, cut a white ribbon through the valley floor. The west side fell away steeply into a narrow canyon. Near the bottom, about a mile from camp, the San Juans were building line. The Jackknife had burned most of the opposite slope. The new line was to stop it once it crossed the gully.

Stephen started down, litter on his shoulder. Anna, wearing the yellow pack and hard hat required on the fireline, carried the jump kit. There was no trail to speak of. At six thousand feet the mountains were choked with ponderosa, Jeffrey, sugar pines and white fir. The few open areas were nearly impassible with manzanita, a sturdy bush with tangled arms clothed in red bark and shining green leaves.

Facing west, the slope caught the full force of the afternoon sun. Needles, twigs, downed timber, gooseberry, ceanothus: the mountain was solid fuel and so dry the dust pounded up by each bootfall tickled Anna's nose till it ran. Deer flies, fat and sluggish in the heat, took bites from thigh and back, the protective clothing apparently no deterrent. Anna swore under her breath, afraid to open her mouth lest one crawl in. Though it would've been poetic justice: a bite for a bite.

Trees grew close with dog-hair thickets of young sugar pines fighting for sunlight in the patches of land that in past years had been montane meadows. But for dust and the all-pervasive smoke, Anna could smell very little. Too many summers without rain had baked the juices dry. All that remained was the faint smell of vanilla given off by the burnished bronze bark of the Jeffrey pines. To be in the midst of a conifer forest and not breathe in the heady scent of pine put her off balance. As if one stood at the seashore and couldn't taste the salt air.

A thick blanket of duff crackled underfoot. Coupled with the racket of breathing it was deafening.

In places the hillside was so steep Anna slid down on her butt, preferring the occasional stickers to falling.

Suddenly Stephen stopped and she smacked her head on the end of the litter. "Signal, for Christ—" she began, but he cut her off.

"Lookie there." He pointed to the base of a sugar pine. Still as a statue in the almost realized hope of going unnoticed was a ringtail cat. Wide, dark, lemurlike eyes stared up from a little triangle of nose and ears. Its long striped tail was curled in a question mark behind it.

"First one I've ever seen," Stephen whispered.

Anna had seen a couple when she'd worked in Texas. They were nocturnal and terribly shy. It was unsettling to see one so close and in the light of day. Unnatural.

"Displaced by the fire," Stephen said.

" 'The graves stood tenantless and the sheeted dead did squeak and gibber in the Roman streets.' " Anna quoted from *Hamlet*.

"Cut that out."

"Right."

The cat seemed paralyzed and a man with a broken leg was waiting, so they pushed on.

Halfway to the canyon bottom, maybe three-quarters of a mile from spike camp, Anna and Lindstrom found the fireline, a six-foot-wide trail rudely scratched into the landscape. On either side trees had been clear-cut and thrown back. Duff and scrub had been scraped away by pulaskis, the double-duty tool with an axe on one side and sharp hoelike blade on the other that most firefighters carried.

To the left, Joseph Hayhurst, his squat frame and strong back suited to the work, was swamping for a sawyer Anna recognized but didn't know by name.

As trees fell and were bucked up into manageable chunks, Joseph dragged the pieces clear of the line. Anna recognized the Apache by his hair and stature. Both men were faceless behind handkerchiefs tied bandit-style over the lower half of their faces in an attempt to screen out dust and soot. Surgical-style painters' masks were far more effective filters, but every culture bows to fashion. Firefighters would no sooner trade their bandannas in for white conical masks than Texans would trade their Stetsons for parasols.

"Joseph!" Anna called when the chainsaw gave them a moment's peace. He pointed farther up the line and Anna and Lindstrom headed north toward the head of the canyon. After the slide and scramble down the hill the "improved" surface was like a stroll in the park. Long after grasses flourished and trees returned the cut would mar the hillside, growing more rutted, wider, as rain and snow runoff took the easier course they now followed.

Dust and smoke were held close by the trees and the air in the ravine was stifling. Rivulets of sweat tickled between Anna's breasts and shoulder blades. Salt drops burned her eyes and puddled at her temples—wading pools for the deer flies.

"Wait up," she told Stephen.

Obediently he stopped while she pulled off her stiff leather gloves and mopped beneath the band of her hard hat.

"Our nose getting a wee bit shiny?" he asked.

"Fuck you," Anna said amiably.

Radio traffic interrupted with another bulletin on the cold front forecasting high winds.

"I wish it'd get here," Stephen said as Anna screwed her hard hat back on. "We could use a break."

"High winds. LeFleur'll be pulling the squad out."

Howard Black Elk, a pulaski held loosely in his downhill hand, walked down the line toward them. "We're bumping back up to spike," he said. "I'm passing the word. Everybody's bumping up. John doesn't like the forecast. John, Jennifer and Lenny Nims are waiting with Newt. He's a hurting unit. Soon as I get word out about the bump, I'll grab somebody and come back, help with the carry-out."

"Thanks," Anna said. "Hamlin's big."

"Damn big. Not far." Howard raised a massive arm and pointed north. "Just outta sight, maybe two hundred yards." He squeezed onto the uphill side of the line to let Stephen and Anna pass.

Hard hats and gloves off, Jennifer and John knelt on either side of Newt Hamlin. Leonard Nims stood up the line leaning on a shovel, looking like he couldn't decide whether to stay or go. Hamlin, a beefy, square-headed boy, maybe nineteen or twenty, sat rigid, his face white and his lips pinched into a thin line. The muscles in his broad jaw worked constantly. Grinding his teeth, Anna noted. Probably to keep himself from crying. Tears made his eyes glitter but not one fell.

The boy's right knee was bent backward, the lower leg pushing up at about a twenty-degree angle from anatomical position. Short or LeFleur had immobilized it, splinting from hip to ankle joint with branches trimmed for the purpose.

Anna dropped to one knee. Hamlin's boot was unlaced. Evidently the pain of removing it had been so intense, leaving it in place had been deemed the lesser of evils. She reached as far into the boot as she could.

"So what happened?" Lindstrom asked as he began unslinging the litter.

"Len was cutting. Newt swamping. Got downhill of a fall. A log rolled and nailed him," John said.

By the careful neutrality of the crew boss's voice, Anna guessed one of the two had been careless. Negligence on the fireline was not taken lightly. There was too much at stake. She glanced up at Nims. His face was crimped into defensive lines. Mentally he was digging foxholes, falling back. Newt was either unaware he could fault anyone but God or too wrapped up in his pain to worry about placing blame.

Anna's fingers found the posterial tibial pulse behind Hamlin's ankle. It was strong and his skin was warm to the touch. "Good job," she said to LeFleur and Short. "Let's leave it like it is and haul him out."

Lindstrom had the litter down, the straps laid out to the sides. "Did you get tired of working and fake a fall just to get a free ride out?" he asked Hamlin.

"How'd you know?" the boy said with a ghost of a smile.

Stephen said: "Me and John will lift Newt. Anna, you and Jen move his leg. On three."

In one smooth motion they slid the kid onto the litter. A barking cry escaped the press of his lips.

"Yeah, yeah, yeah," Lindstrom said. "Trying to get sympathy from the women. Some guys'll do anything to get laid."

"You got me figured out," Newt managed.

"John, take the head. I got the foot," Lindstrom said. "Anna, Jen, take a side as long as we've got the room. Len, get the tools. When Howard gets back we'll switch out every few minutes. On three."

"I'm sorry I'm so big," Newt said as they heaved up the litter.

The apology brought a lump to Anna's throat that annoyed her. "Not a problem," she said. "We can field amputate that leg right here. What do you figure that'd save us, Stephen?"

"Seventy-five pounds easy. Cut it off high."

"Go ahead," Newt said. "I don't think it could hurt any worse. Just leave the family jewels."

"Sure," Stephen agreed. "They couldn't weigh more than a gnat's Adam's apple anyway. Little enough I bet even old man Nims could carry them up the hill without breaking a sweat."

Even with the joint immobilized it was clear every jolting step they took was causing Hamlin pain. It was equally clear the boy would staple his lips shut before he'd let on.

"He's big as a horse," Anna said to Jennifer. "And his leg is broken. Think anybody'd care if we just shot him?"

A gust eddied up the trail, a vortex of ash and dirt whirling in a tiny tornado. Dust devils, Molly and Anna called them when they were children. They moved like sentient creatures, the tails tracing patterns in the earth that could be tracked only to see the creature that made them disassociate, dissolve into nothing but air.

This devil stopped a yard or two in front of them, its tail twitching restlessly in the dust. For a few seconds it hovered as if deciding whether or not to tell them something. Apparently the answer was no. The wind veered and the devil disintegrated into the grasping arms of a manzanita bush hacked out of the ground and lying close to the fireline.

The wall of clouds that had been on the horizon when Anna and Stephen started down was on the horizon still but now the horizon was scarcely a mile above them. Anna was getting a bad feeling.

LeFleur jerked his radio out of his belt. The litter rocked as he held it with just one hand and a tiny squawk escaped Newt's control. Anna pretended not to hear but she moved her hand slightly on the litter so it touched Hamlin's wrist, hoping the contact would give him some little comfort.

"Black Elk, LeFleur." The crew boss was shouting into the radio. His adrenaline level was rising too, Anna guessed.

"Black Elk," came back with a hiss of static.

"Status?"

"Everybody's bumped up. They're halfway up the hill by now. Me and Hayhurst are coming back for you."

"There's enough of us for the job. Head on up. Keep those guys moving. The wind's getting squirrely. No sense anybody getting hurt on this one. Clear 'em out.

"Hang onto your hat, Newt," LeFleur addressed the boy in the litter. "We're going to head up the hill."

"Sorry I don't have a bullet for you to bite on," Anna said as they started up the incline and Hamlin's weight shifted, forcing pressure on the ruined knee.

"I got a lipstick," Jennifer offered. "But I don't s'pose it's the same."

Newt was beyond banter. His face was the dirty gray of ash and sky, all his will needed to form a wall around the pain in his leg.

The slope was close to thirty degrees but the forest was comprised of slightly older growth than farther up. Trees were six to eight feet apart and there wasn't too much undergrowth. Anna's boots dug deep in the duff as she hauled up, one step at a time, the side of the stretcher in one hand, the jump kit in the other. The position was awkward and she knew she wasn't helping much with Hamlin's weight.

Across Newt's chest she could see Short struggling to maintain her end of the bargain. Jennifer's strength was all from the waist down, good wide hips and strong thighs like a figure skater. Anna knew her shoulders and arms would be aching with the strain as she fought to take some of the weight up for Stephen and John.

Cool air gusted from behind. Though it caressed her sweaty skin, it made the little hairs on the back of Anna's neck crawl.

"Dump the jump kit," LeFleur ordered as he picked up the pace. "Len, give a pulaski to Anna. Keep moving."

Anna dropped the medical bag and used Nims's pulaski like an ice axe, clawing up the hill. LeFleur's breathing rasped deep in his chest, the cords of his neck distended and the flesh between the rim of his hard hat and his collar was a deep red.

"Switch out soon," she said to Stephen. He nodded. The foot of the stretcher weighed less and he was both bigger and younger than the crew boss. "Next flat spot. I take the head, Nims, you get the foot. Got that?"

LeFleur grunted.

The vegetation closed in, branches scratching at their faces and arms. The pounding of her heart was the only sound Anna was aware of. Oblivious to anything but the pain in her left shoulder from pulling Hamlin and the small square of real estate directly in front of her boot toes, she trudged on. Quite independently of conscious thought, her mind clicked through numbers trying to find a rhythm to pass the time, keep cadence. Waltz time: ONE, two, three, ONE, two, three.

A place not deserving of the name "clearing" opened up slightly at the base of a ledge of volcanic rock about eighteen inches high and fifty feet long that formed a brow half a mile below spike. Long ago soil had laid down a blanket covering all but the lip and the rock was hidden by a dense cover of waist-high shrubs.

Momentarily free of the trees, they stopped. Short fell to her knees, sucking in lungfuls of air. Hands on thighs, LeFleur tried to catch his breath. Even Hamlin was gasping, fighting pain and shock.

"Sounds like a TB ward around here," Stephen said. "Switch out." The EMT grasped the front of the litter. "Nims?"

Leonard Nims was sweating and his breath was coming fast but he was the freshest of the five. He handed LeFleur the tools and lifted the foot of the litter. Anna and Jennifer switched sides.

"Got to stretch out the other arm," Short said to Newt. "I'll still look like a gorilla but leastways both sets of knuckles'll be draggin'."

"Let's do it," Stephen said.

The words were followed by a low rumble. Faint, visceral, it was like the sound of a freight train coming down the tracks. The noise welled up from the bottom of the canyon. They looked back as one.

The far side of the ravine blossomed in fire. A mushroom cloud poured up in a deadly column and fire spun a tornado of destruction through the forest's crown, pulling oxygen from the air and creating weather of its own. Flame boiled down into the canyon bottom.

"Jesus fucking Christ," Lindstrom whispered. "Firestorm."

4

Never had Anna seen anything so beautiful. Raw, naked power blooming in red and orange and black. Tornadoes of pure fire shrieking through the treetops, an enraged elemental beast slaking a hunger so old only stones and gods remembered.

Exhilaration rose in her throat, a sense of revelation, of sharing the divine. "Whoa," she said, and heard the bubbling laughter of her voice mixing with the roar of Armageddon.

A scream brought her back and the fire of the holy spirit turned to fear that coursed through her with such violence she felt her bowels loosen. The scream had been ripped from Hamlin when Len Nims dropped his end of the litter. Anna could see him barging up the hill through the manzanita. She grabbed up the foot of the fallen stretcher. Hamlin's weight pulled a cry from her, the movement an answering groan from Newt.

"Deploy?" Lindstrom was shouting.

"Not a good place." LeFleur. "Too much brush. Run. Go for the ridge. Run."

Lindstrom held the head of the stretcher, Anna the foot. Both stared stupidly at Newt Hamlin, his only safety between their hands.

"We can do it," Lindstrom screamed.

The hell we can, Anna thought, but she held on to the litter. Newt said nothing. His brown eyes stared into her face, then Lindstrom's, and Anna knew she was witnessing an act of courage. Not bravado—he couldn't loose his jaws to tell them to go—but the courage to keep them closed against the words that would beg them not to leave him.

"We can do it," Anna said.

"Get the fuck out of here," LeFleur shouted. The roaring pushed his words like foam on the tide. "Go." The crew boss brought the handle of the pulaski he carried down hard across the bones of Stephen's wrists. The litter fell. Anna couldn't hold on and her end dropped as well.

"Go. Go." LeFleur was striking at them with the handle, herding them like goats. Jennifer started up the hill, slowly at first, then beginning to run. "Go, God damn it!"

Anna started to climb, Stephen with her, pounding up the slope. Fear took over. John, Newt, everything behind was blotted out but for the fire. She wanted to turn back, to look at it, but an odd memory from Sunday school of Lot's wife turning to a pillar of salt stopped her.

Loping on all fours like a creature half animal, half human, she scrambled over downed logs crumbling with rot, plowed through brush. Ahead of her, in that narrow scrap of world between eyes and hands that still existed, the ground turned red. She thought of "Mars," a short story her sister had written about the red planet. Close on that thought came another: how strange it was that while she was running for her life, she was thinking of Mars.

And she was running for her life. The idea snapped sharply through the sinews of her body and she became aware of the stretch of the muscles in her legs, the hardness of the ground, the slipping as her boots tore at the duff, the strain in the big muscles of her thighs and that slight softening that heralded fatigue. She wondered how long she could keep going.

A scrap of trivia surfaced. Fire, unlike anything else known to man, defied gravity. It traveled faster uphill than down. The length of a football field in a minute, that stuck in her mind. How long was a football field? A hundred yards? Fifty? Third grade. Johnstonville Elementary. She'd won a blue ribbon for running the fifty-yard dash in ten seconds flat. She was older now. Stronger. Older. Maybe only the young would make it.

A thicket of manzanita filled her vision and Anna plunged in. No time to find another way. Breath was cutting deep, each pull of air tearing a hole in her side. Branches scraped her face, plucked hanks of hair from under her hard hat. Nothing registered, not pain, not impediment. Anna felt as if she could claw her way through a mountain of stone.

Then her feet went from under her and she was down, her jaw cracking against a stone or a root. Her head swam with it, her mouth was full. She spit and blood, colorless against the flame-drenched earth, spilled out. She wondered if she'd bitten her tongue off.

"Up, goddam you, up."

LeFleur. He pulled at the back of her pack and

Anna came to her knees. "Go. Go." Anna ran again. The thickets were close to the ridge. Close. If she could make the ridge, maybe . . .

Roaring drowned even thought. Heat scorched her back, she could feel the burning through her left sleeve below the elbow. Air, sucked deep into her lungs, scalded and she screamed without sound. Her legs were growing heavy, sodden. Instead of carrying her she now had the sense of dragging them.

The ridge top rolled beneath her as if she'd flown in. Suddenly she was aware the way had grown easier: the beaten earth of the old camp. Paula's truck, the hood up, was parked where they'd left it. Two gasoline cans sat by the front wheel. Both were puffed up like roasted marshmallows, ready to blow. It crossed Anna's mind to move them before any of the others reached the ridge but she knew if she touched them she would die and she kept running.

Across the camp, clear of the pines, and over the crest of the ridge, Anna could see Jennifer ahead of her crashing down the slope toward the creek bed. Anna stumbled after, falling and pulling herself up time after time. Like a woman in a nightmare, she thought, like the Japanese maidens in monster movies.

Howard Black Elk ran out of the trees just above. He'd lost helmet and gloves. His hands were over his ears trying to protect them from the burning. Both arms were seared, the flesh hanging in ribbons.

Anna caught him by the shoulders.

"The creek," she gasped. "Fire'll slow when it reaches the ridge." While she talked she ripped her bandanna in half and bound Black Elk's hands. The last of the water from the bottle on her belt she poured over the bandages.

"The creek," she repeated.

"Safety zone," Black Elk said. He hadn't panicked. He knew where he was going. Together they ran again, flying downhill on legs that felt made of rubber and sand. Anna slid on rocks, fell over bushes and swung around trees. She heard the gas cans explode and looked back to the ridge top.

Flame was cresting in a wave. Burning debris shot over, tumbling down and starting new fires. A hundred yards and Anna would reach the creek. She turned to run and felt a sharp pain shoot through her ankle.

Fuck, she thought, I've broken it. Fear narrowed to that one place in her body and she put her weight on it. It held. The pain melded into the others as she ran.

The creek was sunken, the banks several feet high and she tumbled over the lip into the sand. Already it was hot to the touch.

"Deploy!"

Maybe it was LeFleur. Smoke blinded her. Hacking coughs tore the air from her lungs. Fumbling behind her back, Anna pulled her plastic-encased shelter from its pouch. She hadn't checked it in years. They were supposed to be checked every two weeks but no one did it. No one thought they would have to use them.

Ripping it out of the plastic, she clawed it open; a small silver pup tent. Firefighters called them shake 'n' bakes. It no longer struck Anna as funny. Scorching wind snatched at the flimsy shelter, threatening to wrench it from her grasp. Fire poured down the mountain, burning embers exploding in its path.

Anna dragged the silver tent over her and anchored it with her boots to hold it down. Pulling it along her back and up over her head, she gripped the front edges in her gloved hands and fell face forward into the sand.

The roar engulfed her. Scouring sand and debris rasped on her shelter and she felt the skin on her back begin to burn. Pressing her face into a hollow in the sand, hoping for air cool enough to breathe, she thought of her sister. If she didn't get out of this alive, Molly would kill her.

5

Footage of the firestorm was on the six o'clock news. The shots were from a distance of several miles and cut short when the helicopter carrying the cameraman hit rough weather. Still the explosive sense of power carried through, the might of nature unleashed.

Frederick Stanton relaxed in the living room of his one-bedroom apartment in Evanston, Illinois. An overstuffed couch, bought for comfort, not looks, dominated the room. In the grate of a defunct fireplace, a television took the place of logs. The hearth of the nineties. Hardwood floors, recently refinished, picked up the reflection from the screen. No other lights were on.

Long legs draped modestly in a battered terry-cloth robe, Stanton lounged with his feet up and a glass of scotch—neat, no rocks. His bifocals were pushed down to where he could see over them. An aqua budgerigar with black tail feathers hopped down the length of one of Stanton's long arms, murmuring and pecking as if the man were made of delicious crumbs.

In the fireplace flames burned silently behind the anchorman's head as he read the news: "The storm front blamed for the blowup brought snow and sleet in its wake, damping the fires and grounding air support. Due to the weather and hazards caused by burned snags falling across the twenty miles of steep and twisting logging road that leads in to the remote spike camp thought to be in the path of the blaze, no machinery will be sent up until morning. A ground crew carrying food and medical supplies has been dispatched up the beleaguered fire road on foot. At present ten firefighters are listed as missing."

The anchor turned and looked expectantly at a blank wall behind him. After a second's delay film of a base camp in northern California was shown.

Frederick sat up. The budgie twittered in annoyance and flew several feet before landing on a bare knee to continue its foraging. One of Stanton's hands strayed to the black receiver of an old-fashioned rotary phone, a movement as unconscious as it was natural to a man who lived by the exchange of information.

The station cut to a commercial for fabric softener and Frederick pawed through a disintegrating hill of newspapers and magazines obscuring the coffee table. Outraged, the budgie flew back to his cage with a noisy flapping that metaphorically slammed the wire door behind him.

"Sorry, Daniel," Frederick said absently. The magazines began to slide and an avalanche of paper cascaded down around his ankles and over long white feet half concealed in slippers trod flat at the heels.

The disturbance uncovered the remote control. Stanton caught it up and began clicking through channels. National coverage was over for the evening. All he could find was Chicago news.

For a few minutes he stared at men in blue-and-white football jerseys running from other men in purple and white. The Bears and the Vikings. Usually Frederick forced himself to watch the highlights and memorize the scores on the off chance he had to pass as one of the boys at some point the following day. Now he wasn't aware of what was on the screen. Behind his eyes he watched a small-framed, middle-aged woman, streaks of gray through the infernal braid she used to incarcerate her hair, crumpled naked in a shower crying and swearing at him.

More fun than petting a bobcat, he thought, and smiled. Somewhere in the heap of materials he'd dumped on the floor was a letter from her. He'd put off answering it one day at a time for three weeks. Too much to say and no way to say it that was guaranteed to charm and amuse. Several drafts had already been consigned to the trash as sophomoric. With Anna he had to use his best material, the new relatively honest stuff. From the beginning he sensed she'd spot anything glib—or worse, would know if he tried too hard.

In the short time he'd known her, he'd had the heady sense of being an angler with a particularly wily and powerful fish on his line.

Not that Frederick fished, except as a less than biblical fisher of men, but this was how he imagined a deep-sea fisherman might feel with a muscular iridescent marlin on the end of his line. A glimpse of rainbow sparkling through the gray of an ocean wave, a sense of triumph. The line suddenly slack;

the prize eluding. Exhilaration at feeling the tug once again.

Frederick felt that tug now. Sipping delicately at the scotch, he wondered who had whose hooks into whom.

His right hand strayed back to the telephone. Pushing a button on the remote, he muted the television. He didn't turn it off. Whenever he was home the TV was on. Sound, color, the electronic simulation of life kept him company. Over the years he'd grown so used to it the place felt cold, haunted without it.

He dialed the Bureau's number from memory. Timmy Spinks answered and Frederick was relieved. Spinks was young but he was sharp and, Stanton hoped, just inexperienced enough not to realize Frederick was about to use Bureau equipment and personnel to his own ends.

"Timmy, Frederick Stanton. Get me everything you can on the firefighters caught in that burn out in California. Do you know what I'm talking about?"

"Yes, sir. It was all over the news."

"That's the one. I want to know what anybody else knows. Who is missing. If anybody's dead and who. What's being done. Everything."

"Yes, sir."

Sir. Timmy made Stanton feel old but since it was old and revered the FBI agent let it pass. "Call me at home. I'll be in all evening."

Stanton hung up and looked at pictures of beautiful women and shiny cars move silently across the television.

The San Juan Plateau crew would be out of the Colorado/New Mexico area. That much was obvious. Anna had mentioned in her letter that half the rangers in the park were fighting fires out west.

What were the odds Anna was on a fire? On the Jackknife?

A thousand to one. With Anna those odds didn't settle Stanton's nerves.

He could always phone her. There couldn't be too many Pigeons in southern Colorado. Information should have no trouble tracking her down.

I'm curious, not concerned, he told himself. If I reached her I wouldn't have much to say. But it was the specter of saying it badly that stayed his hand.

He fixed himself supper and ate in front of the TV, placing bits of food on the edge of his plate for Daniel to share. The little bird kept up a running conversation in a low and liquid warble but Frederick was lousy company.

Until the phone rang, and it occurred to him he had no recollection of what he had eaten or what he was watching, he didn't realize he had been waiting.

"Agent Stanton," he said as if he were at his desk in the office.

"Hi, Dad. It's Candice."

Frederick forced the disappointment from his voice. "Hiya, sweetheart. What's up?"

There followed a long and rambling account of triumphs and political coups on the student newspaper at the University of Minnesota in Minneapolis. After she hung up, Frederick scanned his memory. He was relatively sure he'd made all the right noises but he hadn't really been paying attention. Parental guilt prodded. A gentle poke: Candice was his one success out of three children. Through the divorces and the moves the two of them had managed to stay close.

"I love my girl," he said to Daniel.

The bird cocked its head and looked up out of one bright beady eye expecting attention, but the exchange was over. Frederick's eyes were back on the television, his mind in neutral.

When the phone rang a second time half an hour later he answered "Hello," cognizant of where he was.

"Agent Stanton? It's Timmy. Tim."

Stanton felt a familiar tightness in his belly. He'd first noticed it after he'd become a father for the second time. Driving home late—back in the days when home was populated by more than a bird and TV set—the last block before he turned onto Oakland Avenue where he could see his house, he'd get a slight clutch wondering if good news or bad news or no news awaited.

The house had always been standing, no burned-out shell, no roofless statistic in the wake of a tornado, no children with scarlet fever or black plague. But the tightening was there till he'd closed the door behind him. It was a game he played with himself.

"What've you got for me?"

"Not a whole lot. Events conspired, you might say."

Frederick crushed mounting impatience. "Begin at the beginning."

"Evidently the fire was a bit of a sleeper. It'd just been creeping along for several days. Pretty routine. About two this afternoon a cold front came in. The National Weather Service forecast it. They were counting on the precip to put the fire out. That's what gets most of them out—not as glamorous as I'd thought. This time the winds got bad, sheared in a canyon, fuel was dry and boom! The thing just exploded. Like a bomb. A squad—half the San Juan Plateau crew—was building line on about a two-hundred-acre finger of the fire. Sort of a thumb-shaped burn. When the wind sheared it blew up from two hundred acres to thirty-five hundred acres in less than an hour. Must've been awesome." Timmy's youth crept through the professional recital.

Frederick was pushing the receiver against his head, bruising the delicate if generous ear tissue. He loosened his grip. "The crew?"

"They were cutting back the whole operation. The San Juans were camped out a ways—twenty miles or so from the main camp. One squad had already been taken off the fire as well as two other guys, one with bronchitis and one with back problems. The other squad—about half the crew—was finishing up a section of fireline they'd been building. They may have gotten caught in the path of the fire when it went out of control. They're the ten missing."

"May have? No one's checked?" Frederick was angrier than he had a right to be and it bled into his voice.

Affronted, Tim was all business when he responded and Frederick made a mental note to be effusive in his thanks once he'd gotten what he wanted.

"No, sir. They can't. The fire burned over the camp, the heli-spot and the road for they don't know how many miles. The storm pushing the winds came in with snow at the higher elevations and sleet and rain in the valleys. Winds are still high. Visibility nil. Aircraft are grounded and they can't get machinery up the road. Some have started up on foot but there's no news yet and there's been no radio contact from the missing crew. Word is they have hand-held radios but they're only good for line-of-sight. They're meant for the crews to talk to each other. The commander said they might be able to reach the Incident Base camp if they were high enough. So far they haven't called in or responded. I talked with Gene Burwell. He's the incident commander. He said as soon as the weather breaks they'll get helicopters up there. According to the National Weather Service it should start clearing mid-morning tomorrow."

Frederick digested that. Tim Spinks waited silently.

The incident commander, not the information officer; Timmy must have cloaked himself in the armor of the Bureau. Frederick felt a small stab of embarrassment. He'd headed up enough bad situations to know how costly and irritating it was to have to shift mental gears to talk with other agencies. Especially those not directly involved.

"Good job, Tim," he said, and meant it. "Have you got a list of the missing crew members?"

"John LeFleur, Crew Boss, Newton Hamlin, Leonard Nims, Howard Black Elk, Joseph Hayhurst, Jennifer Short, Lawrence Gonzales and Hugh Pepperdine."

No Anna Pigeon. Frederick felt a wave of relief so strong it surprised him and he wondered why he hadn't asked for the names first. Mentally he wrote it off to the orderly progression of his mind but he suspected it was pain avoidance.

"Read them again." Jennifer Short rang a bell. He'd worked with a ranger with that name in Mesa Verde. "Again." This time he counted on his fingers as Tim read off the names. Eight.

"How many in a crew?"

"Twenty, sir."

"A squad?"

"Ten."

Twenty total, ten demobed, two invalided out.

That left eight. "You said there were ten missing. Who are the other two?"

"Emergency medical technicians running the medical unit. A Stephen Lindstrom out of Reno, Nevada, and an Anna Pigeon from Colorado."

There it was. Frederick felt the tightness harden into a knot. "Are you on all night, Tim?"

"Yes, sir.

"Keep an eye on things. Call me if there are any changes."

"Yes, sir."

"Thanks a bunch, Timmy. You've been super," Frederick added sincerely, remembering his promise to himself. Vaguely he wondered why he always waxed dopey in gratitude. It disarmed people. He'd used the technique so long it had become habit. A self-made nerd, he said to himself without rancor. Whatever worked.

Absently he turned the sound back on the television, banishing the emptiness of the room. Danny hopped along the back of the sofa and onto Frederick's head where he chirped happily, picking through the fine dark hair.

Of course Anna was on the Jackknife. Never had Frederick met a woman with such a propensity for disaster. In high school he'd known a kid like that, Desmond Gallagher. He hadn't thought of Desmond in twenty years but now he was clear and lively in Stanton's imagination. Desmond himself was a slight, pleasant, intelligent boy but he seemed a vortex for strange events. If Desmond walked by a liquor store there was a ten to one chance it was being robbed. If he sat too long at a bus stop odds were a nearby water main would break or a passing Brinks truck would lose its brakes and careen into a fruit stand.

Anna apparently had that lightning-rod quality.

She attracted you, Frederick thought, then wondered why he equated himself with a natural disaster.

Danny still on his head, Stanton rose and shuffled into the tiny kitchen. Dishes were washed and dried and put away and the stove top wiped clean. The one-man breakfast table, like every other flat surface in the house, was piled with papers and magazines.

Frederick had to read them before he allowed himself to throw them out. Information: one never knew what might be important. Stanton tried to assimilate it all and he was blessed—or cursed—with an excellent retention and retrieval system. At Trivial Pursuit he was unbeatable.

He dumped his unfinished scotch in the sink, then washed and dried the glass. Alcohol didn't hold a tremendous appeal for him but it seemed a man ought to have at least one vice to come home to and he never took to tobacco.

He put the glass in the cupboard with four others exactly like it stacked two by two, and stood staring into the shelf as if waiting for a floor show to begin on a miniature stage.

He was worried for Anna's safety, for her comfort, for her life. To a lesser extent, and perhaps more impersonally, he felt a kernel of sadness for the others, Jennifer Short, the Newts and Johns and whoevers. Those were the honorable emotions floating up into the dark of his mind like the messages that used to float up into the black window of a "magic" eight ball he'd been given as a child.

Less than honorable and more compelling was anxiety for himself, for his future. "Future" wasn't quite right. Destiny, Frederick thought, and smiled without being aware of it. To lose Anna Pigeon would be to lose some elusive possibility, some potential fate that was grander, more satisfying than the one that trickled in through his windshield and across his desk every day.

The woman represented a chance.

A chance at what, Frederick wasn't sure. Maybe the all-encompassing "brass ring." A chance he couldn't bear to lose. At forty-four, twice divorced, there might not be many chances left.

6

A roar filled Anna's ears. She didn't know if she was screaming or not. Probably she was. A terrible fear of being crushed by the immensity of what was coming poured through her and she had to fight down a panicked need to throw off the flimsy aluminum shelter and run. Nowhere left, she told herself. And she remembered her father's voice from childhood telling her if she ever became lost to stay put and he'd come find her. Stay put, she told herself.

She must have spoken the words aloud because fine, burning grit filled her mouth and throat. Each breath scorched the membranes of her nose and fired deep in her lungs.

Wind grabbed at the shelter, tore up the edges, thrusting fistfuls of super-heated air beneath. Pushing her elbows and knees against the bottom of the shelter where it folded under, Anna fought to hold the shelter down, the fire out.

Her mind rattled, grabbed onto a prayer long forgotten: *now I lay me down to sleep*—The end flashed like a telegram behind her eyes before the first words were formed and she jettisoned the rest as too prophetic.

I pledge allegiance to the flag of the United States of America . . . She filled her mind with soundless shouting. An impotent wizard fending off genuine magic with a barren incantation.

All hell broke loose above and around her.

Fire pierced the aluminum tent in a dozen places. Sparks were falling, burning through: the shelter was a scam. Soon she would burst into flame. Spurts of adrenaline racked Anna's insides. With the odd unpleasant thrill came a stray thought: how much of the stuff could one gland secrete? Surely a quart had been pumped through her veins in the last hour.

Red, burning, a spark fell on her sleeve. She flicked her arm but couldn't dislodge it. No smolder of cloth followed, no burning through to the flesh. With a jolt of relief that brought tears to her eyes she realized the sparks were not sparks, not embers, but pinholes along the folds in her shelter. The orange light was the light of the fire, but outside glowing through. Classes in fire behavior she'd thought long forgotten came back to her. All shelters had these pinpricks, signs of wear and age. Normal. Okay. Normal. *One nation under God, indivisible . . .*

A slap as of a giant hand smashed down on her shoulders and breath gusted from her lungs. She sucked in fire and clamped her jaws closed against it. The shelter pressed down on her back, the saving pocket of air squeezed away. The yellow pack she wore protected her spine but the skin on her shoulders bubbled and Anna bucked. The tent was pushed up off her back and the searing dropped to a tolerable level.

Her nose and eyes were packed with ash and dirt.

Through the thick leather gloves the little fingers of both hands, flat on the ground and holding down the shelter, began to throb. They kept the tent down, the devil out, and Anna didn't dare pull them away from the heat.

With liberty and justice for all.

Burrowing blind as a mole, she pushed into the sand and blessed all events social and geological that had formed the creek bed and led her into it before the storm broke. Sand wouldn't burn. A mental image of the creek bed melted, a ribbon of molten glass with their bodies burned into it like flies trapped in amber, flickered through her mind and she started again: *I pledge allegiance . . .*

The blessing hadn't extended to Hamlin. The ledge they'd left him on was covered in brush, half a foot deep in leaves and litter. LeFleur: maybe he'd cleared a space for the boy, covered him with a fire shelter. But it was no good. It would only prolong the burning. Newt Hamlin was toast. A ludicrous cartoon version of Wile E. Coyote burned to a crisp sprang up from Anna's subconscious.

And to the republic for which it stands . . .

The air was too hot to breathe. Anna pressed her lips to the sand, sucking slowly as her grandmother had once taught her to suck tea through a sugar cube. The little fingers of both hands hurt so bad she would have wept but there was no moisture in this convection oven shroud. No sweat, no tears. What was the temperature, she wondered. Five hundred degrees stuck in her mind but she didn't know if she'd read it, heard it or was making it up.

Five hundred degrees. Anna pushed her mind back to the days when she was still a meat eater. Chicken was baked at three-fifty. Roast beef at maybe four hundred. Twenty or thirty minutes for each pound. One hundred and eighteen pounds at five hundred degrees Fahrenheit—two thousand minutes. Numbers scrambled and Anna gave up the exercise. It would be a while before she was fully baked.

One nation . . .

Pinpricks of light on the right side of her tent swelled, the burning orange pushing through with such intensity they painted her sleeve like the beams from the laser sight on a high-powered rifle. The skin on her little fingers burned. In her mind's eye she saw it curling away, blackened and seared, leaving only the clean white of finger bones.

Noise crested, became solid, clogged the machinery of her ears and mind. Her head filled with the roar till it seemed it must explode. Her lungs were crushed with it, the bones of her body shaking, softening as if the molecules vibrated against each other. Anna hunkered into the sand, thought, like breath and sight and hearing, blasted away.

When Anna had grown accustomed to the idea of death the roaring seemed to lessen. She sensed it not so much with her ears as with her body. An infinitesimal lifting of the weight, a tiny shift in the crush. That something in the eastern sky that, while not yet light, somehow flaws the perfect hue of the night. The black of the noise was flawed. The firestorm was past the creek. And Anna was still alive.

This is good, she thought. This is good. Elation brought hope up from the depths of her soul and hope brought fear. Anna was sick with it.

Prying open grit-encrusted eyes, she rolled her head to one side. Within the shelter the sparks had moved like stars across the night sky. Orange glared through pinpricks, the small imperfections in the shelter, on her left side now. The fire had jumped the creek bed; it was moving on.

Anna held what fragments of painful breath there were left in her lungs, irrationally terrified that should she move, make even the smallest of sounds, this ravening beast that was fire would turn back, dig her out of her lair and devour her as wild dogs would devour a rabbit.

"Get a grip," she said through cracked lips.

Most assuredly she was alive. Her lungs hurt, she had to go to the bathroom—if she hadn't already—her hands and her shoulders burned, her stomach threatened to empty, but worst was the thirst. Dust stuck in her throat till she couldn't swallow. Lips and tongue were as unyielding as old leather. Her very skin and hair and fingernails felt parched. If she could have immersed herself in water she had little doubt that she would soak it up like a sponge, swell up half again, in size.

"Anybody alive out there?"

Anna thought the words were in her mind, in someone else's voice, and she wondered if this was where the angels came or one's life flashed before one's eyes.

The message was repeated: "Anyone alive?"

It was her radio, impossibly far away on her belt. More than anything in the world, Anna wanted that voice to continue. Inching one gloved hand away from the shelter's edge, she tried to get to the Motorola. Winds jerked the aluminum up and a sandblast of heat and ash choked her. She felt the shelter being peeled back, the fire coming back for her. Abandoning the radio she clawed the tent down again.

"Anyone?"

The voice sounded plaintive now and, to Anna's

fevered mind, farther away. Salvation was slipping from her. The rescue plane flying over her raft without seeing it. Rolling to one shoulder she used her weight to pin down the embattled tent. Where she pressed against the shelter wall she burned. Still she held out till she'd wrested the radio from her belt. Facedown in the sand again, she pushed the Motorola up close to her mouth and forced down the mike button with a clumsy gloved finger.

"I'm alive. Is that you, John?"

"Some roller-coaster ride."

Anna wanted to kiss him, cry all over him, marry him, have his children. "Who else has radios?" she asked.

"Howard's got one. Black Elk, are you alive out there?"

Radio silence followed.

"He's alive," Anna said, not because she believed it but because if he was he'd need reminding. "His hands and arms got burned. He probably can't get to his radio."

"Keep the faith," LeFleur said. "I'm on the far side of the wash from spike. It sounds like it's past me. I think that was the worst of it."

"Gee, ya think?" Anna said sarcastically, and the crew boss laughed. A wonderful sound: heaven, honey, nectar. "How long have we been in these things?" she asked.

A second or two ticked by and Anna got scared something had silenced John LeFleur. "Twelve minutes," he replied.

"Bullshit. I was sixteen when I crawled into this fucking thing, now I'm seventy-four."

Again the laugh. Anna had to bite her lips to keep from telling this stranger that she loved him.

"Black Elk," LeFleur was saying, and Anna cradled the radio to her ear for comfort. "Hang in there. This is the worst of it. Don't get out. Nobody get out. It's still hotter than hell out there."

Literally, Anna thought.

"I can still see the fire through my shelter," she said, because she needed to say something.

"We still got fire," LeFleur agreed.

Anna was comforted. She lay hurting in the sand with the radio pressed close to her lips. For the next hour she and LeFleur talked, keeping their courage up, hoping Howard Black Elk still had ears to hear them with. John had seen Joseph Hayhurst and Lawrence Gonzales stumble into the gully. Paula Boggins and Neil Page had been in the wash when LeFleur arrived. He'd shown them how to deploy the shelters Page had had the sense to salvage from the supplies before they'd run from the ridge.

Anna guessed Jennifer Short had made it, she'd been ahead of Anna when she crested the ridge. Stephen Lindstrom, Leonard Nims and Hugh Pepperdine were still unaccounted for. Anna didn't ask about Newt Hamlin.

Every growl and crack of the fire was described and discussed back and forth and slowly, with the flames, the terror passed. In its wake were all the burns, twists, scrapes and bruises that Anna counted herself lucky to be able to feel.

Finally LeFleur said he was going to leave the shelter. Anna was to wait. Science fiction settled over her brain and she laughed at herself, feeling as if she waited in a sealed space capsule while the captain ventured out on an unknown planet. Laughter dried up when images of "B" movie monsters took over her mental landscape and she realized how tired and afraid she was. Close, she suspected, to hysteria. She willed herself away from that edge.

"Come on out."

Briefly, suddenly, Anna didn't want to go. All the safety she'd ever known seemed summed up in the tinfoil shelter. The emotion passed as quickly as it had come and she pushed one hand out from beneath the tent, shoving up the edge. Smoke rolled in but it was no thicker or hotter than that inside. It took all of her strength to push herself to her knees, her house crumpling down over her back.

Then the foil was being lifted away. Again fear pierced deep: the fire was back, ripping at her safety, her flesh. But it was John LeFleur peeling the shelter off of her, helping her to her feet.

"You don't look much the worse for wear. All parts still working?"

"I guess," she croaked, and took the water he offered. LeFleur's face was completely black, like the "darkies" in the old minstrel shows. Mucus and tears had muddied the soot around eyes and nose and a thin trail of blood cut through the black from the tail of his left eyebrow. Through the soot his blue eyes shined bright as opals in whites so bloodshot they showed pink. "You're the best-looking thing I've ever seen," Anna said from the heart. She shed the yellow pack like a turtle crawling out of its shell and started to pull off her hard hat.

"Leave it," LeFleur said. "The Jackknife's not done with us yet."

Anna rebuckled the chin strap and took her eyes from him for the first time to look around.

Science fiction: it was another planet. Where there had been the green of living trees, the gold of needles, the red of manzanita, the blue of the sky, there was only gray and shades of gray and black. Instead of ponderosa, fir and sugar pine, black skeletal bones poked cruelly toward a sky gray with smoke or cloud. The ground was white, as white as death and bleached bone. Feathers of ash smothered everything, burned so deep and hot the soil itself was dead. Smoke, colorless in a colorless landscape, curled into a sky of the same hue, breathed out like the poisoned breath of a dying planet. Here and there, in a mockery of life, bright beautiful orange-red flames licked at what was left of something once living, cleaning the bones of the carcass.

Anna brought her eyes back down from the ruined hillsides. She had deployed her shelter downstream of a fork in the creek. Above where she and LeFleur stood she could see a boulder the size of a trailer house that had originally divided the creek in two. To the right was a silver-black corner of fabric where someone else had deployed. Whoever was within didn't move.

John laid a hand on Anna's arm. She didn't grab onto it but she wanted to.

"Where is everybody?" she asked.

"Some are downstream, I think," LeFleur said. "And there's a branch over there." He pointed south across a hump of devastated ground oozing smoke and heat. "Not far. Five or six yards. It joins the creek at the boulder. Most are there. I think."

For a moment longer they stood without moving. The only two people on this desolate world.

"Let's go," LeFleur said.

Time to see who had lived and who had died.

7

Wind swirled ash around their ankles. In places the sand was completely hidden. Flakes of soot eddied down on air currents as wild and changing as Medusa's locks. Cold drafts struck icy reminders of the storm front yet to come. Warm whirlwinds, sudden and smoke-filled, attested to the firestorm just past.

Clouds and smoke pressed close and the visibility in the bottom of the canyon was limited. Anna had yet to shake the feeling that she walked on an alien planet. Plowing through air so mobile and viscous, it wasn't a great leap of imagination to think it had a will—or wills—of its own.

She wanted to hold John's hand and, from the drawn look on his face, she doubted he'd mind. Too bad they were grown-ups. Side by side, shoulders almost touching, they trudged through the sand. Ahead, where the creek split at the boulder, wind curled around the stone in a sudden gust and formed into a shape that was almost human.

"Hold up," John said quietly, and Anna was

afraid. The shape continued to shift and settle. Finally it coalesced and she caught a flash of yellow.

"Hey!" she shouted as Stephen emerged from the choking mist. They ran and hugged and pounded backs and laughed like old friends meeting after long years.

"Looking good. Looking good," Stephen said over and over. His eyes were too wide. Whites showed all around the soft hazel pupils. Soot and dirt obscured his skin but for a racoonlike patch over his eyes where his safety goggles had clamped out the worst of the grime. This delicate flesh was stretched tight and the same dirty gray color as the ashes that made up the world.

Shock. Anna reminded herself to be on the lookout for the symptoms in herself and the others. If there were others. Shock would kill as surely as fire but it was a cold death.

Lindstrom grabbed Anna's hand, holding it so tightly the roasted pinky throbbed. It would have taken more than that to persuade her to pull away.

The tinfoil hut by the boulder began to stir and they stumbled over it to drag Howard Black Elk from his aluminum cocoon. Howard was in bad shape. The hasty bandaging job Anna had done on the run down the slope had been scraped away by his struggle to keep his shelter down. Without gloves, his sleeves in rags, the man's hands and arms to above the elbow were badly burned. How much of the charred-looking flesh was third-degree burns and how much dirt, Anna couldn't tell without water, light and a closer examination.

"It don't hurt much," Black Elk said, and Stephen and Anna exchanged glances. When a burn didn't hurt the news was bad. The nerves had been destroyed.

"We'll get you fixed up," Anna said, and was appalled at how halfhearted the promise sounded.

"You're looking good," Stephen repeated. He didn't sound any better than she did.

"Thanks for talking," Black Elk said. "On the radio, I mean. It was better than being alone."

"George and Gracie," Anna said. Howard stood there expressionless, his wounded hands held in front of him like paws. The big man swayed on his feet. "Get him down."

Stephen and John helped Howard to sit, out of the wind, his back to the sheltering rock.

"Where are you going?" he asked as the three of them straightened from settling him. Terror was clear in his face and voice.

"Not far," Anna promised.

"John's got to round up the rest of his flock," Stephen said.

Black Elk didn't look reassured. LeFleur knelt beside the injured man, reached down and turned the firefighter's radio on. "There's some down the creek. Watch. Call me if you see anybody. Don't let them wander by, Howard. Don't let them get lost."

The crew boss made it sound as if he was addressing Horatio on the bridge or the little boy with his finger in the dike.

Black Elk pulled himself together. Anna could see it happening: fear and pain pushed aside by strength and purpose.

"Split up?" Lindstrom asked LeFleur.

"No. You and Anna stay together. You've only got the one radio between you. You go on up the creek. I'll go back down where we were."

He pointed toward the arm of the creek meandering off south of the boulder roughly parallel to the section of creek where he'd met up with Anna.

"We'll check there last. And nobody goes far. Anybody you find, you send back here. Howard will field them in, keep them together." LeFleur looked at his watch. To read the face, he had to scrape off the soot.

"Takes a lickin' and keeps on tickin'," Lindstrom said. Anna silently voted him the man she'd most like to survive a wildfire with.

"Don't walk more than twenty minutes. Whoever didn't make the creek before that . . . didn't make the creek," LeFleur finished.

"Got a light?" Anna asked as she and Stephen started up the creek bed.

"Don't tell me you want to smoke?"

"Headlamp," Anna said. "Mine's in my yellow pack."

Lindstrom stopped obediently and Anna dug the battery-powered light out of his backpack for him.

September had brought shorter days. Smoke and cloud robbed the last light of its strength. Though it was only a little after four it would soon be dark. Anna had ambivalent feelings about that. Darkness had been her cloak of invisibility, her protector more than once. When she was a little girl she'd been afraid. Her mother once asked her of what, and Anna answered, "Of the things that jump out at people." Her mother had looked complacent. "I always figured *I* was the thing jumping out," she'd said. Since that time Anna and the dark had become old friends.

"This'll be a night full of ghosts," she said aloud.

"Anna, cut that out."

"Right."

Sneezing and hacking pulled them forward at a faster pace. Jennifer Short staggered out of the murk coughing as if her lungs would spew out onto the sand. "If I got an orifice that's not running, I don't know where it is. I swear I didn't think a person had this much snot in their head. Disgusting. Anybody got a clean hankie?"

"Blow your nose on your fingers," Stephen suggested.

"My, aren't we down-home?" Jennifer drawled. "Shoot. Gotta do something. Don't tell Momma." She cleared her sinuses.

In the strange half-light Anna noted the red of blood through the soot-impregnated glove.

"I'm an EMT, can I help?" she asked, parroting the accepted introduction of emergency medical personnel coming onto an accident scene. Stephen laughed, they all laughed way out of proportion to the feeble pleasantry.

"It's nothin'," Jennifer said. "You can patch it up when we find a spot to perch."

"Anybody back where you were deployed?" Anna asked.

"Lawrence and Hugh. I didn't walk back down. I came toward your voices. They deployed when I did. How close, I'm not sure. I haven't been paying many social calls just recently."

Drawn by the sounds of the living, two more zombies stumbled out of the smoke. Veiled in gray, soot blackening their faces, they were unrecognizable to Anna until Jennifer called out their names. Once labeled, their individual characteristics came back and Anna could see the men behind the dirt.

Lawrence Gonzales was a slight man in his early twenties with soft straight black hair and clear brown skin. If he spoke, it wasn't ever to Anna, but he smiled enough so that she thought him shy rather than sullen.

Hugh Pepperdine wasn't much older, if any—

maybe twenty-three or -four at most. He was soft and white and pudgy. Nobody could figure out how he'd managed to pass his step test to become a red-carded firefighter. Pepperdine talked too much and worked too little, from what Anna had gathered. The crew nicknamed him "Barney" after the treacly purple dinosaur. It was not a term of endearment.

Right now Hugh didn't seem to know whether he was a hero or a victim. While Gonzales coughed and spit and murmured "pardon me," Pepperdine babbled.

Venting, Anna knew, and neither she nor Lindstrom made any effort to stop the flow of words. Blame for the burn-over was cast on everyone from John LeFleur and Newt Hamlin to the National Weather Service and the National Interagency Fire Center out of Boise, Idaho. Somebody somewhere had screwed up and Hugh wanted his pound of flesh. Mixed in with his diatribe was a thread of personal heroics of the tiny real variety: falling down but getting up again, running and getting away. Chances were good the story would improve over time and Pepperdine would undoubtedly dine out on it for the rest of his days.

"Put a cork in it, Barney," Jennifer snapped when they'd all had enough. She shrugged out of her yellow pack. Pepperdine spluttered to silence and the five of them walked back up the creek to where Black Elk waited by the boulder.

Through the dim light Anna couldn't tell who was gathered around the rock but it was a goodly number and she dared to hope they'd all made it. All but Newt Hamlin, she corrected herself. Guilt tried to cut her but she pushed it away. No time for that now. Six dead heroes wasn't a better deal than one dead boy and five living if fallible human beings.

"Gonzales, Short and Pepperdine accounted for," Lindstrom said as they walked up to the others.

Paula Boggins sat near Howard, shivering in a white tee shirt and shorts. Second-degree burns covered the backs of her thighs and calves and the outside of her forearms. Liquid was seeping through the coating of grit.

"Somebody give me a brush jacket," Anna said. Pepperdine looked away as if he hadn't heard. LeFleur dug his from his yellow pack and Anna wrapped it around the girl's shoulders. Lindstrom's went over Paula's legs. Covering so much of her body, even second-degree burns were a serious injury. Hypothermia and shock were very real threats. "We'll get you fixed up," Anna heard herself saying again, and wondered with what. The only medical supplies not burned up in the fire were the personal first aid kits they all carried, wallet-sized plastic containers with a handful of Band-Aids and little else.

Neil Page had fared better than Paula. Long denim pants and a long-sleeved wool shirt had protected him from burns. The lower half of his face was covered in blood and the front of his shirt was stained with it. The blood was from a nosebleed, he said. He got them when he got excited.

"You're entitled," Anna said. No doubt that there had been some excitement.

Joseph Hayhurst had come through with nothing worse than the scratches and bruises they'd all gathered fleeing the fire. He sat quietly beside Black Elk, an alert look on his face and a strange little half smile on his lips. A well-mannered, well-brought-up man willing to lend a hand. The urbane pleasantness was jarring against the blackened face and wild Apache hair.

While Anna and Lindstrom were inventorying the

injuries sustained by the San Juans, LeFleur attempted to contact Incident Base on his hand-held. "No dice," he said as he stepped back into the defensive circle they'd formed. "Maybe from higher ground. Have we got everybody?"

Silence followed. Minds were numb. Too much stress, too little oxygen had made them stupid.

"Everybody," Gonzales said.

"Where's Len?" The question came from Jennifer. "He was with us carrying Newt out."

No one asked where Newt was.

"Len didn't make it," Hugh said.

"Did you see him?" John asked.

Pepperdine opened his mouth as if to say something then closed it and shook his head. "I just figured maybe the fire caught up with him."

Again the silence. They all looked at one another, everyone expecting someone else to speak.

"Last I saw of him was all ass and elbows hightailing it up the hill," Jennifer said. "I didn't see him reach the wash."

Anna looked around. Heads shaking. No one saw him reach the safety of the sand.

"Did anybody check the southwest fork of the creek?" LeFleur asked.

"You told us to meet back here first." Anna knew she sounded defensive but there was no way to retract. She wrote it off to fatigue.

Reluctance to go in search of Nims was palpable. Anna didn't know if it stemmed from the man's unpopularity or if they were all loath to leave this small island of security, the first they'd felt in a while.

"Stephen," Anna said. "Let's go. If he's there—" He might be in need of medical attention was her thought, but without tools and supplies there was little she and Lindstrom could do that was beyond the capabilities of anyone else present.

Lindstrom levered himself up and put on his hard hat.

"Keep trying Base," LeFleur said to Howard Black Elk as he got up out of the sand to join them. Howard's hands were so badly burned Anna thought the task would have been better given to Joseph till she saw the big man's face. Work, being needed, was all that was keeping Howard going.

"Lawrence, you and Hugh go back up the creek and collect the shelters and anything else we've left. We may need it. It looks like we'll be here all night," LeFleur said.

Paula started to cry. "Stop that," Jennifer snapped.

"Fuck off," Paula said, but she stopped crying and Anna was relieved.

Anna switched on her headlamp. Dust and smoke absorbed the light, rendering it virtually useless. Wreathed in glowing gray, she, LeFleur and Lindstrom spread out and began combing the width of the south fork of the creek that ran parallel to where Anna had ridden out the firestorm.

They all saw the shelter at the same moment. It lay perfectly deployed in the middle of the sand. The tent ridge was erect and the edges held firmly down. Ash had blown around it like a drift of dead snow.

"Len!" LeFleur called. Nothing stirred and not one of the three of them moved. "Len Nims!" Cold gray stillness settled back into the silence as the crew boss's voice died away.

"Let's do it," Anna said after a moment, and broke the line they'd formed upstream of the shelter.

Adrenaline hangover, post-traumatic shock syndrome, the dying light, the devastated landscape—something had robbed Anna of her nerve and she approached the silvery structure as if it housed poisonous vipers. There'd been a tent in Texas, where she'd worked backcountry in the Guadalupe Mountains, filled with diamondbacks. She thought of that now and half believed she heard the threatening rattle of tails.

"Len?" she said as she tentatively pinched up one edge of the shelter. A gloved hand in a yellow sleeve was exposed.

LeFleur, unable to stand the suspense, stepped up beside her. Grabbing the tent ridge in both hands, he jerked it up. Straps and edges tangled around the limbs of the man inside and a tumble of green, yellow and silver was stirred into the sand as the man rolled onto his side.

"Christ," LeFleur hissed. Anna and Lindstrom dropped to their knees and began pawing the foil away.

Light had been leached from the sky. The bottom of the gully was deep in a shrouded dusk. Beams from the lanterns on their hard hats danced confusingly across the prone man's shoulder and cheek.

"It's Len, all right," Lindstrom said.

Silence fell on that, the three of them locked up with their own thoughts. "Did he have a wife?" Stephen blurted out suddenly.

John nodded. "Separated, I think. Got six or eight kids. Good Catholic boy. His yellow pack is gone," the crew boss added.

Anna had taken her glove off and pressed her fingers down on the carotid artery in the side of his neck. "Nothing." She tried again. "Nope."

"This is a hell of a note." LeFleur was leaning over, his lamp shining on Nims's face. Like their own, it was blackened, the blue eyes staring from red-rimmed eyes.

"Smoke inhalation?" Lindstrom offered.

"The rest of us made it," the crew boss said.

"Heart attack?" Anna tried.

"Could be." LeFleur straightened up, dug a Pall Mall out of his shirt pocket and struck a match. "Christ!" he said as the match flared. He dropped it, the cigarette unlit. Fumbling, he pulled his hard hat off and the light from it. Rolling the body onto its belly he shined his lamp on Leonard Nims's back.

A knife handle was sticking out just below the man's left shoulder blade. Blood, mixed with soot and dried to a brown crust, colored the shirt and the sand.

Anna looked to Lindstrom, Lindstrom to John. The crew boss shook his head, struck another match and lit his cigarette. His hands were shaking.

"No way this could have happened," he said as if that would make the situation go away.

Anna turned off her headlamp, whether to save the battery or shut out the dead man she was unsure.

"What now?" LeFleur said.

"You're the crew boss," Anna returned.

"You're in charge of security."

"Damn."

8

Wind snatched up a handful of ash and blinded Anna with it. Somewhere on the far side of the ridge, probably melted into a puddle, were her safety goggles. She thought of them now and remembered the scrape of manzanita across her face. She must have lost them in that thicket.

Anna hung her head and tried to blink the grit away.

"What're we going to do about this?" LeFleur pointed to Len Nims.

"I'm thinking," Anna grumbled. The open eyes of the corpse were slowly filling with grit. "Pull the shelter over him, for Chrissake."

LeFleur drew the aluminum tent up over the body. Ash from his cigarette joined the feathery relics of pine and fir in Nims's hair. Ashes to ashes, Anna thought. Nims was beyond caring. Anna was too, she realized with a pang of guilt. Nims in life was a coward and a pain in the ass. In death he continued in the latter function. His staring eyes were a vicious reminder of mortality, his body a logistical problem, his murder a horrific complication. Anna hated him. Sorry, Len, she addressed the spirit world above the wash. It's just that I've had a real bad day.

LeFleur smoked. Anna's eyes finally cleared and she looked at Stephen. In the uncertain light of the crew boss's headlamp his face looked strained, exhaustion dragging down his cheeks and the corners of his eyes.

"We can't stay here," Anna stated the obvious. "It's too cold to mess around and too dark to do any good. I guess this is a crime scene. Shit. We'll leave it as is. Let somebody deal with it in the morning."

"Sounds like a plan," LeFleur agreed. None of them made any effort to leave. The sheer impossibility of the knife, the dead man, held them to the spot waiting for some rational explanation to manifest itself.

"Somebody must've knifed him when he got to the wash," John said, flicking his cigarette end into the darkness beyond their little cabal. "Maybe a fight of some kind over something—space—something. Len lost."

Anna could tell John liked that explanation. Both hope and finality colored his words. She liked it too, but it wouldn't fly.

"He's in the shelter," she said. "Even if the murderer got an attack of remorse and decided to stick the body in its shake 'n' bake, the thing would have blown off. I had a hell of a time holding mine down. Nims's shelter wouldn't've lasted five minutes without him alive inside."

Silence was agreement. Lindstrom and LeFleur had battled the fire's winds.

"After the fire passed us somebody must have

killed him," LeFleur said. "Jesus. You'd think they'd be too glad just to be alive."

"Blood is all dried up, brown and crusty," Anna pointed out. She didn't lift the silvery shroud to show them. They would remember.

"What of it?" LeFleur was belligerent.

Anna didn't blame him, her voice was sharp when she answered. "So it didn't happen in the last twenty minutes. The heat from the fire dried it, cooked it."

LeFleur stuck his hands in his pockets and looked toward the ridge where spike camp had been. Out of reflex, Stephen looked too. They were all wishing themselves elsewhere.

"Let's get the hell out of here," LeFleur said finally.

The meeting was adjourned. Using stones, they weighted down the shelter that covered Nims's body then trudged up the creek without light or conversation, saving their batteries figuratively and literally.

Clearly not before.

Definitely not after.

Nims had been knifed during the firestorm.

Since that was not possible, there didn't seem to be a whole lot left to talk about.

"What are you going to tell the crew?" Lindstrom asked LeFleur.

"The truth."

That was easy, Anna thought. Too bad nobody had the faintest idea what the truth was.

Gonzales, Pepperdine, Black Elk, Hayhurst, Paula Boggins, Jennifer Short and Neil Page were clustered in the lee of the boulder. Some clear-thinking individual—Joseph Hayhurst, probably—had begun to organize a bivouac. Two of the shelters Hugh and Lawrence had retrieved were spread to make a drop cloth to keep out the chill of the ground. The others were pressed into service as blankets. Temperatures were dropping rapidly. Mid-forties, Anna guessed. With the wind it felt colder.

Paula Boggins huddled miserably under the two brush jackets, shivering and hot at the same time. Tracks of tears streaked the black on her face and her jaw was clenched to keep her teeth from chattering. Sucking on a cigarette and letting the smoke trickle out his nose, Neil Page sat beside her, the blackened silver of a shelter pulled around him to shut out the wind. At every drag he coughed deep in his chest, mouth closed to keep in the smoke.

Paula and Neil concerned Anna. Paula was hurt but it was more than that. No firefighter expected to run from a holocaust the likes of which had caught them, but it was understood that there would be nights on the line with little or no comforts. Everybody got stuck out occasionally. Most times there was the luxury of a "Good Boy" box, a box of provisions helicoptered in for the night. Sometimes there wasn't. That was the deal. Firefighters tacitly agreed to discomfort when they signed on. The same was not true of Paula and Neil. Mentally unprepared, they were at a disadvantage. The mind could keep the body going a long time on will alone. Or it could shut it down.

Black Elk, cloaked in another shelter, cradled the radio on his lap between his elbows. Someone had draped a filthy neckerchief over his hands. Probably more to hide than protect them. That was good, Anna noted. A man at a car wreck she'd worked had been up and functional, talking, then went into shock and died when his left arm, severed at the elbow by a cable, was placed on the stretcher next to him by an idiot EMT. It was better Howard didn't see the ribboned flesh of his arms any more than he had to.

Jennifer Short sat cross-legged on the edge of the shelter used as a tarp. The yellow of her brush jacket, kept relatively clean inside her pack, provided a cheery note. The animation surviving the fire had lent her was gone. Her eyes were unfocused and her mouth crunched into a sad line. Only this morning, Anna recalled, she had heard her brother was dead, killed in the same fire that had taken its best shot at them.

Lawrence and Joseph had emptied the contents of the yellow packs—with the exception of Hugh Pepperdine's—onto the makeshift ground cloth. From the closed bitter expression on Hugh's pudgy face and the care the others took not to look at him, Anna expected there had been words over his hoarding.

Her brush jacket was on the heap they were inventorying and Anna leaned over Jennifer's legs to get it. "I'd offer it to you guys," she said to LeFleur and Lindstrom, their jackets gone to cover Paula, "but it's an extra small."

"Yeah, yeah, yeah," Lindstrom returned.

Anna folded herself into the sand beside Jennifer and dumped her hard hat and gloves in front of her. Jennifer came out of her stupor enough to look up. She shined her headlamp in Anna's eyes and mumbled, "Sorry," when Anna winced. "You look just about as awful as a woman can look and not be dead," Jennifer commented. "Do I look that bad?" Anna opened her mouth to reply but Jennifer cut her off: "Don't tell me. Anybody here got mirrors, you keep 'em to yourself."

That burst of life spent, Short sank into herself again.

In an attempt to get warm, Anna shoved her

hands deep in jacket pockets. Her fingers closed around something disgusting and she jerked them back out. Brown ooze coated her fingertips. For a second her mind blanked, revulsion the only emotion registering. Too much horror for one day. Then she stuck her fingers in her mouth. Chocolate. Sugar hit her bloodstream like a drug and she realized how hungry she was.

"We need to get some food into us," she said.

"Can I lick your fingers?" Stephen asked.

"You can lick my pocket. What have we got?"

Lawrence drew back from the cache of goods he and Joseph had collected, looking to Hayhurst to speak. Joseph tossed out two MREs—meals ready to eat—that someone had the foresight to carry in their yellow packs. LeFleur and Black Elk: the old-timers carried tools, socks and food. There was hard candy as well.

"That's enough to keep our blood sugar up," Anna said. "Nobody will starve by morning."

"Did you find Len?" Black Elk, easily the most severely injured, was holding up better than half the others.

"Bad news," LeFleur said. He pulled out his cigarettes. Two left.

"Give me one of those," Page said.

LeFleur tossed him the pack. To take a man's last cigarette; Neil Page, never high on Anna's list, slipped down a notch. Disaster brought out the best and the worst in people, she reminded herself. She'd not exactly been Little Mary Sunshine over the past hours.

The men lit their smokes while the rest waited for LeFleur's bad news. There was little tension. They could guess Len Nims was dead. Just not how.

One knew, Anna realized with a jolt. One of them

had knifed Nims in the back. Because her mind was overloaded and because what had happened was impossible—nothing flesh and blood could have moved through the firestorm to commit murder—it hadn't come home quite so graphically as it did at this moment that Nims had been killed by one of the people sitting in the sand.

In her career as a park ranger, Anna had dealt with murderers several times but never with such immediacy. Before she'd confronted them, the killers had time to regroup, begin—or finish—their justifications and rationalizations. The thin veneer of civilization had reformed over their faces.

As LeFleur shook out his match and, still standing, began his recital, she studied the faces of the others. Surely, had one of them done the unthinkable—not to mention the impossible—in the last few hours some remnant of the deed would remain.

Anna was disappointed. Hugh Pepperdine registered something resembling peevish annoyance. Neil Page sucked on LeFleur's last Pall Mall as if he hadn't heard. Maybe Paula's shock deepened slightly but Anna couldn't really tell. As for the others, they met it much as Anna had, with disbelief. It was too absurd to fit into an ordered mind. And they all fought in their own way to restore some kind of mental order.

Ever the good host, Joseph Hayhurst passed around hard candy as the crew boss explained the knife in the ribs. His story finished to the quiet crackling of cellophane as they unwrapped their butterscotches. LeFleur sat down. Small snacking sounds defined the circle. Overhead the winds whistled.

"Somebody's got to radio Base. Nobody knows if we're alive or dead." Pepperdine's voice was a whine. He gave them someone to focus their fear and anger on. Anna could feel the group warming to the idea of a scapegoat. Hugh Pepperdine was born for the role and Anna felt like giving him a swift kick herself but couldn't see that it would further any cause.

"It's beginning to look a lot like Christmas," a sweet tenor voice sang. Anna looked up to see who had slipped the surly bonds of earth. It was Joseph. "Snow," he explained.

Mixed with the windblown ash were icy flakes. Minute hissing sounds as the sleet hit hot coals corroborated his assessment. Bad weather could give their adventure another ugly turn.

Anna sighed. " 'Scuse me," she said. "I'm going to go find what's left of the ladies' powder room."

By the time she got back LeFleur had worked wonders with their makeshift camp. Shelters were rigged into a tent attached to the elbow of the boulder providing shelter from the winds.

Lawrence and Stephen had taken shovels into the burn and brought back live coals that they'd heaped in a sand fire pit inside the tent and the temperature approached comfortable.

"Not much left in the way of fuel," Lindstrom said. "But we can mine coals from now till doomsday. Even with the snow, it's a hot motherfucker out there. Pardon my French," he said to Jennifer. Stephen didn't wax obscene from habit, it was by design and for effect. This time he'd evidently hoped to get a rise out of Jennifer but she didn't come out of her lethargy enough to acknowledge him.

When the chores were done, Anna told herself she should talk to Short. Or, better yet, make Lindstrom do it. He was a touchyfeely nineties kind of guy.

LeFleur and Hayhurst were rigging one of the shelters to improve the natural windbreak created by the boulder. Paula and Black Elk had been moved to the snuggest corner. Food and water, not enough to satisfy but enough to survive, had been salvaged.

Anna cannibalized all of the first-aid kits and came up with seven rolls of one-and-one-half-inch gauze. She used a quart of water to cool and flush some of the debris from Howard's hands and arms. His palms and the spaces between his fingers were in decent shape. The back of his left hand and arm was swollen, the blisters ripped open and liquid oozing from tattered flesh. Regardless of what the man would admit, this one had to be hurting like a son of a bitch. The knuckles of the third and ring finger of his right hand were burned down to the bone. His right forearm was charred along the ulnar bone, the meat burned black in a strip an inch wide and three inches long. Around the third-degree burns were blisters the size of silver dollars and heavy with pus.

Anna dressed his hands and arms with hope, a couple of nondenominational prayers and five of the rolls of gauze.

"Don't bust open the blisters," she told him.

"Got to let 'em drain," Black Elk said.

"No you don't. Don't do it. Are you going to quit doing it?"

"You betcha."

Anna saw the twinkle in Howard's brown eyes and knew he was pulling her leg. He wouldn't mess with these blisters.

Paula's burns weren't nearly so severe but they covered a good chunk of her small body. Anna recalled the rule of nines from her EMT training. Second-degree burns were considered minor if they covered less than fifteen percent of the body and the face, hands, feet and genital areas weren't affected.

Arms were nine percent of the body, legs eighteen. A little mental arithmetic let Anna know Paula barely retained her minor status. Between ten and twelve percent of her body was burned. Barring any unforseen incidents Boggins should be all right. Anna was careful to drum that into the girl's head lest her own fear be her undoing.

Jennifer's left palm had a nasty cut where she said she'd fallen on the blade of her pulaski. Anna cleaned it, closed it with butterflies and bandaged it. Unless infection set in, it would heal.

By the time they'd finished it was full dark. Joseph distributed the food. Anna scored a can of beanie-weenies and marveled as she wolfed it down what a wonderful sauce hunger was. Lindstrom made Jennifer eat a can of Polish sausages, then set her to work feeding Howard slimy cold chop suey from a plastic MRE bag. Being of service would probably do Short more good than the nourishment would the big Arapaho.

When they'd finished eating, the firefighters threw their trash into the darkness beyond their enclave. Littering went against the grain for Anna but, with a touch of childish rebellion, she threw her empty tin toward the smoldering Jackknife.

"I'm going to try and make the ridge," she announced. "See if I can reach Base."

"Wait till it's light," LeFleur said.

The rebellion in her soul wasn't quelled and Anna could feel her metaphorical heels digging in.

"Somebody should go," Hugh said. Everybody ignored him. Pepperdine had dined in solitary splendor out of the sanctity of his yellow pack. Any shred of credibility he might have retained was destroyed in that instant.

"It's not more than a quarter of a mile," Anna said. "Maybe a hundred yards to the heli-spot. There's a road from there."

Silence argued for her. The rest of them craved contact with the outside world as much as she did.

"You're not going alone," the crew boss told her. LeFleur didn't want to leave his crew and nobody else wanted to leave the safety of the creek.

"Stephen will go with me."

"Thanks a heap," Lindstrom said, but he was stirring himself up out of the sand as he spoke.

"Go slow," LeFleur warned. "Test each step before you take it. Those stumps are still burning underground. You wade into one, you'll know it."

With that blessing and a pair of borrowed goggles, Anna and Stephen took two of the headlamps and walked out of the circle of light. At the bank of the creek they stopped. Around them the murmur of the wind and the hiss of sleet on the burn pushed the dark close. Cold crept down the collar of Anna's brush jacket and chilled her wrists between the leather of her gloves and the canvas cuffs.

"This might not turn out to be one of your better ideas," Lindstrom said.

"I'm open to suggestion."

"Let's go snuggle in with our compadres and wait till morning."

"Not that one." Though tired to the bone, with a backache that made her stomach roil and two booted feet that felt like hamburger, Anna was pushed by the need to take some sort of action. There'd been a blowup. A boy was burned to death. A man knifed in the ribs by a means she could not make heads or tails of. To sit, to wait, to try to sleep was beyond her. No rational act left, she'd chosen the least irrational. With luck it would even prove productive.

"Tractability is considered an attractive quality in a woman," Lindstrom said as she sank her pulaski into the bank and pulled herself out of the wash.

After half a dozen steps Anna was beginning to doubt her decision as well. It would be easy to get lost. All they had to navigate by was the slope. Ahead, the teeth of the fire were bared in hollow logs and stumps, glowing coals defying the petty attempts of the sleet to quench them. As winds eddied and shifted the coals brightened hungrily.

More unsettling was the fire that lived high in the burned-out snags. The forest was still there but it had been stripped of skin and muscle. Bare bones, charred a shade darker than the night, rose all around like macabre grave markers. High in many of the snags the fire gnawed at the marrow. An occasional crack or fall let them know that a lingering branch had been chewed off, brought down.

Anna kept climbing, pounding each step with her pulaski as John had told her. Behind her she could hear Lindstrom. He whistled "Ring of Fire" between his teeth.

Visibility improved as they gained altitude and their lamps began to be of more use. The ground flattened out and Anna stopped to catch her breath. So changed was the landscape it took her a minute to realize they'd reached the heli-spot.

"Home free," Lindstrom said as he came up beside her. "Wind's picking up."

A curtain of ash and grit blasted by them and they turned their backs.

"One damn thing after another," Anna groused.

A dirt road had been hacked from spike to the heli-spot and the going was easier. Lindstrom took the lead and she fell in behind him, relieved only to have to step where he stepped.

On the ridge the wind was shrieking. Without the sough of needles and leaves to soften its voice, the whistle was sharp and unkind. Stephen's light picked out the hulk that had been Paula's truck. The tires were burned off the hubs. One of the fenders was gone, blasted away when the gas cans exploded. The cab was gutted and the glass gone. In extremis the vehicle had been rendered black and elemental. It no longer looked out of place.

"Maybe it's still warm," Anna said hopefully. Brush jackets were made of unlined canvas, designed to protect from the scrape of branches and the wind. Now that the exertion of the climb was behind them, Anna was feeling the cold.

Using the truck shell as a windbreak, Anna dragged the radio from under her jacket. On the second try she reached Base. The line was etched by static but still readable. The two EMTs found themselves laughing from sheer relief. They weren't alone.

Gene Burwell, the incident commander, spoke with them and Anna sensed a hushed reverence awaiting her every word. Caught up in surviving, the rest of humanity had slipped her mind. Mothers, fathers, brothers, sisters, friends were waiting by radios and telephones, the television tuned to CNN, hoping for news. The drama of what they had been through hit her and she was proud even as she mocked herself for feeling heroic. It was with sadness and an unpleasant sense of failure, slipping from her recently acquired pedestal, that she told them of Newt Hamlin, of Leonard Nims.

News of the murder was met with a static-filled silence Anna couldn't break. Burwell had his mike button down and, she imagined, his mouth open.

Three times he made her repeat the information. Anna was shouting now, her face and the radio shielded by the truck's engine block and Lindstrom's body. Rising wind competed for air time. "What do you want us to do?" she asked.

Burwell was quiet so long she began to be afraid they'd lost contact. Finally his voice cracked back: "Can you last out the night?"

"I think so." Anna had told him of injuries sustained and supplies available. It was a rhetorical question. Could rescue have been sent it would already be on its way.

"The National Weather Service thinks this'll break tomorrow. We'll send the helicopters in for you. We've sent a crew up the road but they won't be there anytime soon. If this sleet holds, the fire will be out by then or close to it. One way or another, we'll get to you."

When the conversation was terminated, Anna felt abandoned. Lindstrom took the radio and relayed their information to LeFleur.

From far away, through the howling of the wind, came soft thuds, the sound a giant's footfalls might make in ash and dirt. Anna grabbed Stephen's arm.

"What the hell . . ."

"John, do you hear that?" Lindstrom barked.

Bile backed up in Anna's throat. The pounding was directionless. It came in intervals of a few seconds to a minute and seemed to be on all sides.

"Put your hard hats on and hunker down somewhere solid," the crew boss said over the radio. "The wind's felling snags. It'll be like a war zone out there till it lets up."

Lindstrom sat down in the ash, leaned back against the engine block and spread his legs. "A little ninety-eight point six?" he offered. Anna squirmed between his knees and he held her close, retaining what body heat they had left.

His hard hat clanked against hers as he leaned his head down. "I sure wish you were fatter. No offense."

"None taken. I sure wish I was home—no offense."

"None taken."

9

Timmy Spinks called Stanton a little after nine P.M. Chicago time. Frederick put down a block of cottonwood and the carving knife, muted the television and answered. As Spinks relayed information he'd received of a radio call from the surviving firefighters, the windstorm and the consequent recall of the rescue crew Base had dispatched up the mountain, Stanton saw the same news marching soundlessly across the TV screen.

He didn't take notes while Spinks talked. Names, dates, places, all the details would be remembered. He wasn't born with the talent. Like a waiter in a fine restaurant, over the years he'd trained himself to use his short-term memory. Later he would make lists. The lists served to make tangible his thoughts. Lists could be thumbtacked on maps, moved around, compared, rematched like puzzle pieces or decorators' samples.

For now Stanton listened, his eyes on the talking head on channel 4, his fingers running absently over his carving. Emerging from the block of wood was a chimpanzee in a cowboy hat and six-guns. Stanton remembered seeing one dressed that way in an old movie. Monkeys in various activities and ensembles cavorted on the windowsill behind the sofa. Stanton had taken up carving in hopes it would do for his hands what the television did for his brain; keep it occupied in harmless pursuits from day's end till bedtime.

The sculptures were good. He knew it without taking much pride in his achievement. Cynicism, carefully weeded out of his daily dealings with mankind, dripped from every knife cut. His monkeys weren't fun, not even a barrel full of them. Slyness, stupidity, greed, envy, arrogance, lust, deceit: seven sometimes deadly but certainly ubiquitous sins marred the simian faces.

Stanton's first carvings had been of people but they had proved unsettling. Too much disappointment was revealed. With monkeys the whimsy somewhat balanced the cruelty.

"What's closest to Lassen Park and the Caribou Wilderness?" he asked when Spinks had finished. "Reno?" Stanton didn't wait for an answer. A map of northern California and Nevada had risen from some recess of his mind. "Book me a flight out of here to Reno."

There was no hesitation before the "yes, sir." Spinks, deliciously damp behind the ears, wouldn't know Stanton wasn't godlike in his powers, that he didn't choose his assignments nor did he prioritize them.

Careful not to scatter wood shavings, Frederick folded up the newspaper laid across his lap. The air ticket he would put on American Express. The days on either sick leave or annual leave. He'd accrued so much of both, come December he'd be on Use or

Lose status anyway. The murder was a bit of unexpected luck. Stanton might even wangle official status with pay.

The thought of seeing Anna again gave him a thrill of adolescent proportions. The corpse was a fitting touch. He never saw Anna unless somebody died. If that wasn't the stuff True Love was made of he'd read all those Thomas B. Costain novels for nothing.

Setting his reading glasses down by the half-finished carving, he made squeaky sounds through pursed lips. Danny squeaked back and Stanton located him in the shadows on top of one of the bookcases. "Come, my little bird-brained friend. Time to return to solitary." As he put the budgie back into its cage it crossed his mind that he ought to buy Danny a companion. He could never tell if baby budgerigars were male or female but perhaps it wouldn't matter. Just somebody to pass the time with, twitter to in the dark.

"Maybe when I get back," Frederick promised.

Timmy got him on a red-eye out of O'Hare, through Salt Lake City, arriving in Reno at three-forty-eight A.M. Seven hundred and twenty-three dollars. Frederick abandoned American Express at the airport counter and put it on an already overburdened MasterCard. This would have to be paid off one month at a time along with Candice's college tuition.

Long legs jacked up against the seat back in front of him, Stanton cinched his seat belt down, then opened the envelope of computer printouts Spinks had given him: data on the Jackknife, maps of the area and background checks on the survivors and the two deceased still up on Banyon Ridge just east of Lassen Volcanic National Park.

He started with the report of the fire. Not because it held the greatest interest, but because it was going to be a long flight and he was saving the best for last. Last was Anna's background check, on the bottom of the pile. She wasn't a suspect, he was just being nosy. Law enforcement computer networks weren't the all-knowing, all-seeing, long, strong, electronic arm of the law that the various agencies would have the public believe, but they housed more dirt than a Hoover. A professional gossip's dream come true. Frederick had the highest regard for gossip. It showed people still cared what their kind did or did not do. It shored up the illusion of self-importance and morality that separated man from the monkeys he carved.

With a pleasant sense of anticipation that claimed him at the outset of most investigations, he began to read.

The Jackknife had been spotted on the twenty-seventh of September by a fire lookout in the Lassen National Forest. The burn had originated near Pinson Lake, California. Lightning, the cause of a majority of wildland fires, was not in evidence. The first victims, Joshua Short and his dog, were suspected of starting the blaze.

Frederick noted the plural and wondered what role the dog was thought to have played in arson. Maybe in the vein of Mrs. O'Leary's cow.

In eleven days the fire had grown to fourteen thousand acres of public land, thirteen thousand five hundred on National Forest land and five hundred acres in Lassen Volcanic National Park. An Incident Base camp of a thousand-plus firefighters had been established on the edge of the Caribou Wilderness east of the park and a spike camp within the wilderness area on Banyon Ridge. The fire had burned steadily but unremarkably until the cold front moved in over the Cascades. The blowup was a spectacular swan song, bringing the total acreage burned to over seventeen thousand.

Precipitation and cooler temperatures were thought to have stopped the fire. It was still being monitored and, though the crews were being demobilized, Gene Burwell, Incident Commander, would head the rescue effort to bring the stranded squad down off the mountain.

Chain of events, cause and effect, never ceased to fascinate Frederick. A cold front rolls over a mountain range; a brother is burned to death; a man named Nims is knifed in the back; Frederick notices he may be falling in something—"love" for lack of a better word; Joshua Short, alleged arsonist, sets a fire that overruns a spike camp where his sister has been dispatched. The world was a house of cards.

Stanton met Jennifer Short, a seasonal law enforcement ranger, when he worked a homicide with Anna in Mesa Verde National Park. Her steel-magnolia persona delighted him. He had a secret envy for those with colorful ethnic roots. Accents and cultural eccentricities provided good cover, a touch of mystery and romance. A middle-aged, middle-class, middle-western white boy had only his expected naïveté to fall back on when the emotional roads got rough. He hoped Jennifer's steel predominated over the magnolia for the duration. News of her brother's death, the trauma of the fire, might be enough to render her useless to Anna.

Through the musings and mental exercises it was never far from Frederick's mind that somewhere on the flank of a mountain, Anna was snuggled down with a murderer. It was so like her it made him smile.

Spreading out Timmy's maps, he noted with approval that the area of the fire and base and spike camps had been marked with colored pens. Somewhere in the circle of fluorescent orange was Anna. It wasn't hard to picture her in mud and trees and other uncivilized accoutrements. He'd never seen her anywhere else and wondered if he'd be disappointed should she ever turn up in Chicago in pantyhose, pumps and perfume; if the Calamity Jane aspect of the woman piqued a palate that had become slightly jaded.

Frederick had never been handsome enough to be vamped by cheerleaders, but he was single, straight and employed. It got him enough offers that he sat home nights by choice, not necessity. Danny, the monkeys and Tom Brokaw: not a bad life if one sent out for pizza.

He tried to picture Anna in his home and failed. Oddly, it disappointed him. He desisted and turned his attention to the background checks. The pages were run together on perforated computer paper. Stanton tore them neatly into sheets. Maybe the next generation wouldn't require the familiar comfort of rectangular white pages, read left to right, top to bottom, but Frederick found it helped organize his thoughts.

LeFleur, John Alvin, forty-five, white, male, five-foot-eleven, one hundred sixty pounds, brown hair, blue eyes. No wants. No warrants. Criminal history: felony draft evasion, 1971. Charges dropped. Possession for sale of Quaaludes in 1972. Two years' probation.

Timmy had tapped into personnel records and Frederick skimmed LeFleur's employment history:

high school education, independent contractor, carpenter, bartender. Before signing on with the Bureau of Land Management it didn't look as if the man had ever held a job for longer than eighteen months running. Firefighting was the one constant: summer '81, '82 and '83 with the Forest Service in Colorado; '86, '87 and '89 on the Angeles in California; '91 and '93 with the National Park Service at Rocky Mountains. Since 1993 he'd been a permanent resource management technician with the BLM out of Farmington, New Mexico. A GS-5, Frederick noted. No money in that. If the man's tastes ran to anything grander than beans and rice he needed the fires to make ends meet.

Nims, Leonard Lynn, forty-three, white, male, five-foot-nine, one hundred fifty-eight pounds, gray hair, blue eyes. No wants. No warrants. No criminal history. Served in Vietnam in '71 and '72. Honorable discharge. Graduated with an AA in Forestry from Lassen Junior College in 1977. Worked for the Bureau of Land Management in Susanville, California, from '79 to '90. A GS-9.

Stanton pulled the map across his knees and looked up Susanville. On the edge of the desert sixty or seventy miles south of Lassen Volcanic National Park was a small town of that name. Lots of public lands surrounding it. Either a logging or mining town, Stanton guessed.

Since '93 Nims had worked on oil and gas leases for the BLM in Farmington, New Mexico. A GS-7's pay grade.

There was a story there. Frederick could smell it. Three years with no employment history, then another job halfway across the country at a lower pay scale. It could be as simple as moving home to care for an aging parent or a love affair that tore up roots. But something.

Nims was the man with the knife in his ribs, Frederick reminded himself, and he reread the file to cement it in memory. Unless Nims had been killed by a psychotic, something he had seen, done, said, been or tried for had gotten him killed. If the reason wasn't too obscure or too bizarre, Frederick would probably find it. Professionally, he only struck out about fourteen percent of the time. In baseball he'd have been a star. In law enforcement he was just a good cop, better than most, not as good as some.

But I'm not above asking for help, he thought with a smile that was only a little bit bitter. That's part of my charm.

Pepperdine, Hugh Clarence. Age twenty-three, white, male, six feet, two hundred fourteen pounds. No wants. No warrants. No criminal history. Graduated cum laude from New York University with a degree in Environmental Studies. New-hire law enforcement ranger out of Aztec National Monument near Farmington, New Mexico.

Frederick had been to Aztec sightseeing after the Mesa Verde assignment. An Indian ruin and a visitors' center on a small plot of land constituted the whole of it. Delightful as it was to visit, he didn't imagine Hugh got much hands-on law enforcement experience. Chipmunks in the garbage would constitute a crime wave at the sleepy little ruin. Unless there was something that didn't show up on his records, Pepperdine would probably be of little help to Anna.

Short, Jennifer Katherine. Stanton started to move her to the bottom of the pile because he knew and liked her. Law officers had an aversion to believing someone they thought well of could commit murder, wanting to believe that somewhere in their heart of hearts they would *know* a murderer when they met one. Gut instinct, training, intuition, insight—something would tip them off.

Sometimes it did. Sometimes it didn't. In a former incarnation—one he was none too proud of—Frederick had invited a murderer to Thanksgiving dinner with his kids. Since then he'd learned to bake the turkey himself.

Shoving his reading glasses closer to the tip of his nose, he studied Short's file. No wants. No warrants. No criminal history. Graduated from Memphis State in accounting, 1985. From '85 to '94 she worked as a computer programmer for a local firm. Summer of '94, having completed a one-semester course in law enforcement at Memphis State, she was hired on as a seasonal law enforcement ranger at Mesa Verde.

Ran away with the Park Circus, Frederick thought, and envied her slightly. Should wild urges knock on his door, child support, alimony and tuition would see to it he sent them packing.

Black Elk, Howard Lawrence. Thirty-one, Native American, male, six-foot-one, two hundred ten pounds. No wants. No warrants. Criminal history: two driving under the influences and one drunk and disorderly in 1986. Nothing since. Undergraduate degree in archaeology from the University of New Mexico in 1989, master's degree in history from the same institution in 1991. Black Elk had worked in cultural resources for the Bureau of Land Management in Dove Creek, Colorado, until the present time.

Hayhurst, Joseph Charles. Thirty-three, Native American, male, five-foot-seven, one hundred fifty-two pounds. Black hair and eyes. No wants. No warrants. No criminal history. Bachelor of Arts from San

Francisco State in Renaissance art history. Employment record: 1988–1990, high school art teacher in Los Gatos, California. Summers with the NPS in Yosemite. 1990 to the present, Interpreter, GS-7, for the National Park Service at El Malpais in New Mexico.

Gonzales, Lawrence David, Hispanic, male, twenty-two, five-foot-nine, one hundred sixty pounds, black hair, brown eyes, high school graduate, A. D. Durango. Frederick frowned in annoyance, then looked to the bottom of the page. Timmy, bless his thorough and ambitious little heart, had penned in an explanation. An A. D. was a direct hire, not through any agency, that was often used when fires were bad and extra personnel were called for.

Wants and warrants. Frederick started out of the lethargy into which the sound of engines and the small print of strangers' lives had lulled him. Gonzales was wanted in Washoe County, Nevada, for aggravated assault, assault on a federal officer and grand theft auto. According to the map, Reno was in Washoe County. Gonzales might be dangerously nervous finding himself so close to home. Frederick set the Gonzales file aside. Before he landed, he'd have Spinks do some more checking. That in mind, he eyed the flat plastic AT&T phone outlet pressed into the seat back in front of him. He'd never used one, never seen anyone else use one. He hoped he wouldn't make a fool of himself when the time came.

Lindstrom, Stephen Marshal. White, male, twenty-seven, six-foot-two, one hundred eighty-seven pounds. Criminal history: arrested 1989 for obstructing traffic, fined and put on six months' probation. BS in biology from Nevada State University, ski instructor at Tahoe winters 1989 to 1993, wilderness guide for Outward Bound summers '89 to '93. 1993 to the present dispatcher for the U.S. Forest Service out of Reno, Nevada.

The two other reports were slim. Neil Page wasn't on anybody's computer that Tim could find. He'd been hired on locally. He had no record. The woman, Paula Mary Boggins, had two previous arrests but since they'd been when she was a juvenile, the records were sealed.

Frederick leaned his head back against the seat and closed his eyes, collecting his thoughts. Newly acquired information was shuffled through his synapses like cards through the hands of a contract bridge player. Categories and cross references fell into place: LeFleur, Nims, Gonzales, Pepperdine, Short, Black Elk and Hayhurst were from the Four Corners area. Close enough they could have had contact before the fire.

Lindstrom, Nims, Gonzales, Hayhurst, Boggins and Page, and possibly Short because of her brother, had a connection to northern California.

Nims, Gonzales, Short and Hayhurst fell into both geographical categories. In a field where transience was a way of life—and many seasonals and firefighters led a nomadic existence—this was not in itself suspicious. It was just more information and Stanton filed it.

There were two questions about most murders: why was the victim killed and why was he killed when he was killed? Anna might have some thoughts on that.

Murder was such a good icebreaker.

He opened his eyes. Anna's file, the only one left, was on his knee. Had his legs been six inches shorter, he could have used his tray-table as a desk. With the new "efficient" seating in the 727s, he couldn't fold it all the way down without straddling the plastic tray.

Pigeon, Anna Louise, forty, white, female, five-foot-four, one hundred eighteen pounds, brown hair, hazel eyes. Frederick remembered her hair as more red than brown and, at a guess, would have said her eyes were blue. So much for the credibility of eyewitnesses. No wants. No warrants. No criminal history. He was relieved and laughed at himself, unsure of what he had expected. A Bachelor of Arts in communications from the University of California. Seven years with the National Park Service in Texas, Michigan and now Mesa Verde in southern Colorado. That was it: no secrets, no insights. Closing his eyes again, Stanton rested his hands on her file.

He was a father, a government bureaucrat—albeit one with a tad of glamour still attached to his profession. He had a girlfriend of sorts—a woman he saw occasionally who would probably consider herself a girlfriend.

Jetting halfway across a sleeping continent to save a damsel in distress struck him as impulsive and not a little bit ridiculous. Particularly a damsel who may or may not wish to be rescued by him and who would undoubtedly have the ill grace to rescue herself before he could arrive triumphantly on the scene, spurs jingling, armor flashing and whatever else men were required to jingle and flash in these cynical times.

Still he wasn't sorry he'd started the quest. Opportunities to be a Fool for Love didn't come along every day.

10

Anna's fists were clenched on the front of Lindstrom's brush jacket and his were clamped around her neck, their hard hats jammed together like mating turtles.

Darkness was absolute and breath hard to come by. Soot and ash, galvanized by the rising winds, bonded with the air till it seemed a solid thing. Anna blessed LeFleur for the loan of the goggles and hoped the man wasn't suffering too badly in their absence. The kerchief she'd tied over the lower half of her face was so impregnated with dirt it served more to slow particles than filter them out.

The giant had gone mad. Footsteps melded into a cacophony of cracks and falls like thunder. The ground shook as ruined snags fell before the onslaught of wind. A dead forest, black monoliths burned by the hundreds and thousands and hundreds of thousands, many as tall as telephone poles, tons of charred wood and ash and cinder, was toppling. Every time the pounding came near, Anna cringed, though she knew she would never hear the one that crushed her.

A crash came so close it shook her insides. Chunks thrown from a shattered snag rained down in a visible shower of sparks striking holes in the night. For an instant Anna thought her eyes were playing tricks until points of fire pierced her cheek.

Ponderosas that had thrived on the flat-topped ridge, winter snows providing ample moisture and nothing between them and the sky, were being taken down. Orange fireflies swept by on the winds, battered against the metal. Pieces of burned debris, some large enough to rattle the darkness with their passage, exploded into the storm as the giants were felled.

A convulsive clutch cracked her hard hat against Lindstrom's as he jerked her to him. They were cuddled as close against the engine block of the truck as the laws of physics would allow, their legs pulled in, wrapped together. Anna's feet and butt were so cold they hurt and her back ached from being crimped into a bow. Muscles in her calves had begun cramping but she was afraid to stretch her legs. Anything she stuck out was liable to get squashed.

"It's the end of the fucking world," Lindstrom hollered in her ear. "We've got to get under this truck."

Again the ground shook. Anna pushed her face into the front of Lindstrom's jacket. "You first," she said.

"I may be too big. You go. You're little and scrawny. I'll get as much of me under as will fit. Go."

Boggins's truck rested on metal rims, the rubber of the tires lying in still-smoldering heaps. Clearance between the undercarriage and the ground felt like eight or nine inches—no more. Anna doubted she could squeeze beneath.

A wrenching blow from an airborne branch striking her right shoulder convinced her to try.

She threw herself back, shoulders on the ground, and tried to scoot along the edge of the truck's shell. Cramped so long in one position, her legs refused to work. Her feet felt as unresponsive and heavy as wooden blocks. Lindstrom was shoving against whatever parts of her anatomy he could lay hands on in the dark, trying to stuff her beneath the chassis.

Pushing and floundering brought pins and needles to her numbed limbs and, whining like a lost kitten, she began to thrash through the ashes.

Running had always made her more afraid. Looking in closets and under beds for the bogeyman seemed to make it almost a surety that, one day, he would be there. Fear, kept at bay from pride or necessity, ripped through her as she squirmed under the frame. Oblivious of the buttons on her jacket catching and bits of flesh snagged away by sharp edges of metal, Anna writhed in a frenzy of terror.

Then she was under. The fit was tight. Something metal and round pushed down on her chest. Darkness weighed heavily, even the small frightening relief of sparks was denied her eyes. An old horror of small enclosed spaces crushed the air from her lungs. A short segment of imagination's videotape played through her mind: her bloodied fingers clawing at a coffin lid. It was right out of a horror movie about premature burial she'd seen as a kid. Her mother had told her it would give her nightmares. Absurdity watered down panic and she willed herself to lie still and breathe deeply.

Scrabbling at her left elbow announced Lindstrom's attempt to join her and Anna was ashamed. She'd forgotten Stephen utterly. In her privately constructed hell she would have left him to die had that been the option. Once more she'd gotten lucky: human frailty shown, no damage done.

With the crippling darkness and noise, it took her a moment to grasp what Stephen was doing: digging, burrowing under. She almost laughed at the obviousness of it and began pushing ash and duff, protected from the fire by the body of the vehicle, away from her. Lying on her back she felt as helpless as an upended beetle, but it wasn't long before enough of a trench had been excavated that Stephen wormed his way in beside her.

A jarring crash robbed her of any voiced welcome. She felt his hand close over hers and they lay together like frightened children as the remnants of a tree hailed down around the truck.

Beneath the undercarriage the air was more breathable. Stretched flat, muscles uncramped, blood began to flow and some of the awful cold went out of Anna's bones. Conversation was impossible and she squeezed Lindstrom's hand to let him know how glad she was to have his company. Not much time passed before she felt his fingers relax, go limp. He was asleep or dead. Either way there was nothing she could do about it. Exhaustion weighed down her limbs, her eyelids and the soft stuff of her brain, but sleep would not come. The adrenaline cocktail mixed in her blood held onto the edge of consciousness even as the body fought for rest.

An idle mind is the Devil's playground, Anna thought as she sensed renewed cavorting of demon fear. To keep evil at bay, she tried to fill her skull with nontoxic thoughts: Piedmont, her pumpkin-colored tiger cat; Molly, her sister in New York;

Frederick. Frederick brought with him the baggage of her husband, Zachary, nearly eight years dead, and derailed that train. For a while she tried clothes, food, sex, raindrops on roses and whiskers on kittens, but they all fell away and claustrophobia returned.

Finally she latched onto murder. Not a pleasant subject, but one sufficiently captivating to hold her attention. And, since the death wasn't her own, heartening in its own way. Anna was surprised at how little thought she had given Nims's slaying and at long last understood how soldiers emotionally survived a war. Human comprehension was finite. For each thing added, something had to be taken away. Sometimes that something was grief, loss or fear, its place filled by the need to take the next step, hurdle the next fence.

Time passed, shock was worn away with busyness. Leonard Nims's death was just a puzzle as devoid of life as the corpse in the ravine. It provided the little gray cells with something to do other than conjure horrors with which to annoy her adrenal glands.

Why should anyone want to kill Leonard Nims? Without even reaching, Anna could think of half a dozen reasons. If this had been the Orient Express and Nims the body with the myriad wounds, the mystery would have been a lot simpler. Finding the person who *didn't* want to off him would have been easier than sorting through those with good reason in hopes of finding the one who was willing to walk through fire to accomplish the task.

Still, to crowd out the Devil, Anna listed motives. LeFleur had fought with Len. Over what, she wasn't sure, but John had gotten a fat lip out of the deal. Nims had come in with scratches. At the time

Anna'd thought they'd come from a branch. In retrospect, coupled with his surly manner, they may have been inflicted in some altercation, maybe over a woman. He had expressed his hatred of women at the time, at least those not "in their place." That was reason enough for Anna to kill him. Maybe it was good enough for Jennifer as well. Paula Boggins would probably find it sexy.

Stephen, John, Jennifer—any one of them might hold Hamlin's death against Nims. Anna doubted the rest of the San Juans knew yet that Nims had dropped the boy's stretcher and run.

We all dropped it and ran, she reminded herself. Hamlin's death was shared by the five of them. Unless Len had caused the accident that broke Newt's leg. Who would have known about that before the fire blew up?

Black Elk. He was a squad leader, LeFleur had called him down the line to help. If Anna had been able to pick up on where the blame was being laid, Howard was sure to. He was better versed in crew politics than she. Black Elk could have told Joseph Hayhurst; there would have been time before the firestorm.

Guilt could move mountains, unhinge psyches. She, Short, Lindstrom and LeFleur must each in some way feel responsible for Hamlin's death. Might the need to shift blame—push a perhaps intolerable weight off onto another—be enough to justify murder in someone's mind? Lindstrom could be unforgiving of those who failed to measure up to his standards. Jennifer had been known to carry a grudge.

Anna made a mental note to see if anyone had been special friends with Newt Hamlin.

That vein mined out, she moved on to physical

evidence. As an investigator, she'd pretty much bollixed that. The crime scene had been so thoroughly contaminated, any good defense lawyer could probably get a notarized confession found pinned to the corpse with the murder weapon suppressed.

I've had a lot on my mind, she excused herself, and tried to bring the scene into focus. The darkness was so unrelenting she wasn't sure if her eyes were open or closed and she couldn't move her hand to her face to find out.

Don't think about that, she cautioned as panic reared its ugly head. She squeezed her lids shut on the off chance they weren't.

She was lamentably bad about remembering names and faces but she was good with scenery. Nims's murder scene fell into this category. Background came into focus first: low hanging clouds, smoke, ragged black fingers poking at the sky, a manzanita bush burned so fast and hot the perfect shapes of the leaves were still embossed on the ash. The creek bank where a bit had fallen away, the simple brown of earth looking alive and colorful in the gray landscape. Around the shelter ash smoothed by the wind, no tracks but hers, LeFleur's and Lindstrom's. Sand. The silver shelter so carefully erect and tidy.

Anna stopped the film there.

The shelter was textbook perfect, like the drawings of how a shelter should be deployed. She remembered noting that at the time, being bothered. But events rushed on and she'd not had time to analyze why. Nothing was textbook perfect. Though she'd not had the opportunity to view her shelter from the outside, she expected it was crushed and rumpled, not creased neatly along its little pup-tent spine, corners all aligned. She'd seen Black Elk in his shelter. He looked like a baked potato somebody had been using for a soccer ball.

Ergo, whoever killed Nims had neatly put the shelter up around the corpse after the firestorm. Had it been earlier, the classic lines would have been mashed by the elements. The murderer knifed Nims during the firestorm and exited the shelter after the firestorm.

A very mortal human thing to do, Anna was relieved to note. Visions of a demonic creature of flame and smoke darting about with a knife in its paws during the blowup were exorcised. Considered in the light of reality, a commodity Anna felt had been sorely compromised by nature over the past hours, the murderer had therefore to enter the tent before the burn, remain inside with Nims, murder him, wait out the storm with the corpse, then exit and reconstruct the tent.

Cozy.

Why would Nims let anyone in his tiny shelter? He wouldn't, not even if their life depended on it. He'd let them die as he had let Hamlin die.

As they had all let Hamlin die.

Give it a rest, Anna told herself sharply.

Physical evidence. Screwing her thoughts down tightly against stray emotions, she contemplated blood: good, tangible, necessary blood. With a knifing there was often an impressive amount of the stuff. She'd seen it on Nims and where else? Page: Neil Page's shirtfront. He'd claimed nosebleed. Worth looking into.

Jennifer. Her left glove had been bloodied. She said she'd cut her hand. Something in Anna was loath to consider Jennifer a suspect and she had to remind herself murder was an equal opportunity employer. Jennifer was there when Len dumped

Hamlin. Jennifer had a brother just killed by fire. Under duress could she have slipped a mental cog and plunged a knife between Nims's ribs?

Literally if not metaphorically the woman had blood on her hands. Worth looking into.

Anna switched on the mental video again and watched herself lift the edge of the shelter: Nims's arm, the gloved hands; LeFleur shaking the tent like a housewife with a dusty rug; Nims's body, tangled in the straps, tumbling into view. Anna stopped the action there and tried to concentrate on the picture.

At a crime scene in a normal place she would have had at least the rudimentary investigative tools at her disposal. A camera, for one. There were a number of reasons to photograph a crime scene, not the least of which was that often, after the dust had cleared and one viewed the event through the perspective of the camera lens, details not noticed at the time became apparent.

Holding the image behind her eyes, Anna tried to do that now. Nims had been poured out of the shelter on his side, left hand above his head, the right palm up near his face. Anna tried to see if there was any expression but the soot that blackened all their faces masked his as well. All she could recall was the startling opalescence of his eyes.

She tried to see the entirety of the body: the right hand, the left—glove caked with blood—hard hat knocked askew, yellow shirt, drab trousers, blood, brown and crumbly on his back and left side beneath his arm.

The picture wavered, disintegrating under so much scrutiny. There was something wrong but Anna wasn't seeing it. Tomorrow—or today, she had lost all sense of time—she would make a proper study of the scene. At the moment the adrenaline had been reabsorbed and her body was claiming its right to rest. She drifted into sleep so deep and hard even dreams were shut out.

11

Anna woke from a nightmare and tried to sit up. Metal held her flat. Dream became reality. She was suffocating, life was being crushed out of her. Desperately, she began fighting for space and air.

"You're okay. You're okay. You're under a truck. I'm here. God damn it, Anna, cut it out!"

Stephen Lindstrom tweaked her ear hard and she began to put two and two together. The sum was not much more comforting than the nightmare had been. But there was light at long last and where there was light there was hope.

Faint gray pushed in around the sides of the truck's undercarriage but there was nothing to see: no stumps or ash, burned rubber; nothing but blank even-toned gray-white with light behind it.

"Snow?" she croaked through dry lips.

"Not much. I poked my fingers out. Maybe six inches or so. It kept us snug as the proverbial rug bugs."

Anna realized she wasn't terribly cold. The earth

and the metal chassis had retained some heat from the fire. Snow had held it close overnight. "Probably the only reason we woke up at all," she said. Freezing to death in a fire would have been just the touch of irony the gods delighted in.

"I've got to get out of here." Long hours—even those free from consciousness—of suppressing the claustrophobia were over. Now that she could escape, it became imperative that she do so. Working through the shooting pains in her hips and shoulders, she forced the joints through their first movement in God knew how long, crabbing her way from under the truck.

Snow broke free, fell in clumps down the collar of her brush jacket, jammed up under the edge of her gloves. The bite of cold brought Black Elk and Boggins to mind. Their burns would weep, robbing their bodies of fluid, of heat, opening the door to shock and hypothermia.

Nothing she could do about it at the moment.

She took a mouthful of snow and held it on her tongue, letting the melt wet her parched throat and lips. Shuffling her feet and swinging her arms to pump life back into them, she watched Lindstrom crawl painfully from beneath the truck, his left glove clutched in his bare hand. Elbows out, body flattened, he put her in mind of a giant insect in a Jules Verne novel, something trapped in lava, released by the fires.

Oddly, it made her nervous and she looked away.

The world was much changed from when they'd gone under the truck. Like Rip Van Winkle, it seemed as if she must have slept for a hundred years. What had been a world of black was now so white it was hard to distinguish between hill and hollow. A white sky, sifting fine flakes of snow through utterly still air, pressed down on snow-shrouded ground. Here and there the black skeletal arm of a tree thrust up, often capped with a rakish point of snow. Tree trunks, ten, twenty, a hundred feet long, were scattered like jackstraws, crisscrossing each other in ragged confusion.

Nowhere was there any color; not a scrap of green or yellow or brown or blue. Even the red-orange of stray embers was quenched, replaced by steam as colorless as everything else. What had once been a living forest, a kaleidoscope of life and color, now resembled a Chinese brush painting. Black ink on white rice paper; starkly beautiful but without welcome.

Lindstrom pushed himself to his hands and knees and Anna grabbed an arm to help him to his feet. "Did we die?" he asked, yanking his glove on with jerky irritated movements. "I'm pretty sure we did. God, but I feel hung over. What a bender we must have been on." He began to imitate Anna's shuffling dance, moving with the clumsy inexperience of a new-made Frankenstein's monster. "Not dead," he said after a moment. "Got to pee. Ghosts moan and rattle chains but I've never heard of one taking a piss. My, but this *is* good news."

Anna obligingly turned her back. It was the one instance in life where she credited Freud's much-touted theory of penis envy. With the snow and the cold she didn't relish the dropping of drawers that was becoming more necessary with each passing minute.

"Bet you wish you had a handy-dandy picnic device," Stephen said.

Anna heard the workings of a zipper and turned back. "My wish list is longer than Santa's at the moment. A bath, breakfast, pancakes, coffee—"

"Cut that out."

"Right." Anna pulled the radio from her belt and turned it on. Hand-helds worked on clamshell batteries. They weren't meant to run indefinitely. When it came down to it, she could cannibalize the batteries from her headlamp but she doubted they had much more juice in them than those in the radio.

Static pulsed as she monkeyed with the volume and the squelch. "Damn."

"Losing it?"

She nodded and placed a call to Base. Nothing came back but static. "What time is it?" she asked.

"Just before six."

"They're up. We'll try again when the weather lifts or maybe with another radio."

"Anna." Her radio crackled the name in LeFleur's voice.

"We're still alive," she told the crew boss. "Howard? Paula?"

"Everybody made it down here. Lawrence and Joseph kept the home fires burning. They're beat." Anna could hear the pride in his voice. "I heard your call to Base. Any response?"

"Not yet."

"Sounds like your battery is going. Save it when you can. What kind of shape are you two in?"

Anna looked to Lindstrom and he shrugged. "Good. We're in good shape."

"Could you check on Newt? It's a long shot, but if . . ."

"I'd forgotten all about Newt," Stephen said in a stricken whisper.

So had Anna.

"Will do," she replied. If Hamlin had survived the fire only to die of exposure because of their neglect it would be unconscionable. There were enough bad dreams to go around as it was.

Hamlin wasn't only merely dead, but, as Anna couldn't help parroting Munchkinlike in her mind, really most sincerely dead.

They brushed off enough of the snow to determine that the lump beneath was indeed a human form. During the firestorm his shelter had blown off. The body was burned till it was unrecognizable.

Fire had robbed the corpse of all the trappings of life: hair and flesh and eyes. There was no odor but the clean, slightly acrid scent of dust and Anna didn't find the body as upsetting as she'd feared she might. In fact, she was strangely untouched by it personally, feeling rather a generic sadness for those left living who had loved the boy.

Mostly, as she and Lindstrom slogged back up through the snow, climbing over downed snags heaped together like pickup sticks, Anna's strongest feeling was of hunger. Life asserting its dominion. After a grilled cheese, fries and a vanilla shake she would be better fortified to contemplate the great beyond.

From the ridge she radioed John and told him the news. It was expected. "Thanks" was all he said, and: "Had to make sure. Try Base again," he told her. "Meanwhile, I'll get another radio up to you. Pepperdine needs airing off anyway."

Anna called Incident Base again. The Motorola bleated static and she was surprised to hear Gene Burwell's voice rasp back.

His words were hard to understand and harder still to accept. Winds had felled snags across the logging road. How many miles he didn't know, but estimated the burn had covered at least four. The ground rescue unit had been recalled. Crews were already clearing away the deadfall but trees had come down by the hundreds. Weighted by six inches of new wet snow, more were falling all the time. Conditions were hazardous and the going slow. A helicopter was on standby. As soon as there was a break in the weather it would be dispatched. Till then the crews would keep on working but rescue by road wouldn't be that day. Possibly the next.

Disappointment, as strong and petulant as that of a child, swelled in Anna's chest and she had to keep her mouth shut to avoid saying something snippy.

"The weather will lift before then," Burwell promised.

"Does he think he's Willard Fucking Scott?" Lindstrom hissed.

Stephen's pique helped Anna rise above her own. "We're fairly stable up here, considering," she shouted into the radio as if volume could cut through the interference. "Hungry mostly."

"Stand by."

A long silence followed and Anna felt herself irrationally wishing for a reprieve.

"Maybe the cavalry arrived," Stephen said hopefully, and Anna laughed.

"My thoughts exactly. Not bloody likely. The cavalry's out clearing deadfall."

"Spoilsport."

The radio came to life again in a series of squawks and hisses. "Anna, this is Frederick, Frederick Stanton of the FBI."

If Anna had believed in prayer and believed they got answered she would have had to admit that at least this once the answer had been "yes." A hundred questions came to mind. The need to bawl and babble like a child threatened to overwhelm. Frederick Stanton.

Anna's throat closed and her eyes filled with tears. When she'd been in second grade, she'd broken her leg in a sledding accident at school. Brave and jaunty, she'd allowed herself to be towed in from the playground and carried to Mr. White's big oak desk. Then, when her mother arrived, she'd dissolved in tears. Because she could afford to.

"Ten-four," she said idiotically.

"Are you clear to copy?"

"Yes," Anna said, wanting his voice to go on.

By the time it dawned on her that "Are you clear to copy?" was NPS code for "Is the bad guy standing there ready to clobber you the moment his cover is blown?" the damage had been done.

12

Stanton finished relaying the criminal histories from Timmy Spinks's background checks.

"Anything more to transmit?" Anna asked politely. Receiving a negative, she made arrangements to call in every three hours and turned off her radio to preserve what was left of the battery. Depression settled over her in a palpable cloud, filling her lungs as surely as the smoke had. Safety, home, was held only by a tenuous channel forged through unstable air by a wave it took faith to believe existed. Withdrawal, Anna thought: the high, the crash. Hope and cocaine.

Any comfort she'd gotten from the first strains of Frederick Stanton's voice was blasted away. Suddenly, irrationally, she was angry at the man. Trundling through the friendly skies with hot and cold running stewardi, warm dry clothes and food, to broadcast criminal histories up to her private patch of purgatory.

Trapped on a ridge in the Cascades, one did not wish to know one's fellows that well. Untold secrets were the safest. Anna would keep her eyes open, learn what she could. None but a lunatic, armed with only a Swiss Army knife, her backup a grieving seasonal and a pudgy neophyte, would go hammer and tongs after a murderer.

Knowing would be dangerous.

Not knowing would be worse.

Stephen was standing close, shoulders hunched, his hands deep in his pockets, looking as forlorn as Anna was feeling. "I really, truly, deeply, honestly want to get the fuck out of here," he said morosely. "I promised God I'd never put my peas on my brother's plate and tell Mom I'd eaten mine if He'd just get me an Egg McMuffin this one time."

Anna laughed. "Obstructing traffic? I can't remember if that's a venial or a mortal sin. We're probably all being punished for your transgressions."

"He didn't mention indecent exposure, did he?"

Anna shook her head.

"They must have dropped that charge."

"I wish I'd seen the booking photos."

For a moment they stood staring at their feet. Soot-covered boots had trampled the snow into a gritty pack. Anna's toes were growing cold and the heat she'd generated on the expedition to find Hamlin had turned to a fine sheen of sweat rapidly chilling her skin. Without food it would become increasingly difficult to stay warm. A furnace had to have fuel to burn.

"Damn it." She kicked a grubby clod of snow.

"Fuck," Lindstrom said, and kicked it a second time. "Validating your feelings."

Anna nodded absently.

"Things are looking pretty grim for our intrepid band of adventurers, are they not?"

"Fair to middlin' grim," Anna agreed. "It sounds

like we may be stuck here at least another twenty-four hours, maybe more."

"Unless I'm given absolution for obstructing."

"And flaunting. So long as the snow lasts water is not a problem. No food, fear, cold, Dr. Death sleazing around in everybody's mind."

"Exposure," Lindstrom said. "Shock."

"Pudding, Barnaby, pudding!"

Lindstrom looked alarmed, then concerned as he studied Anna for incipient signs of insanity.

It annoyed her. *"The Matchmaker,"* she snapped. *"Hello Dolly*. 'Pudding' was the code word agreed upon so the boy from Yonkers would know when he was having a bona fide adventure. This is an adventure."

"What tipped you off?"

"Extreme discomfort." Anna shook free of self-pity, a physical act marked by a shrug and a shudder. "We're going to be fine. We focus on keeping everybody warm, hydrated and calm. That's all we've got to do."

"I've got a barn! We could turn it into a burn ward!" Lindstrom said in such a wonderful imitation of Andy Hardy Anna felt an uncharacteristic surge of optimism.

"Hey! Hey, you guys! I've been trying to reach you on the radio for five minutes." Hugh Pepperdine lumbered through the snow, his face red and gleaming with sweat. On his back was his yellow pack.

"What do you bet he's got food in it?" Lindstrom said.

"Failing that we could always eat him," Anna replied.

Gasping for air, Pepperdine came up beside them. "You gotta monitor your radio." He cocked a finger pistol-like at Anna. "You ought to know that."

Hugh was having way too much fun handing out advice and it crossed Anna's mind to snub him but she didn't. She was too hungry, too tired and too cranky. A snub might set off a chain reaction she'd regret. "Saving batteries," she said pleasantly.

Hugh pulled a radio from the pocket of his brush jacket. "Confiscated this from Howard. He's not law enforcement. I heard Base," he puffed. "I was about halfway up the hill. You should have waited till I got here. Didn't you hear him ask if you were clear to copy?" Pepperdine elaborately avoided looking at Lindstrom. This was secret cop stuff.

Anna was irritated on two counts: one, he was right, and two, he was Pepperdine. "What makes you think I'd've been clear to copy with you listening?"

Hugh ignored that. "What are we going to do about Gonzales? I've had my eye on him. I knew something was hinky. Assault on a federal officer. I go to the mat for my people."

Hot air pumped Pepperdine's ego with each word. He literally puffed up, the chest going out, the belly in.

"Nothing," Anna said flatly. She waited a moment for that to soak in. When Pepperdine opened his mouth to argue, she said again: "Nothing. We are not going to do anything. We are going to stay warm and dry and calm. We will be polite and helpful and when we get out of here Lawrence Gonzales will be the county sheriff's problem."

Hugh looked appalled. "He assaults a federal officer, murders Len and we're supposed to look the other way. That's pretty shoddy police work, Anna. Gonzales could just walk out of here anytime."

"That's right. And we don't know if he had anything to do with Nims." Anna was trying to drill some kind of sense into Hugh Pepperdine but had the feeling she was making no headway. Armed with a little information against his fellows and a little authority from the badge at home on his dresser, Pepperdine was learning that power corrupts.

"I think we ought to arrest the dude."

Dude. Anna doubted Hugh had ever used the word before in his life. He seemed fairly pleased with the effect until Lindstrom echoed "Doooowd" in diphthong-laden valley speak.

"Arrest him with what?" Anna asked reasonably. "And do what with him? Tie him to a snag with our belts? Lawrence may not want to be arrested. Have you got some sort of black-belt, kung-fu training I don't know about? We've been working, sleeping and eating with the guy for two weeks. Nobody seems to have suffered overmuch."

"Nims," Pepperdine said.

"We don't know that. Leave sleeping dogs lie. And give Howard his radio back."

Pepperdine hugged the Motorola protectively against his chest. "Howard's not law enforcement. It's just you and me."

"Jennifer's law enforcement," Lindstrom pointed out.

"She hasn't been to FLETC," Hugh snapped.

FLETC was the Federal Law Enforcement Training Center in Georgia where all permanent law enforcement rangers with the National Park Service went for training. Pepperdine was so fresh from its hallowed halls he was going to be a major pain in the ass. Anna suppressed a sigh.

"We'll work things out," she said. "You want a radio? Take mine."

Forgetting his trek up the hill had been to replace the radio with the dying battery, he snatched it eagerly, as if it was somehow invested with special authority. Immediately he switched it on and stowed it in his pocket. Anna clicked off the one she'd traded for, saving the battery.

When the three of them reached the wash, Anna told Stephen and Hugh to inform the others of the rescue efforts, cautioned Hugh to keep his mouth shut about the background checks and excused herself to do "girl things."

She wanted another look at the body.

Anna rocked back on her heels and sat quietly in the snow. Flakes, fine as silt, continued to drift from the air, more as if they were formed from the matrix of fog than falling from a distant cloud. Light was evenly spread, air and snow uniformly glowing. There were no shadows.

The shelter they'd used to cover Leonard Nims's body had been disturbed, the snow shaken off when the aluminum cloth had been peeled back. Someone had been messing with the corpse.

Anna surmised someone rather than something not because all animals had perished in the fire—many would have survived—but because there were heavy, human, fire-booted tracks. They neatly skirted a car-sized boulder in the stream bed as if this obvious sidetrack could obscure their origin. The trail came from the bivouac, stomped around the body and returned the way it had come.

Something had been removed or something added to the scene: incriminating evidence taken or misleading evidence planted. Cop-thinking, Anna realized. The obvious was more human and mundane:

curiosity. Somebody just wanting to see the dead guy. Cheap thrills. The fact that she'd said the corpse was not to be visited notwithstanding. Who was she? Some lady EMT with the word "Security" typed in after her name on her red-dog, the term used to describe the pink paper firefighters' time was recorded on. Out here the trappings of rank were stripped away. Nature was a great equalizer.

By the look of the drift in the tracks, they were several hours old. More than that Anna couldn't tell. Everyone but Paula wore fire boots. The tracks looked too big to be Jennifer's but Anna wouldn't even swear to that.

Having learned all she could from the outside, Anna moved to unveil the body. Nims had been dead sixteen to eighteen hours. With rigor mortis and the cold, his body was stiff as a board. Where it wasn't black, the skin was a dirty gray. Len's right cheek was dark and mottled. Blood, no longer moved by his heart, had settled in postmortem lividity. The blue eyes were still open but the orbs had begun to dry and they no longer had that startling brightness. Anna tried to close the lids with a gentle sweep of her hand the way she'd seen it done in a thousand movies but they wouldn't stay down. She found herself pressing too hard, felt tissue give beneath her fingers and made herself stop.

With the cold, the hunger, the isolation, a scary edge was being neared. That place where nightmares and reality become indistinguishable. They were all somewhere in the neighborhood of that chasm. Some closer than others. Anna rocked back on her haunches, made herself look away from the body and let the peaceful desolation of the landscape calm her febrile mind.

There were times it was not good to be too much

alone, she thought, and wished she'd made Stephen come with her.

At length her brain settled and she pushed on.

The footprints were most plentiful behind Nims's right shoulder and slightly to the rear. Anna moved to stand in the same place, leaned down and rolled the corpse back and toward her. It came up all of a piece and was surprisingly heavy. Sand beneath the body was compressed into the shape of chest and limbs as if Nims had tried to squeeze himself into the earth to escape the fire or his assailant. A thin layer of ice had formed where the body's heat, leached out slowly in the hours after death, had melted blown snow. Nims should have been frozen to the ground but whoever had stood here before had rolled the corpse up just as she was doing and rifled the pockets of the shirt. The button flaps were undone and the fabric pulled away from the body where ice had once adhered it to the flesh.

Since Anna had failed to search the corpse when they'd first found it, she could only surmise something had been taken rather than left. Cursing herself for a fool, she made a careful search of the body. Compass in the left shirt pocket. Right pocket empty. Len carried a leather knife sheath on his belt beneath his left arm. The sheath was empty. Dollars to doughnuts the knife was in his ribs, Anna thought. The handle of the weapon was of metal with holes cut out either for weight or style. By the size of the hilt and sheath, the blade was close to six inches long. Judging from the angle, the point of the weapon had been driven into the heart. There were no signs of a struggle.

Nims's trouser pockets yielded nothing of a telling nature: lint, Chap Stick, gum, a spare handkerchief. Somewhere along the line he'd shed his yellow pack—probably as he fled the fire—but the square canvas envelope that housed his fire shelter was still on his webbed belt.

The snap was closed and it struck Anna as peculiar. She was willing to bet there wasn't a person among them who'd taken the time to resnap the case after deploying their shelter. She opened it and looked inside, not sure what, if anything, she expected to find. It was empty but for a handful of crumbs. On a hunch she put one on the tip of her tongue: a cookie crumb. A number of things fell into place. When Anna returned to their bivouac she would count the shelters but she knew there would be only eight.

Nims might not share his shelter to save another's life but not everyone was so single-minded. In the 1980s, Anna remembered, winds had snatched a fire shelter from a man's hands. His buddy had made him lie beneath him, sharing his own shelter. Both men survived.

The crumbs in Len's shelter envelope: too lazy to carry the added weight of the aluminum tent, he had probably jettisoned it in favor of extra food. Just as nature was about to cull the idiot from the gene pool, someone had taken pity and let Nims into their shake 'n' bake. That would account for the deep depression in the sand beneath the corpse. Someone had lain on top of him.

Why save a man's life at the risk of one's own just to stick a knife between his ribs? Surely it would be simpler to let him burn to death? No investigation, no prosecution; just one little secret to carry to the grave.

Unless Len forced himself on his benefactor.

No signs of a struggle, Anna reminded herself.

With the firestorm bearing down it would have required utmost cooperation to survive.

An impulse killing, then. Something had happened in the shelter during the storm that had caused savior to turn executioner, driving Nims's own knife into his heart.

Anna remembered trying to breathe, to think, not to think, to remember the pledge of allegiance and keep her pinky fingers from being roasted. She doubted she could have focused on anybody else long enough to bother killing them.

She pulled the shelter back over the corpse. Nims's left hand with the blood-encrusted glove protruded from beneath the covering, reaching out as if for help. Anna grabbed the thumb and pulled. The glove slipped from the dead hand. She remembered noting when he'd come to the medical tent how small his feet were. His hands, too, were delicate and well formed. On a corpse they were unpleasantly human, touching. Anna wished she could tuck the hand under the tarp but it would mean breaking the arm and she wasn't up for that. Feeling she'd done something irreverent, she tugged the glove back in place.

The bloody glove argued against the instantaneous death other factors pointed to. To soak the glove so completely, Nims must have grabbed at the knife as it went in. Anna tried reaching her left armpit with her left hand. It was devilishly awkward but in great pain or fear might have been accomplished.

Having weighted the shelter with rocks once again, she followed the path of the grave robber back to where the others waited by the boulder.

The shelter LeFleur had rigged was surprisingly cozy and Anna had a strange sense of hearth and home when she saw the familiar faces.

Paula had been dressed in a spare fire shirt and wool trousers someone had had the foresight to stuff into their yellow pack—Black Elk, by the size of the clothes. And Anna recognized a pair of her own blue wool rag socks on the girl's feet. Lindstrom was sitting close, jollying her, and she was laughing. Better medicine still. Howard Black Elk leaned against the boulder, eyes closed. He'd gone a bit gray around the mouth. Though he was a strong man, his injuries were taking a severe toll.

The fire pit was well stocked with embers and Joseph Hayhurst had converted helmets into vessels to hold snowmelt. While Anna approved the Apache's enterprise it depressed her slightly. It was an admission they might be there awhile.

Pepperdine was haranguing John LeFleur about posting twenty-four-hour watches. The crew boss's mouth was clamped shut and his eyes fixed beyond the younger man's shoulder.

Back to the others, Jennifer sat staring out at the nothing peeling away above the creek bank. Her eyes were hooded, unseeing, and Anna knew she was at as much or more risk than the two burn victims. Most people at some time in their lives lose the will to live for a minute, a day, a week. It was possible Short's survival instinct had chosen the wrong place and time to abandon her.

Pepperdine saw her approach and turned from LeFleur to what he clearly hoped would be a more sympathetic ear. "Gonzales is gone." His tone made it clear he considered Anna to be at fault. "I told you we should've radioed John."

He hadn't but she let that pass. "Hey, John, what's Hugh been telling you?"

"Gonzales went to take a dump," LeFleur said bluntly. "Barney's got a problem with that, I guess."

"He's gone," Pepperdine insisted.

"Looks like Neil's gone too," Anna said mildly.

"Nature calls," Hayhurst put in, "and man answers. I kind of envy their regularity."

Hugh looked from Anna to John and back again. "I think somebody ought to go bring him in," he insisted. Color had come up in his fat cheeks and he was balling his fists.

"Suit yourself," Anna said and, sitting down, pulled her wet gloves off to warm her fingers over the embers.

A high ululating wail, like a child in terrible pain or a man in an extremity of fear, cut through the bickering. Little hairs on Anna's neck began to prickle and she could feel adrenaline pumping into her overtaxed system.

No one spoke. Paula clutched the sleeve of Stephen's jacket and Jennifer pushed a palm to her lips as though to stifle a scream rising in her own throat.

Again the cry came, high and clear and cutting to the bone. Paula began to whimper.

"Gonzales—" Pepperdine began.

"Shut the fuck up." Lindstrom. Silence, deep and awful, followed.

"Want to go see what it is?" LeFleur asked, and for the first time Anna heard a quaver in the man's voice.

"Not particularly," she returned.

Again the cry.

This time something cut it short.

13

Dawn never broke. With fog and drizzling snow the quality of the light never changed. Impatience gnawed at Frederick's innards like the Spartan boy's stolen fox, but he bore it less heroically. Gene Burwell, a well-groomed man of Santa-like girth and facial hair, was patient and understanding. Stanton realized it took a true gentleman to ignore his fidgeting.

Incident Base was still surrounded by statuesque ponderosa and fir, the manzanita still green. Snow gave the scene a holiday feel; white drifts on evergreen needles. But for two crews with six sawyers, the camp was devoid of the one thousand souls who had called it home for the last couple of weeks.

A low-boy with a D-8 Cat had been dispatched from the Forest Service office out of Chester, a logging town twenty miles to the south. Seven miles down highway from Base a helicopter sat at ready, fueled and loaded, with two EMTs standing by.

Burwell, Stanton and Lester Treadwell, a lean, wiry man in his fifties who was in charge of clearing the deadfall, had taken a four-wheel drive truck up the logging road toward spike camp as soon as it had gotten light.

The first few miles were clear, then the road turned along the side of a mountain and wound up through the black—part of the burn left by the Jack-knife. There they'd had to stop. Charred snags from a foot in diameter to some grand old trees that must have measured eight or ten feet across and a hundred feet long had blown down in countless numbers. The road and the land surrounding were crosshatched with black. Logs tumbled like wind-blown straw lay in a tangled mat. Even a man on horseback couldn't pick a path through the devastation.

Cigarette dangling from his lips, Lester Treadwell stomped around muttering, his grizzled hair sticking out from beneath his hard hat where he'd pushed it back on his bony skull in a frenzy of thinking. "These're big boys," he said. "There'll be fire in 'em for a couple days. Hell on saw blades. Keeps things interesting though. Six sawyers. I'll send them up to cut anything looks like it'll bind." For Stanton's benefit he explained that downed trees, piled like these were, created strange tensions. When cut there was always a danger of one of those tensions being released too suddenly and part of a tree snapping loose and killing or injuring the sawyer.

"That'll get us started but we need heavy metal. With that D-8 Cat we'll push this mess aside," Treadwell said.

"How long?" Frederick asked.

"A D-8'll push a lot of weight," Lester said, flicking a spent cigarette and pausing to light another. "It's a hell of a machine. We can clear a mile a day easy."

Burwell had estimated four to six miles of the road fell within the black. Frederick rubbed his forehead, knocking the borrowed hard hat askew. He hadn't asked Anna if she was hurt. She hadn't reported any injuries to herself but then she might not. He found himself thinking how small she was. Though she carried herself like John Wayne, she was only five-four. No fat to keep her warm.

Unless the weather broke, it would be four to six days until help could be gotten to the stranded firefighters, to Anna. Cloud cover kept temperatures from dropping much below the mid-twenties, but without food and shelter it would be a rugged few days. Perhaps deadly. Especially for a crew harboring a scorpion in its bosom.

"Up higher the fuel load's not so thick," Burwell said kindly. "It'll go faster the higher we get."

Frederick noted the man's concern and knew he wore his heart on his sleeve. Stanton was being obvious and he didn't like being obvious.

"We'll get cracking," Treadwell said.

Frederick had never handled a chainsaw in his life and Treadwell wasn't going to let him start now. Stanton knew Occupational Safety and Health Administration regulations as well as anyone; still he chafed at the enforced inaction till Treadwell took pity and signed him on as a swamper.

For two hours he dragged and rolled chunks of burned timber bucked up small enough it could be muscled clear of the road. Stanton's office-softened hands blistered. His back and shoulders ached. Time and again he had to leave a log for the other swamper because he hadn't the strength to shift it without help.

It had been years since he had felt like a ninety-eight-pound weakling. As he'd moved up in the organization, his mind and what amounted to a passion for detail had brought him honors. Brain over brawn, the pen over the sword. He couldn't even bench press his I.Q.

Shortly after nine A.M. Stanton's impatience, though still alive and well, had been tempered by hard physical labor. Nearly three hours of it had cleared less than fifty yards of road. Exhaustion brought with it some clarity of thought and he knew he would prove more useful in the less manly pursuits and wondered at himself for waxing so hormonal over a woman he'd known only a short while and kissed only twice.

Making his excuses, he borrowed an all-terrain vehicle from the incident commander and followed the logging road down to Base. The Command tent, Communications and Time Keeping kept the home fires burning. Portable space heaters powered by a generator in the back of a semi-truck trailer held winter at bay. Frederick was doubly glad of the warmth and fresh coffee. Glad for his chilled and tired body and glad, in a moment of pure unreflective selfishness, that it was not he who huddled hungry in a wash.

While he drank his coffee, thick with Cremora and three spoons of sugar, he allowed himself a small pleasant fantasy: warming Anna's square capable hands between his own, massaging feeling gently back into her little feet. Residual hormones kicked in, heating the dream too rapidly, and he shelved it. The time would come, he promised himself, when he could afford the luxury of distraction.

Four phones were hooked up in the Communications tent. Frederick took over one line to begin a series of calls. A spark of envy burned him as he thought of the wide-shouldered men with leathered faces running chainsaws and bulldozers and he quashed a sophomoric image of himself, newly Paul Bunyan-like, scooping a grateful Anna from the jaws of death.

Think, Frederick, he told himself. Think. It's what you're good at.

Nine-forty California time. Ten-forty in New Mexico; he would start with the Bureau of Land Management in Farmington.

One receptionist and one bum steer later he was talking with Henry Valdez, the head of the gas and oil leasing program for the three million acres of federal gas and oil reserves in New Mexico and southern Colorado.

Stanton was winging it. Without visiting the murder scene, viewing the corpse, interviewing the suspects or examining the physical evidence, he was at a distinct disadvantage. Anna would have to find out how it was done, who had means and opportunity. Motive was the only angle he could pursue. Until something that smelled like a lead turned up, he decided on the simple expedient of gathering information. As much as he could get.

Valdez sounded genuinely sorry to hear of Nims's death. Whether he personally liked the man or whether because the wheels of the Office of Personnel Management ground so painstakingly slow Nims's position would go unfilled for six months, Frederick couldn't tell.

Henry Valdez was disappointing, at least in terms of giving up personal information on his employees. Clearly the man disliked gossip and had little imagination where his fellow mortals were concerned. Nims was a good worker, well liked by most of the Bureau's oil and gas lessees. He was an avid hunter and fisherman and on good terms both professionally and personally with his clients.

Valdez was more forthcoming about the nuts-and-bolts aspects of Nims's job. Nims did the Environmental Impact Statements for proposed wells or the extension of leases on already existing wells. His background was in forestry but he'd acquired a solid understanding of geology.

Whether Nims was liked by his co-workers, Valdez didn't feel he was in a position to say. He was also not in a position to say why Nims had left the BLM in Susanville, California, to accept a position three years later at a lower pay grade. He did volunteer that, though it wasn't common practice, neither was it rare. Often government employees left to try their hand in the private sector or transferred because of personality conflicts.

What personality conflicts?

Valdez wasn't in a position to say.

Frederick scribbled down a few notes and moved on to John LeFleur.

Valdez seemed more than happy to gossip about the crew boss and Stanton guessed either his earlier reticence sprang from a sincere attachment to Nims or his sudden forthcoming attitude bespoke a pointed dislike of LeFleur.

According to Henry Valdez, John LeFleur was a dog in the manger. Always discontent with his lot and jealous of those around him. A dinosaur, Valdez called him, a man still crying because the college boys got promoted faster, because a man could no longer start in the mail room and become CEO. LeFleur had the firebug, he told Stanton. With some it's like an addiction. All John wanted to do was fight fire. He was getting too old to work the line but lacked the organizational and people skills to move up into overhead and hated anybody who did.

That smelled like the lead Stanton had been sniffing around for. "What about Nims?" he asked. "Did LeFleur hate him?"

"Hate might be laying it on a bit thick," Valdez said. "But they don't get along. John thinks Len gets all the breaks—that old song and dance. John just can't face up to the fact he's not manager material and never will be."

"Were he and Nims in competition for the same jobs, promotions, any of that kind of thing?"

"John may have thought they were for the fire management officer position we've got opening up, but John never had a snowball's chance in hell of getting it."

"Does he have a snowball's chance with Nims dead?" Frederick asked bluntly.

A moment's silence deadened the line. "A snowball's chance," Valdez said carefully. "But only just."

Frederick thanked the man and hung up. On a yellow notebook he'd begged from Time Keeping he wrote MOTIVES. LeFleur's was weak at best but perhaps the man didn't know that. If he believed Nims was all that stood between him and professional advancement it would suffice. Especially if a golden opportunity was dropped in his lap.

Under MOTIVES Stanton scribbled "JL firebug bites Nims" in a galloping hand.

Howard Black Elk's supervisor was out sick. No one answered the phone at the number either Paula Boggins or Neil Page left and neither had filled in the box under "Previous Employer." The head of dispatch at Forest Service headquarters in Reno, Nevada, Stephen Lindstrom's boss, wouldn't be in the office until after lunch. The Washoe County Sheriff's Office couldn't tell Frederick any more about Lawrence Gonzales than Spinks had already uncovered but promised to do some digging and call him back. No one answered the phone at all at Aztec National Monument where Hugh Pepperdine was purported to work.

Estelle Parker, the superintendent at El Malpais National Monument in New Mexico, was only too happy to talk. She didn't even pretend she had more pressing matters to attend to. She had been instrumental in hiring Joseph Hayhurst, she said, and was proud to have him on her staff. Words ticked out with the smooth assuredness of a paid political announcement. Superintendent Parker mentioned Hayhurst's Apache heritage three times and Frederick began to wonder if she thought he had something to do with the Equal Opportunity Hiring Program.

"What does he do?" he interrupted. The woman didn't reply right away and Frederick fancied she didn't have that answer quite so carefully scripted.

"He runs our cultural resources program."

Frederick waited. "Better fill me in," he said after a moment.

Again Parker hesitated. Stanton wished he was sitting in her office where he could watch her face. Over the phone he had no idea whether there was something fishy about Mr. Hayhurst or the superintendent simply didn't have the foggiest notion of what her employees did with their days.

"Well, I know he does evening programs," Parker said. "I hear they're excellent. And he is the curator for our museum—does the cataloging and so forth. He's in charge of preserving the cultural resources inside the monument's boundaries."

It's a small, small world, Frederick whistled under his breath. Leonard Nims wrote Environmental Impact Statements, the documents that, in essence, granted or denied commercial interests permission to dig, drill, ditch or otherwise disturb culturally sensitive areas in northern New Mexico. Joseph Hayhurst preserved Native American cultural resources. The two men probably knew each other.

"Does Mr. Hayhurst do any work for the BLM in resource management?" he asked.

"No . . . no. Why?"

The superintendent sounded confused and Frederick was reminded how little communication, much less cooperation, there was between government agencies. Fighting wildland fire seemed one of the few places they worked and played together nicely. Sort of like law enforcement agencies and the War on Drugs, Stanton thought. A politically safe and extremely well-funded bandwagon to jump on.

"Is he active in any preservation groups or movements outside the confines of his job?"

"I shouldn't think so. No. I wouldn't know." Either Superintendent Parker was a past master at stonewalling or she had no idea what went on in her park. Stanton suspected the latter. Unless she and Hayhurst were running drugs, such an elaborate show of ignorance was overkill.

Having made sufficiently polite and grateful good-byes, Frederick set down the phone receiver and stared blankly in front of him. What was missing? A hollow unsettled feeling swelled behind his breastbone, psychological heartburn. It was the feeling he got the night he forgot and left Candice standing in a tutu outside a ballet school in a bad part of town for three hours, and once when he'd refigured his taxes and discovered he owed fifty-two hundred dollars more than he thought.

Closing his eyes, he tried to clear his mind. One

of the phones rang and someone answered it. For a second he listened to see if it was for him. It wasn't.

That was it.

He checked his watch: twenty past ten. The radios had been silent but for the low-grade chatter of the dozer operator.

Every three hours, they'd agreed. That would have been around nine-forty-five.

Anna hadn't called in.

14

Anna realized she'd stopped breathing and consciously drew air deep into her lungs. The others were paralyzed as well. Screams, so viciously aborted, had rooted them in the sand. Paula's whimpering whetted the edge of the silence. Lindstrom put a protective arm around the girl's shoulders. From the look on his face, he was almost as frightened as she.

Black Elk gulped air only to expel it in a wet-sounding cough. Howard was in trouble: bronchitis and third-degree burns. For the first time it occurred to Anna that he might die. Injuries like his wouldn't prove fatal in the sterile and supportive confines of a modern medical facility. In the snow, in the Cascades, the outlook wasn't so bright. Not if they didn't get rescued soon.

"It's too fucking much," LeFleur whispered. Absently he pawed at his shirt pocket. When his fingers didn't find the expected smokes he spat into the snow. Pepperdine had squeezed in under the shelter, his back pressed against the boulder. "Really ups the old pucker factor, doesn't it?" LeFleur needled him.

The crew boss's smile was shaky but it was a start. Anna broke out of her state of suspended animation and stood up. Her legs trembled but she told herself it was due to fatigue and too little food.

"I guess somebody ought to check it out," she said, but she didn't move.

"I guess," LeFleur agreed. He didn't move either.

"I'll go if somebody'll go with me," Joseph Hayhurst offered. He got to his feet and carefully brushed the sand from the seat of his pants—as if anybody would care where he was going. This accomplished he looked at Anna with his strange little smile and gestured to the ruin of the forest. "Ladies first."

LeFleur had collected himself and, to everyone's relief, took control. "Joseph, you and Anna follow Gonzales's tracks out if you can. Me and Stephen'll try and pick up Neil's. See what we come up with. You've got a radio?"

Anna did.

Numbers seemed to reassure Pepperdine. He stepped forward importantly. "I'd better go after Gonzales."

"Stay here," Anna said curtly. Hugh would be of little use in a fight but that wasn't why she snapped at him. He got on her nerves and they'd been stretched a little thin lately.

"Jennifer can stay," Hugh said.

"Jennifer hasn't been to FLETC." Anna meant it unkindly but Hugh took it as a compliment.

"Roger. I'll be monitoring if you need backup."

As Pepperdine settled close to the warming embers, Anna looked past him at Jennifer Short. Her fist was still pushed against her teeth as if her brain had failed to shift gears when the alarm wound down.

Not good. Short was not a coward. In fact, her tombstone courage had nearly gotten both of them killed in an incident at Mesa Verde. To see her so diminished scared Anna. As soon as she got back, she promised herself, she would do something. What eluded her.

"Um, excuse me, but the trail grows cold," Joseph said, and Anna realized she'd been woolgathering.

Snow around the bivouac was heavily trampled but on the far side of the boulder Joseph found a fresh set of tracks. With more faith than certainty he and Anna began to follow them up out of the creek to the north.

Once clear of the wash the confusion of footprints thinned out to be replaced by a confusion of snow and felled snags. White humps gave way to blackened holes. What appeared to be solid ground would suddenly collapse, a pit of smoldering wood beneath. The going was slow but not impossible and Anna preferred it to sitting with too much to think about and too little to do.

Joseph, despite his earlier invitation, led the way. He was ten years younger than Anna and his eyesight that much better. In this landscape of sharp contrasts and directionless light, he was better able to pick a trail between hazards.

Anna was glad to leave him to it. Free from having to watch where she put her feet, she scanned the area. Snow draping over crosshatched piles of trees, unexpected open places, hummocks higher—or lower—than they seemed; she combed the broken landscape for any scrap of color or movement that would indicate life.

On such a surreal stage, monsters didn't seem impossible or even terribly unlikely. She and Joseph moved through a world that looked much like Anna imagined the inside of Dean Koontz's or Stephen King's mind might.

Surreptitiously, she crossed herself. She wasn't Catholic—or even necessarily Christian—but it seemed like a good idea.

Occupied as he was by navigation, Joseph failed to see the flash of yellow when Anna did. He was a couple of yards ahead of her, pushing against a forty-foot snag that had weathered the windstorm. If it was going to fall it was healthier for him to choose when and where than wait for a capricious Mother Nature to drop it on the unwary.

Anna slipped up behind him and touched his shoulder. With a startled gasp, he swung at her. Had she been taller and slower, his fist would have taken out several of her teeth. As it happened, a pratfall, functional if not stylish, saved her bridgework. For an art historian he was fast with his fists.

"Sorry," she whispered as Joseph, his face arranged in apologetic lines, helped her to her feet.

"Likewise, I'm sure. Why are we whispering?"

Anna was on her feet, Joseph sweeping her backside free of snow like a concerned valet. "Fire shirt," Anna said, and pointed. "Somebody's over there."

"Want me to go first?"

Anna did but since he'd asked she couldn't say so. "At least you didn't scream," she muttered out of spite.

"Our mothers covered our mouths when we were babies so the yellow legs wouldn't find us," Joseph whispered at her shoulder. "Didn't your parents let you watch *Wagon Train*?"

"Shhh."

All she could see of their quarry was a piece of

NoMex maybe six inches square—a shoulder or elbow—showing from behind a tumble of deadfall.

Torn between the urge to hurry to a man very possibly injured and the need to go slowly lest danger still lurked, Anna repeated her early EMT training: First make sure the scene is safe. That was always a good answer on a multiple-choice test.

Skirting a fallen snag, Anna got far enough around the piled debris so that she could see most of the man. He was seated on a downed piece of timber, his back to them. One green leg and hip, yellow arms and shoulder and the back of a head covered with a blue bandanna tied pirate-style low over the forehead were visible.

"Neil," Joseph whispered as Anna called: "Neil!"

Page squeaked and turned. When he recognized them he bent over at the waist, his head and shoulders disappearing behind the burnt wood. To Anna it looked as if he were picking up a small article and hiding it. Maybe in the snow or the logs. Maybe in his pocket.

In a few seconds it was done and Neil Page was trotting toward them, a mixture of relief and alarm on his face. "Holy shit. Did you hear that . . . that whatever? What was it? Somebody else killed? Fuck. A murderer's on the loose. That's all I need. It sounded like a girl—a kid maybe." Incongruous as it was in this torched wilderness, Page was pumping Joseph's hand with a grip a used-car salesman would have been proud of.

Whatever he was up to by himself on that log, the man had definitely had a scare. If not the strange cry, then something else. He was babbling and his hands trembled. Sweat mixed with soot glistened like fine bugle beads at his temples.

"Are those your tracks?" Anna pointed to a set of

prints leading across the small clearing at a right angle to the trail she and Joseph had followed, but from the opposite direction.

Page looked around as if the question taxed his cognitive powers, then nodded. Yes, they were his.

"We'd better keep going," Anna said to Joseph. "Since nobody has doubled back on the trail we were following, there's a good chance it's Gonzales."

"You can't leave me here by myself." Page was dangerously close to whining.

"Come on then," Anna said.

He liked that only a little better but fell in step behind Anna as Joseph led the way up the track they'd recently abandoned. Neil Page was a careful man. He hung back far enough he wouldn't lose them but too far to be of much assistance should the need arise.

The short burst of strength lent by fright had worn away and Anna was running on empty. Without food to restore strength and proper rest to restore sanity, she could feel muscle and nerve being drained with each log they climbed over, each stump hole they avoided.

Vision narrowed and concentration wavered. Soon she was just putting one foot in front of the other, seeing only the prints Joseph Hayhurst left in the snow. When he came to a stop, she almost tread on his heels before she realized it.

"Listen," he said.

Anna could hear her own breathing and his, the faint crunch of boots in the snow from where Page walked behind them.

"There," Joseph said.

A thump, something pounding into the snow, the dirt, a body—something soft enough to absorb most of the sound of the blow. Then a shout, a whoop, joyous, victorious.

"Wherever we're going, I think we just got there," the Apache said softly.

Ahead was a clutter of downed trees blanketed with snow. Beyond, as best as Anna could tell with the fog and the vague light, was a ditch or ravine backed by a steep hill. In places trees had blown down, pulling root systems out of the hillside. Great gouts of brown, living dirt spilled down over the apron of white.

The track they followed circled the piled timber and vanished down into the ravine. The scene was picture-perfect for a trap. All that was missing was a nice little bit of cheese set in the trail.

Anna looked behind her. Page had stopped twenty yards back. Waiting to see which way to run, she guessed.

"Let's do it," she said.

15

A second shout galvanized Anna. She moved past Joseph and down the trail. Mobility restored courage and she was surprised that she'd let the heebie-jeebies soak so deeply into her soul. Still, when yet another cry came she flinched and her step faltered. Lest Joseph notice, she walked faster.

A minute brought her to the end of the pile screening the ravine. She looked over her shoulder. Hayhurst was right behind her. She nodded and he raised his hand, slowing and falling back slightly. There were those with whom communication was effortless, even without words. Maybe especially without words. And then there were the Pages, the Pepperdines, the Bogginses who seemed impervious to all the words in the world. Like lovers, Anna thought. Some understood the merest touch, others even Dr. Ruth couldn't get through to.

Careful to step only in existing tracks so the noise of her footsteps wouldn't broadcast their approach, Anna moved into the crook where the trail hooked around the timber: the place the cheese would be were this indeed a better mousetrap.

From that vantage point she could see into the wash, a shallow creek, five or six feet wide and half that deep, carved by spring runoff. Black snags had fallen across, creating fragile bridges dusted with snow. Beneath were the tracks they'd been following.

Crabbing down the steep bank Anna lost her footing and slid the last few feet. So much for the element of surprise.

"Are you okay?" Joseph whispered from the top of the bank.

Anna made the "okay" symbol with thumb and forefinger.

"Can you see anything?"

Crouching, she looked under the burnt timber spanning the creek bed. For several yards the snow was crushed and trampled. Drops of red, startling in a landscape devoid of color, were spattered in a wedge-shaped pattern.

"Blood."

"No kidding?" Joseph slid down the bank, squatted in the snow beside her and shouted: "Hey, Lawrence! Are you in there?" Maybe it was a tactical error but Anna was glad to have the tension broken.

Footfalls crunched toward them, slow and labored as somebody frog-walked under the downed pines.

"Lawrence?" Anna echoed because she needed to do something.

Another whoop and Lawrence Gonzales crawled from beneath the tree trunks on hands and knees. Blood stained the cuff of his NoMex shirt and he pushed a shovel ahead of him. The blade left a red trail on the snow where it passed.

Lawrence grinned up at them, his teeth white and perfect, then reached back and Anna tensed.

"Breakfast," he said, presenting them with a badger dead of severe head trauma.

Joseph started to giggle, high and sweet like a young girl. Anna became infected and laughter bubbled out.

Gonzales looked from one to the other, a tentative smile on his face as if he was willing to join in if only someone would share the joke with him. "What? What's so funny?" This innocuous phrase tickled Anna and Joseph all out of proportion.

Anna could hear the hysteria, feel it hard in her rib cage. It was out of control but it felt good.

Gonzales was hailed the conquering hero by everyone but Hugh Pepperdine. He made a sullen remark about the Great White Hunter that brought the blood into Lawrence's cheeks but Anna thought she saw it for what it was, good old-fashioned envy.

Lawrence and John cleaned and skinned the badger with Black Elk's Buck knife. The San Juans, it seemed, went for the most part unarmed.

Just for something to do, Anna watched for a while, but the steaming entrails and the casual gore of men used to dressing game got to her and she retreated back to the relative civility of camp.

Howard and Joseph were talking quietly. Paula appeared to be asleep. Jennifer hadn't moved from where she sat back from the fire pit. Anna settled close to her, closer than she normally would, hoping to share some of her warmth with the other woman.

Jennifer's bare hands rested on her knees. Anna pulled off her glove and touched the back of Short's fingers. They were ice cold.

"Jen," she said softly. A second or two elapsed before Short responded to the sound of her voice. Jennifer's eyes were unfocused, her cheek muscles sagging like those of a much older woman.

"After we eat, we've got to talk," Anna said.

"I thought you were a vegetarian." Short spoke in a monotone.

"Under duress I've been known to eat my little friends. Jen, you've got to snap out of it," Anna said.

Jennifer's eyes were glazing over. Clearly, she just didn't give a damn.

Anna changed tack. Softness left her voice. "A man's been murdered. The only person I really know is you. I can't afford to trust anybody else. You've got to help me."

A flicker, the merest gleam of interest, enlivened Jennifer's blue eyes. From the distant past, Anna remembered her sister telling her one of the few things other than drugs and exercise that could help pull someone out of a clinical depression was helping others, virtue its own reward, medically speaking.

"After we eat," Anna said just as if Jennifer had agreed, and scrambled to her feet before Short had time to reject the idea.

Anna wasn't sure she wanted to know who'd knifed Leonard Nims. Even less did she wish the perpetrator to know she knew. But perhaps the puzzle would pull Jennifer out of herself, give her something healthier—if that was the right word given the circumstances—to focus on. If they turned anything up, they could hand it over to Frederick Stanton when they got off the ridge.

Stanton. The idea of rescue, of a savior, of warm caring arms, made Anna weak and weepy. With an unconscious twitch she shrugged the thought off.

* * *

Badger was as aggressive and feisty inside Anna's belly as the animal was purported to be when defending its position in the food chain. Having given up her carnivorous ways for nearly a decade, her stomach found the gamey meat a challenge to digest.

Seeing the look on her face as she carefully chewed each bite Stephen said: "It's fat-free and organically grown."

Anna shot him a dirty look and doggedly chewed on. Stephen's chunk seemed to be putting up a fight of its own. Cursing, he yanked his left glove off with his teeth and tackled the meat bare-handed.

"I'll eat yours, Anna," Pepperdine offered.

Anna scowled and swallowed. Nauseating, politically incorrect, stringy—it didn't matter. Strength was legal tender when the niceties of society were stripped away, and she had no intention of going bankrupt before she had to.

Failing with Anna, Hugh began eyeing Jennifer's meat. Short held the badger without interest.

"Eat that," Anna ordered.

Mechanically, Jennifer bit off a chunk, chewed and swallowed.

"Eat all your badger or there'll be no rat pudding for dessert," Lindstrom said firmly, and was rewarded by a ghost of a smile.

Everyone's spirits were up. Not only because of the food—they'd not been without long enough to suffer more than discomfort—but because they had taken back the reins. Lawrence was a San Juan. He'd brought home the bacon. No longer were they helpless children cowering and waiting for someone to rescue them. They were, as in Brando's famous line, "contenders." Men facing the wilderness. Even the women. Macho was a state of mind.

Though Anna didn't so much as fish—she hadn't the heart to stop that silvery flash of life—and the meat curdled in her belly, she felt it. All for one and one for all: the Musketeer credo permeated the group around the fire. Except for Hugh Pepperdine. He'd not forgiven Lawrence for being the day's hero and tried to build himself up and tear Gonzales down with a series of inane remarks.

They were so close in age some competition was inevitable, and Pepperdine's attributes, assuming he had any, Anna thought uncharitably, didn't translate well outside the city limits. Pepperdine lost on all counts: looks, courage and endurance. Probably the most damaging thing was that Hugh tried desperately to be liked and failed. Lawrence never had to try.

When Anna had forced down all the badger she could and Jennifer had eaten all she was going to, Anna announced: "I'm going to the bathroom," and fixed Short with a pointed stare.

As they walked away, Lindstrom called after them: "Firefighters don't go to the bathroom in groups." Laughter followed them out of sight around the boulder.

Seated on rocks a hundred yards up the creek, an icy fog isolating them from sight as well as sound, Anna told Jennifer everything she'd seen, thought or been told. She recounted the criminal histories Stanton had gathered, how the body was found, the knife, the blood on the glove where Nims had evidently tried to pull it out, the depression in the sand from the weight of the second body. She told Jennifer that the corpse had been searched by someone and of Neil Page's furtive hiding motions. Though Jennifer had been there when LeFleur came in with a split lip, Anna went over that.

Jennifer sat like a lump and Anna couldn't tell if she was listening or not. When she finished the recital, she waited. After a full minute, the younger woman stirred. Pushing her matted hair back off her face, she stared down the creek bed.

"Josh and I were close," she said, the words made visible as her breath steamed in the air. "He was just a year older than me and it was like we were the same age. He got mono when we were kids and got held back a year so in high school we were even in the same grade."

She was talking. Anna didn't much care about what. Cold seeped through the seat of her britches from the rock, stealing what little warmth Lawrence's badger had brought her, but she sat stock-still for fear of interrupting.

"We went to college together in computer science. Josh was smarter than me but I worked harder so we made the same grades. We'd go to parties together and wait for Mr. Right." Jennifer laughed.

There was nothing Anna could say. She thought of her sister and tried to think of the words that would comfort her if Molly died. There weren't any.

"What was he doing in this part of the country?" she asked to keep Jennifer talking.

Tears tracked the grime on Short's face and her nose was running. "Josh got a job programming a new security system for Harrah's in Reno—Reno's where he met Stephen. They were both into computers and hit it off right away. Anyway, the money was good and Josh said he needed to get out of Memphis for a while so he went.

"He fell in love with the mountains. I'm a river girl. I got to be by a big muddy river at least a few months out of the year or I just don't feel right. But

Josh said he'd found his spiritual home. He got all excited about trying to save it—you know, stopping logging or saving those speckled owls—whatever. It wasn't just a social thing with Josh. He really cared. That's part of what got me interested in being a park ranger, though I thought I'd mostly just like playing at it for a while. New places, new people, something different to do. Josh was doing some kind of environmental thing down where the burn started. I guess that place where he was camped was going to be logged off or something."

Instead Joshua Short lost control of his campfire, lost his life and destroyed the forest he was hoping to save. Anna kept her cynicism to herself. Now wasn't the time. There would never be a time.

"I'm sure gonna miss him," Jennifer said simply.

"Yeah."

They sat without talking. Anna tried to massage some heat into her hands. Jennifer fished a bandanna, more black than red, from the pocket of her brush jacket and smeared the mess on her face. Where she managed to wipe it clean she left streaks of white.

"What do you want me to do about Len's murder?" Short asked.

It was working. Jennifer was looking and sounding alive again. Anna rubbed the corners of her mouth with a thumb and forefinger to pull out the smile she felt building there.

"I'm pretty sure Nims was carrying food instead of a fire shelter like he was required to. We know he was knifed during the firestorm, probably by someone who'd meant originally to save the guy's life. We know he was stabbed by his own knife and something was stolen from the corpse. Start with

Neil Page. Go out and see if you can find whatever he was hiding out in the woods. Talk to him. We need to find out exactly where everybody deployed. The only person I actually saw crawl out of his shake 'n' bake was Howard."

"He could have killed Len, then got back into his own shelter," Jennifer said.

"I counted. Eight shelters. Nine people. There's no way of knowing whose is whose. By the time I figured it out all the shelters had been gathered and reused to make the bivouac."

"Okay. Howard's out," Jennifer conceded. "His hands are bad. I doubt he could've held a knife well enough anyway. He can't even close them."

"You do Page," Anna said. "I'll take John and see what I can find out. Be discreet. The last thing we want to do is stir up a hornet's nest."

"Might beat hunting badgers for breakfast."

Anna let the smile claim her mouth. Jennifer Short was coming around.

16

Lindstrom met Anna and Jennifer halfway back to the bivouac. "Sorry to break up the party," he said with no trace of his usual humor. "It's Howard. He's taken a turn for the worse."

Helplessness and fatigue bore down on Anna. The bad news brought back some of the dead look to Jennifer's eyes. Morale had grown so fragile. "Jen, follow up on that stuff we were talking about," Anna said sharply. If the comment aroused Lindstrom's curiosity, he didn't have the energy to pursue it.

Black Elk was lying near the boulder, his breath rattling ominously in his chest. Under the soot his flesh was chalky and dry, the rims of his eyes red. Joseph and Lawrence stood nearby talking in the hushed tones people use around a deathbed. Neil had disappeared again. Hugh and John were gone as well. Paula huddled as far from the sick man as she could get and still remain within the enclosure. The atmosphere of optimism brought on by their unexpected meal had evaporated.

"Where's LeFleur?" Anna demanded as she stooped and pushed under the jury-rigged shelters. There was nothing the crew boss could do but it annoyed her that he'd jumped ship.

"He and Hugh went up on the ridge to radio Base," Joseph said.

Anna glanced at her watch. The badger incident had chased the call from her mind. Aggravation grew along with the absurd notion that calling Base, calling Frederick Stanton, was her exclusive domain.

"Makes sense," she said, and knelt near Black Elk. "Hey, Howard, how're you doing?" Picking up his wrist, she held her fingers over his radial pulse and watched the seconds flit by on her digital watch: one hundred and twenty beats per minute and thready.

"I'm good," Howard said. "I breathe better when I sit up some."

Lindstrom knelt at the man's other side. "I laid him down after he lost his lunch," he told Anna.

"Don't like badger?" Anna laid the back of her hand against Howard's neck.

"Guess not."

Black Elk's breathing was shallow and rapid, his skin cool to the touch.

"Joseph, get me the yellow packs," Anna said. He brought them from where they'd been cached at the far end of the boulder and Anna and Stephen stuffed them beneath the injured man till they'd made a pad that propped him in a semi-sitting position. No longer able to hide his pain, Howard moaned when they moved him.

The bandages on his arms and hands were damp. Anna pinched up the skin on the back of his arm where the flesh was intact. It remained tented for several seconds after she released pressure. He was losing too much fluid.

"Better, big fella?" Stephen asked when they'd settled him.

Howard nodded.

"I've always wanted somebody to call me that," Anna said. Howard smiled for her but it cost him.

"Where's my radio?" he asked. "If I had my radio I could listen for you guys. There might be something."

His mind was wandering and Anna felt a clammy tickle of fear. "It's right here, Howard." She took the radio off her belt and put it on his chest. He cradled it with his ruined arms and seemed comforted.

"I can listen," he said. "You never know."

Anna rocked back on her heels and looked around. Their helmets were of plastic. "Somebody had those old-fashioned metal hard hats," she said aloud. "Where are they?"

"John wears one," Jennifer volunteered, and: "Here it is." The other belonged to Black Elk. They found it half buried in the sand next to him. "Get me some embers," Anna told Joseph. "Fill both these hard hats. I want one at his feet and one close up. We need to keep him warm.

"Paula?"

Paula Boggins looked up through a tangle of filthy hair. Anna had paid little attention to the girl once her superficial burns had been dressed and warm clothes found for her. When a whimper or a word did catch Anna's attention, she had written Boggins off as weak but in no danger. Seeing the dark blue eyes through the haze of hair, Anna noticed something else. Much as she hated the overused term "survivor," she knew one when she saw one. She'd seen eyes like Paula's in old photographs from World War II, and on the six o'clock news. She'd seen them when she'd pulled injured climbers off rock faces. The eyes of the people who made it. They crawled, fought, ate their fellows; they did whatever they had to and they lived.

"Paula, could you do me a favor?" Anna asked with sudden respect.

The girl responded to the unaccustomed tone with a slight straightening of her shoulders. "What?" she asked warily.

"Howard's burns are weeping. He's losing heat and fluid. I'm going to get some snow melted and keep it warm. Could you help him drink a little every few minutes or so?"

Paula looked behind her as if there might be someone else Anna was addressing. "Sure," she said.

By the time Joseph came back with the coals, the water was warmed and Paula had curled up next to the big firefighter with something resembling concern registered on her dirty face.

"Ember mines are getting few and far between," Joseph said as Anna placed the hard hats close enough to warm Howard but not so close they'd burn and banked sand around them to hold them steady.

"Where'd Lawrence take off to?" Lindstrom asked.

"He went to get Anna's radio back from Barney," Joseph said neutrally.

"Jesus," Anna growled. "I'd better go run interference."

She followed the now well-beaten trail up toward the ridge. Fog lay over everything, damp and disheartening. Raw air sawed at her throat as her breath came faster. The temperature hung around thirty degrees, not fluctuating with day or night. White rime was beginning to form on the black carcasses of the trees. Cold soaked through the sweat to chill Anna's skin and she found herself lost in a fantasy of a hot bath and a glass of hearty burgundy.

For a long moment she wished she hadn't sworn off alcohol. It didn't seem fair to feel guilt simply for wanting something when there was no chance in hell of getting it. And she did want it: the bath, the booze. Every cell in her body set up a vibration of yearning that brought saliva to her mouth.

Needing a distraction, she took the same medicine she'd prescribed for Jennifer: murder.

With the exception of Black Elk, any one of them could have killed Len. To push a sharp blade between the ribs of an unsuspecting man didn't require a great deal of strength.

The firestorm had descended in fury and left in a pall of suffocating smoke. Anna remembered seeing several people when she first stumbled into the wash but with everyone dressed alike, masked with bandannas and seen through veils of blowing smoke and ash, she couldn't say who was who. Or where. Or when.

The number of suspects could be significantly reduced by the simple expedient of finding out who was actually seen getting into or out of their shelter. It was possible lies would be told but Anna doubted it. The San Juans got along well enough for the most part, but they weren't close-knit—not enough to lie for one another. Disparate ages, jobs, agencies, backgrounds kept them from forming the esprit de corps often found in hot shots, the elite initial attack crews who trained and worked together for the entire season.

Howard, Joseph and Lawrence seemed to have formed the fastest friendship but even that struck Anna as more a friendship of convenience than a real kinship of like souls. She doubted it would lead to an exchange of Christmas cards.

Neil Page and Paula Boggins had something going but Anna had no idea what. Page treated Boggins with a contempt that smacked more of familiarity than dislike. Paula didn't show an overabundance of respect on her part either but she put up with Page as if she was used to him. Since he'd hired her, Anna assumed they knew each other from before, their affiliation mutually gratifying on some level.

They might lie for each other, Anna thought, and wondered why. Just a gut reaction, she decided. Page oozed sleaze and back in spike camp, Paula had come across as . . . Anna stopped walking and tried to find the right words while she caught her breath. They came to her in the cutting voice of Patience Bittner, a sophisticated hosteler she'd known on Isle Royale. Paula had come across as "low rent, blue collar, waitressy." Never mind that Anna had delivered her share of hamburgers and worked with her hands. The description fit if taken in the truly mean-spirited sense it was meant.

Who would Lindstrom lie for? Maybe Jennifer; they had the dead Joshua in common.

Sounds of a struggle brought Anna out of her reverie and she broke into a run. Just below the ridge she blundered into a shoving match. Lawrence Gonzales had the Motorola radio in his hand and was fending off an enraged Hugh Pepperdine with it. "Give it up, Barney," he was shouting.

Pepperdine, his face engorged with blood, flecks of spittle at the corners of his mouth, was grabbing at the smaller man in weighty but so far ineffectual lunges. His breath came in steaming gasps and he wasn't wasting any on words.

"Break it up!" John LeFleur ran down from the ridge. "Break it up!" he yelled again.

Gonzales heard and in the moment of his distraction, Hugh Pepperdine plowed into him. Both men went down.

Anna and John reached them at the same time and began pulling. Pepperdine's unpracticed fists were pummeling Gonzales's face and upper body. Lawrence wasn't fighting back but trying to protect himself from the blows with his forearms. "Get the son of a bitch off me," he yelled.

"Come on, Hugh. Let it go. Come on." Anna caught hold of one of Pepperdine's arms and tried to lever him off Gonzales. Hugh was out of shape and an inexperienced fighter but he was a big boy and she couldn't budge him.

"Break it up," LeFleur hollered a third time, grabbing Pepperdine by the collar and attempting to drag him backward.

A loose elbow clipped Anna on the chin. Her teeth cracked shut and light sparked behind her eyes. Letting go of Pepperdine, she retreated a few yards, deciding the better part of valor was to let the two idiots kill each other if they were so inclined.

Lawrence continued in a defensive posture but Anna got the feeling of a coiled snake. Barney'd better not push his luck, she thought, as she rubbed the ache from her jaw and checked to see if any teeth had been loosened.

"I'm gonna kill him, John," Gonzales grunted. "Get him off me." LeFleur jerked on Pepperdine's shoulder but Hugh was beyond reason. Anna doubted he could even hear them. He'd gone into one of those berzerker rages seldom seen off the playground. Had he been any good at dealing destruction, Lawrence, forty pounds lighter and several inches shorter, would have been a bloody pulp. This was probably the first fight Hugh had been in since third grade; hence the schoolyard tactics.

Recovered, Anna pulled herself together to give LeFleur a hand. Hugh, astride Gonzales now, pulled back a fist. Just as she caught it in both hers, Anna saw Lawrence's face change. Grimacing stopped, talk stopped, a cold professional look calmed even his dark eyes. In a move as quick and precise as a snake smiling, two fingers shot out hitting Pepperdine in the throat.

Hugh's eyes bulged, horror locked his lips back. Breath stopped with a wet choking sob. His hand jerked free of Anna's fists not to strike at Lawrence but to claw at his own throat as if he could pull out the dent in his pharynx.

Fumbling at his collar, Pepperdine collapsed sideways.

Gonzales scrambled to his feet. "Holy Mary Mother of God," he muttered. "Is he going to be okay?"

"You tell me," LeFleur growled. "Anna?"

She crawled over next to Hugh. "Take it easy," she told him in a voice intentionally laden with calm. "You're okay." She wondered if he was or if the blow had broken the cricoid cartilage. "Just lay back, breathe through your nose. Atta boy."

Pain and surprise had done more damage than Gonzales. As Pepperdine stopped hyperventilating he found he could breathe. Bit by bit his chest stopped heaving and some of the blood left his cheeks.

"Sorry," Gonzales apologized. "He got me mad."

Pepperdine began to sputter, trying to sit up.

"Lawrence, go on up to the ridge," LeFleur ordered. "When I heard you two locking horns, I dropped my pulaski. Get it for me, would you?"

Hovering behind the crew boss's shoulder, Lawrence stayed where he was. The sight of him looking so concerned and unscathed was having a deleterious effect on Anna's patient. "Is he going to be okay?" Lawrence asked solicitously, and Anna felt Hugh twitch under her hands.

"He'll be okay," she said. "Go get John's pulaski."

Lawrence backed away half a dozen steps then turned and jogged up the slope, clods of soot-blackened snow flying off the lug soles of his boots.

"He assaulted me" were Hugh's first intelligible words. "You saw. He assaulted me."

"Looks like you were doing a lion's share of the assaulting," LeFleur said. "Everybody's on edge. Nobody got hurt. But if you two go at it again somebody's damn well going to get hurt. I'll see to it myself. Got that?"

"He assaulted me." Hugh pushed himself up into a sitting position and faced Anna. "You saw. I'm a federal law enforcement officer in the line of duty and he assaulted me."

Anna took a breath, counted to ten in English, then again in Spanish. "Hugh, you have no jurisdiction. You're not in the line of duty. Period. We're all strung a little tight right now. Let it go at that. No harm done."

Pepperdine's face closed down, his eyes hooded. "Fine. If that's the way it's going to be. I'll take care of it myself."

"Drop it, Hugh," Anna said more sharply than she'd intended.

Hugh snorted, contempt sprayed out in a fine mist of spittle. Lumbering to his feet, he started down the hill.

Anna thought to call after him but didn't. Better

to get some ground between him and Gonzales for the present.

"God damn it," LeFleur said. "Why the hell did the worm have to turn on my watch? Shit. We're going to have to do something about that boy before he talks somebody into killing him." He sat back against a charred stump and closed his eyes. "Wish I had a smoke."

"Wish I had a drink."

"Scotch."

"Red wine."

"Lightweight."

"I quit," Anna said righteously.

"Bully for you."

Conversation languished. Anna curled her knees up and hugged them trying to retain what body heat she could.

"Tell me about Len," she said after a while.

"He's dead." LeFleur didn't even open his eyes.

Anna waited.

"What do you want to know?" he asked finally.

"Why did he take a job in Farmington at less pay than he'd had in Susanville?"

"He got in bad odor around these parts is my guess. He's got an ex and kids in Susanville. Maybe she ran him off."

"Was he fired?"

"Nobody's ever fired. They just sort of move on. Usually they get promoted. Bumping some bastard upstairs is the easiest way to get him out of your hair." A lifetime of losing embittered his voice.

"What did he do?" Anna asked.

"Lumber leases, I think."

"I mean to get 'moved on.' "

"Beats me."

"What does he do in Farmington?" Anna tried another tack.

"As little as he can get away with."

This was like pulling teeth. Anna waited.

"Oil and gas leases. He's supposed to do the Environmental Impact Statements. As far as I can see he just rubber-stamps them NSI—no significant impact."

"Do you know any reason somebody might want him dead?"

"Do you want 'em in alphabetical order or just how they come to mind?"

"Did you see anybody getting out of their shelters after the fire?" Anna asked abruptly.

"Just you and Howard, why?"

"Did anybody see you?"

LeFleur opened his eyes. "Oh, I get it. I've gotten a little slow on the uptake in my old age. You think I killed him?"

Anna said nothing.

"Fuck you, Pigeon." LeFleur closed his eyes again. After a minute had ticked by he said: "But I would have if I'd gotten the chance. He was a slimy S.O.B."

Anna had gotten all she was going to. She changed the subject to one closer to her heart. "What did Incident Base have to say?"

"They've got a helicopter standing by and nearly three-quarters of a mile of road cleared. If the weather lifts, we'll be home in time for supper. If not . . ."

"Did you tell them about Howard?"

"I told 'em."

Both of them knew it was meaningless. What could be done was being done. They couldn't clear deadfall any faster because Black Elk was losing ground.

"I almost forgot," LeFleur said. "You're supposed to radio that FBI agent. Secret squirrel stuff. He wouldn't talk to me."

Frederick Stanton wanted her to call. Anna felt an excitement all out of proportion to the event. What was she hoping for? Some clue to the secrets of the people she was marooned with? A key to unlock the murder? Or sweet words broadcast over high band radio for the world to eavesdrop on?

That was it and she mocked herself. People fell in love during disasters. It was provable if one considered statistics as fact. Plane crashes, boat wrecks, plagues, wars—all hotbeds of romance. Something to do with keeping the species going or reaffirming life.

It's the firestorm, the murder, she told herself. Anybody with a clean warm bed was bound to look good.

"Give me your radio," she demanded of LeFleur. Anna was damned if she was going to forswear all her addictions.

17

Frederick sat inside the Communications tent, his feet planted in front of the space heater. Four long metal folding tables were pushed against the canvas walls. Another had been placed directly under the one light bulb, bisecting the fifteen-by-twenty-foot space. Radio equipment and packing cases obscured the tabletops. More, along with manuals, clipboards and myriad forms, were jammed beneath. Idly, Frederick wondered how many acres of trees a crew had to save to make up for those cut down to provide the forms that fed the government's firefighting machine.

Between his hands, Stanton held a chunk of pine—white pine, Burwell had told him. It was lumpy and knotted where the branch had grown up against an unforgiving surface and been forced to make a ninety-degree turn. Bark still clung to it in places and it smelled pleasantly of pitch. Frederick turned it round and round, feeling for the monkeys within. The carving was clear in his mind: two monkeys tied together by a telephone line trying desperately to move in opposite directions. He just needed to find the picture in the wood grain.

Whittling helped to pass the time while he waited for the phone to ring, the radio to come to life.

Investigation was a waiting game: waiting for calls, reports, evidence; waiting in offices, parked cars, restaurants. Waiting in the brush and in alleyways. Frederick was good at it. Waiting was when he unfettered his mind, let the known and unknown tumble around without any imposed order. Intuition, that moment where the whole exceeded the sum of the parts, only came when he let go of his lists and his plans.

Whatever Anna Pigeon's virtues were, he suspected patience—waiting—wasn't one of them. As far as he knew she'd only worked three homicides in her career. Over the course of twenty-four years with the Federal Bureau of Investigation, he had been involved with so many cases he couldn't readily put a number to them. In the early years he assisted, in the middle he ran them. More and more lately he found himself assigning cases. Experience had given him a strong mistrust of people.

Coming to view the world as divided into two groups, Us and The Assholes, was an occupational hazard in law enforcement. Frederick wasn't quite that far gone, but he knew murder led to more murder. Maybe the killers discovered how easy it was. Or how little life really mattered. Some of them liked the power. Some got scared. But somewhere along the line every single one of them had come to the conclusion that the taking of another's life was the solution to their problems. If it worked—and in the short run it usually did—the next time they ran into difficulties they were apt to apply the same remedy.

Anna was first and foremost a park ranger. Stanton had nothing against park rangers. As a group he rather liked them. But they'd never struck him as the cutting edge of law enforcement. Most were too ready to believe the best of people. Not about the little stuff—they knew everybody littered and fed the animals—but they didn't seem to grasp the concept of true malice. Rangers worked on the premise that evil stemmed from ignorance; that John Q. Public could be educated out of his wicked ways.

Anna wouldn't be careful enough. She wouldn't watch her back. Unless she knew who the killer was. Most killers were opportunistic. If Anna knew who it was she could see to it no opportunity presented itself.

Frederick set aside his unborn monkeys and picked up the notepad beside the telephone. His morning had not been wasted and he was forming a colorful police sketch of the personalities Anna contended with. The eclectic nature of fire camp had brought together strange bedfellows. Because of the small-world nature of fire fighting and the regionalism for both local hires and interagency crews, there was a good deal of cross-pollination.

As a young agent Frederick remembered being surprised at how often and successfully the "do you know . . ." game was played. Professional circles were tight. Digging down a layer or two invariably somebody knew somebody who knew you. The same had held true when he'd pursued his investigation of the fire camp personnel.

Gonzales, Lawrence. The Washoe County Sheriff had returned Frederick's call shortly before eleven A.M. The case was before his time but the charges weren't being pursued. There was little interest in hauling Gonzales back to Nevada to stand trial. Gonzales was known to have a quick and violent temper, the sheriff said—he knew the boy's family—but there was no real harm in him. Reading between the lines, Stanton guessed the sheriff believed Gonzales could knife somebody but hoped it wasn't true.

The Bureau of Land Management in Susanville had supplied the tidbit of information Frederick had underlined in his notes. When Gonzales was in high school in Susanville, California, six years previously, Nims had been in charge of the lumber leasing for BLM forest lands. Gonzales, along with a dozen other high school kids, had worked for Leonard Nims marking timber. For reasons nobody knew, Gonzales had dropped out or been asked to leave the project halfway through the summer.

Frederick had pressed the woman in charge of personnel to tell him why Nims had left the Bureau for three years. She dug out Nims's file. It said only that he'd resigned for "Personal Reasons" but she'd been a clerk then and remembered a good deal of tension at the time of his resignation. When Nims worked in Susanville, Duncan Foley had been the BLM forester. He'd since retired. Stanton had the man's phone number scribbled on his pad. It was one of the return calls he waited for.

Frederick had gleaned a little additional information on the Boggins woman. She lived in Westwood, a logging town in the mountains between Chester and Susanville. She had a two-year-old daughter and, though she didn't hold down a job, with the exception of occasional work during fire season, she appeared to live fairly comfortably without welfare or food stamps.

Frederick had tracked down Paula's two juvenile offenses to Chico, California, a valley town about two hours' drive from Westwood. The Chico county officials couldn't release information from sealed records over the phone but they could tell him who bailed her out after both arrests: Neil Page.

There was no background on Page and no connection Stanton could find between Page, Boggins and the murdered man prior to their work on the Jackknife fire.

Two more calls to New Mexico had uncovered some promising information on Joseph Hayhurst. Tandy Oil and Gas was trying to get leasing rights to fifty-seven hundred acres of BLM land near the Bisti Wilderness. Hayhurst was working with the Navajo to get the lease stopped. The Navajo held that the drilling would desecrate an important buffer area as well as sections of the Great North Road left by the Anasazi. The BLM had put the project on hold pending an Environmental Impact Statement. Leonard Nims had been on vacation, then dispatched on the Jackknife, but he was scheduled to write that EIS as soon as he returned.

Stephen Lindstrom's supervisor returned Frederick's earlier call. He had nothing but praise for Lindstrom's work but it was couched in such careful terms Frederick knew there was an undercurrent of personal distaste. Lindstrom was from the Bay Area and some of his co-workers didn't care for his big-city ways, was all Frederick could gather from the mixture of fulsome praise and oblique snipes.

Lindstrom's supervisor had mentioned that Stephen knew Joshua Short, the man credited with starting the Jackknife. He seemed to be implicating Lindstrom in the arson but when pressed he reluctantly admitted that Stephen Lindstrom had been in the middle of a five-day training seminar in Las Vegas when the fire had started and couldn't have had any "hands on" involvement with the incident.

Stanton would pass it on to Anna for what it was

worth. Lindstrom was big and strong and he was an EMT. He'd have no trouble finding the heart in one sure stab.

Hugh Pepperdine and Neil Page were still just headings in Frederick's notebook and he waited for the calls that would help him fill in the blanks.

"Base, this is Spike Camp Medical Unit Leader."

Anna's voice emanated from the hand-held radio Stanton had set near the phone and he jumped. His nerves sang like stretched piano wire. Before he could grab up the Motorola, Burwell answered. Anna asked for him and Stanton thumbed the mike down. He held the radio tightly as if by the force of his fingers he could hold onto Anna. The timbre of her voice was deep for a woman, strong, but she sounded so tired and he wished he had words to buoy her up.

"I've got some information," he said into the transmitter, and was dismayed that his words sounded so cold. "Are you ready to copy?"

A pause followed, scratching through the dead air, and he wondered what was going through her mind. Somehow he felt he had let her down.

"Clear to copy. At least as near as I can tell. I've got John's radio, Lawrence has mine but they should be out of range by now . . . it's a long story," she finished wearily.

Frederick smiled. Rambling, tired, human, it warmed him to hear her lose her professional tone. On one level he knew circumstances had undermined the formality of radio etiquette. On another he chose to take it as a sign of friendship. Clutching at straws, he chided himself.

"How are you doing, Anna?" He pressed his lips close to the transmitter as if that afforded any privacy.

"You sure know how to cheer a girl up."

"Sorry. What have you found out?"

"The big news is Barney. What happened up here anyway? He's got Howard's big ol' Buck knife strapped to his belt and has been swaggering around like Rambo saying he's got to defend himself."

Anna groaned.

"Just telling you," Short said without rancor.

"Okay." Anna thought for a minute. "Here's what we've got. I talked with Frederick. Washoe County doesn't seem too interested in dragging Lawrence back for prosecution on the assault and grand theft auto. It was five years ago and nobody cares much anymore. But Lawrence may not know that. He worked for Nims about six years ago. He quit or got fired. There might be something in that or Nims might have known there was a warrant out for his arrest."

It crossed Anna's mind that Jennifer was younger and prettier than she was and might be able to get more out of Gonzales than she could but she dismissed it. There was a chance Lawrence was dangerous. "I'll check it out.

"Stephen's supervisor has something against him. He seems to think he might have been involved with your brother in his environmental protests."

Jennifer thought it through a minute, then shook her head. "I don't think so. Josh was very left wing, I guess you could say. Stephen's conservative. Josh bitched about it once or twice."

"Do you know if Stephen had something against Len?"

For an instant Jennifer looked startled, then pro-
essionalism took over. This was an inve
ot a birthday party. Everybody was invite

A couple of clicks clouded the air. "Good. I'm good" came back a little too strong and Frederick wondered what he had done to offend. "Black Elk's in trouble," she added. "And morale's a little strained but otherwise we're hanging in there."

Acutely aware of the distance between them and the public nature of this broadcast, Frederick paced the Communications tent. Even his pacing was frustrated. Tables and equipment curbed his steps and the sloping canvas of the roof brushed his hair if he veered from the ridgeline.

"Stand by," he said abruptly. He sounded aggravated and wished he could explain. Forcing himself to sit down he picked up his notes.

18

Back against the body of Paula's truck, elbows on knees, Anna rested her head in her hands. She felt like whining and wouldn't have hesitated to do so if there'd been anyone around to commiserate with her. Constant cold was the worst of it, more debilitating than hunger or fear. Her time in the Trans-Pecos had brought out her exotherm tendencies. If she let self-pity take hold, she believed she would never be warm again.

Scritching at her scalp, rubbing off—or in—the crud that lodged there, she thought about Frederick. She'd managed to forgive him for being comfortable and for doing his job. By the end of the conversation she'd even said thank you with a modicum of heartfelt warmth. When all this was behind her, she would sit with him and talk, tell him all the details of this chapter of her life and he would understand, understand even the things left unsaid. At least that was the fantasy. That was always the fantasy.

Cynicism stole the fun from the dream and, forc-

ing herself to concentrate, Anna worked th
information Stanton had unloaded.

Though he was a good worker, Lindstr
pervisor disliked him and suspected him of
able crimes. The sheriff of Washoe Count
Lawrence though he was a wanted felon. No
to go on. Physical evidence was more reliab
Anna returned to the puzzle of the shelters.
task was to see who'd been seen leaving theirs.
would significantly narrow the playing field
ready it was down by three: herself, Black Elk
by necessity, Jennifer Short. Anna hoped she ha
made a grave error in character judgment.
"you're the only one I can trust" speech had be
pure theater. She couldn't trust anyone and t
thought depressed her. Maybe she'd get lucky, maybe somebody saw Short crawl out of her shake 'n' bake.

Whoever was left would have to be questioned. The safest way would be for her and Jennifer to do the interviews together, but given the inherent anarchy of the situation Anna doubted they would g
any cooperation.

Subtlety and luck were all they had going
them. They'd have to make the best of it.

Heavy breathing caught her attention. Je
was puffing up from the heli-spot. "Over
Anna called, and Jen waved as if there could
mistake about who was talking to whom on t
olate ridge. She trotted over and plopped d
side Anna.

"Least ways I'm warm." Short fanned
with her hand.

"Wait till the sweat starts to cool," Anna
simistically.

"Not so's I'd know. I hadn't met him but once till this fire. He doesn't seem to."

"Okay," Anna said. "Joseph had a beef with Len over some land he was considering for oil leases—Joseph's been working with the Navajo in northern New Mexico to get it stopped. If he's passionate enough about it it may mean something. At the moment it's the strongest motive we've got. John's hating Nims seems a little weak to me. And John's such a firebug I can't imagine him sullying a natural disaster with something as mundane as murder. But he's not ruled out. Nobody saw him getting out of his shelter.

"Frederick found out Neil Page bailed Paula out of jail a couple of times. I don't know if it has anything to do with anything but you should talk to her."

"I got something," Jennifer burst out. Anna could see the pride and excitement on her face and was glad somebody was having a good time. For the moment at least, Short had forgotten about the death of her brother. "I went out to that place you guys saw Neil and there wasn't nothing there. At least nothing I could find. I think he was just hiding out smoking cigarettes so he wouldn't have to share. But I met him coming back and started needling him, pretending I knew he'd killed Len—"

Anna shuddered. "Jesus, Jen, you've got to watch it. You'll get us both killed."

"No, no. I was real discreet."

Anna doubted it but she wasn't going to waste words.

"Anyway, Neil got huffy and said I should talk to Paula. Remember those scratches on Len's face? Well, according to Neil, Paula put 'em there. He swears he doesn't know why."

"Worth following up on," Anna said. "See what you can get out of Paula. See if anybody saw her getting out of her shelter."

"Neil didn't. He said she was already out when he got up. I guess that means she saw him though."

"Check it out." Anna shoved herself to her feet. "We'd better get a move on before we freeze to death."

Home sweet home, Anna thought sourly as they returned to the bivouac. Buck knife displayed ostentatiously on his hip, Hugh Pepperdine paced back and forth, deepening a blackened patch in the snow.

"Nice knife," Anna said.

Hugh shot her a filthy look.

" 'Scuse me, Barney." Jennifer started to duck past him into the shelter.

Pepperdine grabbed her upper arm. "No more Barney," he said.

Short just glared at him. After a moment Hugh let go of her. "Thank you," she said coldly.

Hugh had backed down but Anna noticed his free hand had gone to the hilt of the knife. Pressure was ungluing the New Jersey boy. At a guess she would have figured as much, but she thought the stress would manifest itself a little differently. Pepperdine was turning into a bully. He had the height and weight to make it stick and it was as if he'd waited all his life for the opportunity. He reminded Anna of one of the wretched little boys in *Lord of the Flies*. How many more times would he back down, she wondered.

Forcing all contempt from her voice, she said: "I sure appreciate you giving up the radio. Black Elk's mind is wandering some. The radio kind of ties him to reality, I think."

Pepperdine was stone-faced. Anna couldn't tell if he was mollified or not and she didn't have the energy to lay it on any thicker. She poked her head into the shelter.

Lindstrom and Paula flanked Black Elk. Boggins had tied her hair back with somebody's bandanna and fed Howard tepid sips of water. Jennifer settled in the darkened enclave with a sense of purpose.

Anna left her to worm what information she could from Paula. "Where is everybody?" she asked Pepperdine, who was continuing his self-imposed sentry duty. He looked at her and the hatred in his eyes hit her like a bucket of ice water.

"Why?" he said after a good fifteen seconds of silence. "You want to go crawl in bed with your precious little Lawrence?"

Shock stilled Anna's tongue as well as her brain. It passed and was replaced by a deep sense of unease. "You're slipping a few cogs, Hugh," she said carefully. "The weather's bound to clear and we'll be out of here. Just hold it together awhile. Everything's going to be all right." She laid her hand on his arm in what she hoped was a reassuring gesture.

Pepperdine pushed it off. "That stuff won't work on me." He was so superior, so smug, Anna's good intentions went west.

"Did you happen to see anybody getting out of their shelter after the blowup?" she asked abruptly.

"No. I did not. When I crawled out Sir Lawrencelot was already wandering around. He could have been out awhile for all I know."

"Anybody see you?"

"Lawrence did." Hugh looked both complacent and mean. He knew exactly why she was asking and

Anna reminded herself not to underestimate his intelligence just because she'd taken a dislike to him. A memory of the first minutes after the burn came to mind. When John asked where Len was, Hugh said, "He didn't make it." John pressed him and he'd insisted it was just a guess, but there had been no uncertainty in his voice, no speculation. He'd stated it as fact.

Pepperdine had known Len was dead before they'd discovered the body. Despite this apparent alibi, Anna was keeping him on her active list until she found out how he'd come by that knowledge.

"Where is everybody?" she asked again.

"Looking for coals. John and Neil went downstream. Joseph up."

"Lawrence?"

Pepperdine smirked and pointed to the north side of the creek. "Have fun," he called after her as she climbed the bank. She didn't look back. She allowed herself a small fantasy of shooting him. Not only would it be personally satisfying but it might be the only way to keep him from tearing their fragile society apart.

Events had piled on top of one another with such stunning rapidity no one had yet ventured very far from camp. Close in the tracks and trails were a mishmash. Less than twenty yards from the creek they sorted themselves out distinctly. The constant temperatures preserved footprints in pristine condition.

Pepperdine had pointed north; Lawrence had found his badger north. Pursuing a hunch, Anna followed the old trail. Thoughts blinding her, she walked without really seeing until she reached the clearing where Neil had been sitting earlier in the day. It seemed more like weeks. Time was definitely doing its petty pace thing.

Anna considered rechecking the scene. Hiding out and smoking was believable but there was something about it that rang a sour note. It'll come to me, she promised herself.

Lawrence was in search of embers. She schooled her mind. Steam, smoke, heavy fuel loads, melted snow: those were the things he would be looking for. Squinting against the glare, gray faded into gray, white jarred against black, and she wished she had the eyesight of a twenty-three-year-old.

The constant fog was wearing on Anna. She suspected it was partly to blame for the creeping insanity that darkened their minds: Black Elk's wandering, Jennifer's depression, Paula's sullenness, Pepperdine emerging as a closet bully.

Anna had spent a year of graduate school at the University of California in Davis. She remembered the weeks of heavy tule fog that smothered the campus for twenty-two days in January of that year. Students were jumping from the clock tower. Professors were beating their wives.

Dense unremitting fog filled the brain, chilled and clouded human thought processes.

A hallucination disturbed Anna's field of vision. Past the dry creek where Lawrence had bagged breakfast, over a low ridge, the texture of the world's walls looked slightly different. Asked to describe it, Anna would have been hard pressed to find words. The difference was minute, a mere disturbance of the air, like the first wavering of heat mirage rising off the desert in late morning. If she stared too long or thought too hard she couldn't see it anymore.

A set of boot tracks branched off in that general direction and she followed them. At the badger creek the trail veered again, the new track leading up the ridge, zigzagging around fallen trees. Snow over ash: each print was as clear as the painted footsteps in an Arthur Murray dance studio.

At the top of the ridge Anna could see what had drawn Lawrence so far from camp. Beyond a shallow valley and over another hill, slightly lower than the one on which she stood, the imperfection in the air was pronounced. Steam billowed up in clouds. A faint smell of rotten eggs tainted the air.

The view from the second ridge was considerably more startling. In the valley below a horseshoe-shaped depression cut into the side of the mountain. Steam poured up in veils, sinuous, live, sentient to a tired mind. Snow had melted in a wide irregular circle exposing gray earth and rivulets of smoking water of improbable aquas and oranges and lavenders. The sound of bubbling—bubbles primeval in size—percolated through the steam. Seated on a stone, his back to her, was Lawrence Gonzales, mother naked.

From her work in the northern midwest Anna knew it wasn't uncommon to find people frozen to death, their clothes torn off and strewn around. No one knew for sure, but the theory was that in the late stages of hypothermia, when the body's thermostat was going haywire, the victims felt suddenly hot and so divested themselves of garments.

Almost instantaneous with that thought, the pieces came together. Lassen Volcanic National Park. The entire mountain range from Canada on down was formed by volcanic activity. Lassen Volcano had erupted in the early 1900s, Helens in 1980. Thermal activity was a common feature in the park. Mud pots, fumaroles and boiling springs. Lawrence had found a thermal outlet.

One thought crowded all others from Anna's mind. She forgot she'd come to interrogate the man, she forgot all the dangers, she forgot Gonzales was naked.

It would be *warm*.

"Lawrence!" she hollered lest her sudden appearance startle him and he injure himself in the boiling stream.

"I'm naked," he called as in warning.

"That's okay." Anna hopped the last few feet, unlacing a fire boot as she came. Dumping herself on the rock next to him she finished unlacing and pulled her boots off with a grunt.

Lawrence had dragged his shirt modestly over his lap but Anna was beyond noticing. Thrusting her feet in the thermal pool next to his she threw her head back and laughed. "Who'd've thunk it? Heaven's a fire pit stinking of sulphur. We've got to call the Pope and let him know they've got it all wrong."

To their left a small lake, thirty or forty feet across, hissed and spat. The water backed up against a wall of dirty-white porous soil pocked with holes, some the size of pinpricks, some several yards across. Above the mud bluff were old growth trees, the bark blackened and the needles scorched but the tops still green. The Jackknife had gone around them. They would probably survive another hundred years if no one cut them down.

Steam poured from vents and Anna could hear the dull wet plop of mud pots. For twenty yards around the lake nothing lived, at least nothing larger than the rainbow-hued algae that lined the runoff beds. The ground was as barren and white as an alkali flat.

The thermal lake looked as if it came from one of the seven levels of hell. Colors were bright and unnatural, painted by algae that lived in the differing temperate zones. Water was opaque: milky green, then blue, then white. To the center and rear, where the mud pots boiled, the surface simmered, heat roiling, sending up belches of sulphur-scented steam.

Lawrence's perch was sensibly downstream from the burning lake where the water had been cooled by springs and melting snow.

Anna stripped down to her underpants and shirt. But for Lawrence's delicate sensibilities she would have chucked those aside as well. Sulphur water, stinking and warm, ran from her arms and face in black rivulets. Hot air billowed around her. The rock beneath her bare thighs was pleasantly warm.

"God, this is great," she said for the tenth time.

"Be careful," Lawrence cautioned. "There's a place like this over in the park called Bumpass Hell because the first white guy that found it fell through and got a leg burnt off. These places are weird. The ground is hollow like." Gonzales had spread his trousers around so they covered his crotch and most of his butt. He sat rigid as if afraid any movement would endanger this careful arrangement.

Anna realized she held him captive as effectively as if he were locked in an interrogation room and dragged her mind back to the reason she had tracked him down. Gratitude was getting in her way. A badger and a bath: Gonzales was proving an excellent friend. Anna shelved her generous impulses.

"You know this area pretty well?" she said for openers.

"I grew up sixty miles south of here," he replied.

Anna pondered what to say next. She was acutely aware that she was unarmed and semi-naked within throwing distance of a lake she'd not only never swim out of but from which her body would probably never be recovered.

"Susanville?" she asked, remembering a small red dot on the California road map. "You're a hunter, camper, hiker—that sort of thing?"

Gonzales shook his head. "A city boy without a city. I worked around here. Not up this far—down on the Plumas National Forest south of Westwood."

"For the Forest Service?" Anna asked. She was pushing close to potentially sensitive areas. Reluctantly, she pulled her feet out of the warm water and stepped into her pants. Maybe naked, Lawrence would be too shy to chase her if she had to make a run for it.

"The BLM," he said. A note of caution crept into his voice and he was looking uncomfortable. Unless a suspect was drunk or retarded, and even then about half the time, there came a moment when the conversation got too close to some core truth. Defenses went up. Anna watched for that moment with both anticipation and dread. If it came it meant she was on to something. It also meant they were on to her and getting what she was after became more difficult.

The summer job, the BLM was a raw nerve. She filed that away and backed off for the moment. "Reno's fairly near here, isn't it?" she asked.

Lawrence relaxed. The change in geography soothed him. Anna was interested. Susanville had the history of a lost summer job, Reno of assault and grand theft auto.

"Eighty miles southeast of my hometown," Lawrence said.

"Get over there much? Gamble? Take in a show?"

"I used to. I used to date a girl from Sparks. It bumps right up against Reno." Lawrence laughed.

"What?" Anna prodded. She was just curious. If it was funny to him it was probably of no use to her.

"Nothing." He poked his toes into the flame-colored slime at the bottom of the stream.

"Come on," Anna said. "I'm bored."

"Promise you won't tell anybody?"

He looked so charming and boyish that Anna promised. She could always break it.

"This girl's father was a jerk. A real jerk. I tossed him in the Truckee River. He was spitting water like a whale and he got out this badge he was always flashing to get out of traffic tickets and yelling 'I'm a federal officer, I'm a federal officer.' " Lawrence laughed again. "The guy was a meat inspector."

Anna laughed with him. So much for assault on a federal officer. No wonder the Washoe County Sheriff's Department had no intention of extraditing the perpetrator. "Did he drown?" Anna asked to keep the story going.

"Nah. It wasn't that deep. It was August. He didn't even catch a cold. Me and Justine jumped in his old Thunderbird and left him there dripping and waving his meat badge."

That must have been the grand theft auto. Anna was relieved. There were still a lot of questions about his summer working for Nims but this wasn't the healthiest place to ask them. Anna pulled on her boots and began lacing them up. For the first time in what seemed eons her feet were warm. "Too bad we can't bottle this and take it back to camp," she said. By the time they'd traversed the three-quarters of a mile to the creek bed any water they took with them in their plastic canteens would be cold.

"Could you turn around?" Lawrence asked. "I'm going to put my pants on."

Anna turned her back on the boy. He'd never know what an act of faith it was.

"We could bring Howard up here," Lawrence suggested. "It's warmer. Maybe he'd feel better."

The thought had crossed Anna's mind but she'd discarded it. "I don't think we'd better move Howard until we have to."

"It's bad then?" Lawrence asked, and Anna respected the concern in his voice.

"It's bad."

When they were within earshot of the bivouac, Anna returned to the subject of Leonard Nims. "When you worked with the Bureau of Land Management, what did you do?"

"Marked timber." Gonzales was walking in front of her and Anna noted the slight hitch in his stride.

"You worked for Leonard Nims?" Anna gave up pussyfooting. There wasn't time and Lawrence was already on his guard.

He stopped and turned to face her. Anna stopped as well, keeping ten feet of trail between them. "Checking up on me?"

Anna made no reply. The answer was obvious.

Behind Lawrence's dark eyes decisions were being made. Anna could see them working across his even features. None of the early warning signs of impending violence—tensing, changing the center of gravity, fist clenching, eyes skittering—manifested itself, so Anna stood her ground.

"There was a wildfire," Lawrence said finally. "Somebody lit it on purpose. Len said he was going to say I did it."

"Did you?"

"No. Len told me to but I didn't. He must've got somebody else to do it for him."

"Len told you to light it?" Anna was just confirming what she'd heard. The information was too new to process.

"Yeah. It was a bad summer. Everybody was out of work. Fire fighting's good money. It happens all the time."

"Len wasn't out of work."

Lawrence shrugged. "You think I'm making it up. Len said everybody would. So I lit out."

"I don't think you're making it up," Anna said slowly. She didn't know if he had all the facts straight, but she didn't doubt that he believed his own version. "That must have been hard to take."

"You're going to pin his murder on me, aren't you." Gonzales wasn't asking. His eyes narrowed, weight shifted, fists balled. Fear tuned up Anna's muscles, readying to fight or run.

"I'm not pinning anything on anybody," she said evenly. "I'm just asking questions. Did you see Hugh getting out of his shelter?" More than an answer, Anna needed to change the subject.

"He was already out. He helped peel the damn thing off me."

Gonzales didn't strike Anna as a thinker. He was a doer. She doubted he'd wasted much time figuring out the importance of fire shelters: how many, who was where, who could prove they had one. Pepperdine, on the other hand, was a thinking man, an educated man. He would have figured it out.

Somebody was lying. Given the choice of who, Anna tended to lean toward the man clever enough to come up with a reason he thought he needed to.

19

Anna couldn't remember ever having been so tired. Her wristwatch told her it was close to one in the afternoon. Her stomach reminded her it was way past lunchtime. The gray skies told her nothing. It could be dawn or dusk or anywhere in between. The brief respite from the cold the hot springs had afforded was just a memory. The chill had returned, sunk back into her bones. It would have been worth the walk back up the hill to be warm again but Jennifer and Stephen had gone and Anna stayed to watch Howard.

Soon after she'd relieved Stephen, Howard had fallen into an uneasy sleep. Paula Boggins, faithful to the job Anna had given her, took the opportunity to slip off to the "ladies' room." Anna smiled, the superfluous trappings of civilization suddenly striking her as dear, precious; humankind touching and admirable in its usually futile attempts to rise above a less than divine nature.

John, with Hugh trailing officiously after, had gone to make the call to Base. Anna was just as glad.

She needed time to think. Then she needed to talk with Frederick in private. Or what passed for private over the airwaves.

Leaning against the boulder in the semidarkness of the makeshift tent, she closed her eyes and hoped for rest if not sleep. Both eluded her. Fragments of conversations, images, ideas, drifted through her mind.

Gonzales, boyish and earnest, chucking a meat inspector into the Truckee. Gonzales leaving the summer job because he was suspected, accused of, or framed for arson.

Either Len had falsely accused Lawrence or he had known of the arson. Six years ago: it seemed a little late in the game for revenge but grudges had been held longer and with less provocation.

Nims might have been blackmailing Lawrence, threatening to report the arson.

No. Anna shuffled that card to the bottom of her mental deck. Nims would be in just as much hot water for not reporting it when it happened. Besides, Lawrence didn't have anything but youth and good looks. Sex? Could Nims have been blackmailing Lawrence for sexual favors? Anna could easily see Lawrence killing a man for that. But not six years later in a firestorm. He'd have beat him to death with his fists the first time the subject came up.

Lawrence said Nims ordered the fire set. Could he have been blackmailing Len? That made as little sense as the other way around. Nims was right: nobody would have believed the kid then and even less so now. Unless Lawrence had found proof.

Still, it was Nims who'd wound up dead. Blackmailers didn't tend to kill their victims. No profit in it.

Then there were the lies. Either Lawrence had lied

about Hugh seeing him exit his shelter or Pepperdine had lied. Since Anna put her money on Pepperdine, she decided to grant Lawrence Gonzales at least temporary amnesty and moved on.

Hugh Pepperdine had known Nims was dead before he should have. Hugh had, Anna was convinced, lied about Lawrence seeing him get out of his fire shelter. Pepperdine was a veritable casserole of modern-day neuroses. Anna wished she could turn him loose in Molly's Park Avenue clinic for an hour or two and get a psychiatric profile on him. Insecurity teamed up with conceit, braggadocio with cowardice, selfishness with a need to be admired. Pepperdine was dysfunctional—to put it politely—and he was lying, but Anna couldn't figure out why. So far she'd heard nothing that connected him in any way with Leonard Nims. He didn't appear to have done anything sufficiently interesting in his short life to make him a candidate for blackmail. And Anna doubted he had the muscle memory to shove a knife into another man's ribs.

Violence is learned. She remembered practicing kicking till her back ached, swinging a baton until she could no longer lift her arms. Practicing technique was part of it but just as important was teaching the body to respond without having to wait for orders from a mind that might be otherwise engaged.

Women—and momma's boys like Hugh Pepperdine—had a harder time of it. Movies, books, television, myths and wives' tales taught little girls to shriek and throw up their hands in despair. Mind and body had to be taught to overcome programmed helplessness.

Lawrence Gonzales had the muscle memory. So did Joseph, Anna realized. When she'd startled him, he'd swung on her with a movement so ingrained it was not precipitated by conscious thought. He'd not learned that in art history class.

Stanton said Joseph Hayhurst was working to block an oil lease on what he believed to be a culturally significant site. Surely that wouldn't be grounds for murder. Not that one Leonard Nims more or less was equal in value to an irreplaceable historical artifact, but because Nims was a bureaucrat, a cog in a very large machine. He'd be replaced. There was no way one could kill them all, though Anna suspected activists often fantasized about it.

Removing Len would be, at best, a temporary solution. Unless it was a foregone conclusion that Len would okay the lease where another would not. What had LeFleur said? Nims rubber-stamped oil lease applications "NSI," No Significant Impact. The oil drillers must have been grateful. How grateful? What would it be worth to them in cold, hard cash?

Lawrence said Nims ordered him to light a wildfire, people needed the work. How much? In Susanville Nims had been in a position to hire local firefighters. What would it be worth to a man out of work, trying to feed a family?

Anna opened her eyes. She had a couple of homework assignments for Frederick Stanton next time they made contact. If Nims was in the business of taking kickbacks for favors rendered, Joseph might want him dead.

Who else? LeFleur would be better off professionally exposing Nims than killing him.

Neither Stephen nor Jennifer had motive as far as Anna knew but they didn't have alibis either. Out of necessity Anna had granted Jennifer temporary amnesty. Much as she would like it to, that couldn't include Stephen. Stephen had the knowledge to pierce Len's heart at one go. Anna believed he had the strength of character to share his fire shelter when the chips were down. Odd that in this murder she must first find the person kind enough to save the victim's life—unless the murderer recognized the situation as a dream-come-true from the beginning. Unlikely, Anna thought. Too much going on for detailed plotting.

Black Elk moaned and jerked in his sleep. Anna laid her hand on his chest hoping to comfort him. He opened his eyes and looked into hers but she doubted he was seeing her.

"How're you doing, Howard? Can I get you anything?"

The big man didn't answer. Anna moved and his eyes didn't follow. Whatever he saw, it was not of this world. "Len shouldn't have done it," he said clearly. "Paula wasn't hurting anybody."

Howard was dreaming or delirious and Anna felt a stab of alarm. Curiosity overcame it. Feeling like a heel even as she did it, she pressed him: "What shouldn't Len have done?"

Black Elk hadn't heard her. He closed his eyes and his body relaxed. Whatever alarm had gone off in his fevered brain had been answered and he fell into a doze.

Leaning back again, Anna closed her eyes as well. Unless Howard was totally lost in dreams, Len had done something to Paula Boggins. Perhaps the something over which Paula had clawed his face. Jennifer had been questioning Paula; probably some of the conversation had soaked into Howard's consciousness, hence the outburst.

According to Stanton, Paula had been arrested twice. Page had bailed her out twice. She lived fairly comfortably with no visible means of support. Boggins might be living off an inheritance or alimony but if not she was getting paid for something that went unrecorded. Odds were it was illegal. That being the case, it was possible Len had been blackmailing her and/or Neil if he was in partnership with her. She and Neil had a relationship that spoke of familiarity and tolerance without affection. That smacked of a business relationship based on mutual need or profit.

It made more sense to Anna than the Gonzales/Nims scenario. Boggins could knife someone if she had to, Anna would lay money on it. Paula would do whatever she had to to get by. Page didn't seem an unlikely source of violence either.

Anna had a hunch Paula's means of support might be illuminating. She added to her list of things a suggestion she needed Frederick to track down.

More out of habit than because there was anything she could do for him, Anna checked Howard's pulse and breathing, then settled down to ponder Neil Page. Page acted suspicious, if that counted for anything. He was always creeping off by himself, anxious to cast any particles of blame, however small, on someone else. He'd been quick to deflect interest from himself by telling Jennifer Paula and Nims had quarreled and Paula had scratched Len.

Page also insisted Paula had seen him getting out of his shake 'n' bake. Should that turn out to be true, it effectively let him off the hook. Too bad, Anna thought. So far it was a tossup between him and Pepperdine as to who she'd most like to pin a homicide on.

Scooting as close to Howard as she could, Anna laid her arm across his chest to share her warmth with him. As soon as Jennifer returned they could compare notes. Till then she would try and get some rest.

20

Sleep had finally overtaken Anna and in her dreams she was warm and fed and unafraid. When the sound of fabric rubbing against itself intruded, her mind, loath to desert the comfort it had found, attributed it first to window curtains floating in a gentle breeze, then to the swish of starched petticoats, a sound dredged from so deep in her subconscious all she could come up with to account for it were the ruffled squaw dresses she and Molly had been given for Sunday school when they were children. The picture was so alien it woke her and she found herself slumped under the fire shelters. The arm she'd draped across Black Elk's chest tingled from being too long in one position and her lungs hurt from trying to soak up oxygen around the smoke-borne debris lodged in the tissues.

Jennifer Short had returned. She stunk of sulphur and the top layer of grime on her face had been sluiced to a translucent gray.

"What time is it?" Anna asked, as if it mattered.

Short looked at her wristwatch. "Coming on two."

Anna had slept less than an hour but she felt better for it. Carefully, so she wouldn't wake Howard, she pinched up the sleeve of her shirt and hauled her arm off his chest. He didn't stir but the sleep that claimed him was more akin to trauma-induced unconsciousness than true rest. At least he was still breathing, though ragged gurgling sounds attested to the effort. Anna laid the back of her hand against his neck. He was hot to the touch. Fever boded ill but the over-warm skin felt good and she left her hand there in hopes an exchange would benefit both of them.

Jennifer settled down in the gloom near Black Elk's knees and stretched her hands toward one of the metal hard hats Joseph had filled with coals. Her fingers trembled.

"What did you think of that weird lake?" Anna asked. Jennifer didn't reply. She didn't even raise her eyes. The yoke of depression Anna had thought thrown off was back, pressing down on her shoulders, bowing them till it looked as if it must be causing physical pain.

"Jen!" Anna said more loudly.

Finally the younger woman looked up. Her eyes were as dull and opaque as the waters of the thermal spring.

"You look like shit," Anna said kindly. "You've caved in somehow. What were you guys doing up there?"

"Nothing. Washing. Like that." Jennifer lowered her eyes again and pushed her shaking hands nearer the makeshift brazier. "Coals are near dead."

"We'll find more," Anna said, though she was far from certain they would. The Jackknife had consumed all the fuel for miles. All they had left were her leavings.

"What did you get out of Paula?" she asked, hoping to engage Jennifer's mind.

Short just shook her head. "She saw Neil get out of his shelter. That's about it." That minimal exchange seemed to exhaust her and she hung her head, staring sightlessly at dead embers.

Anna sat up straight and looked Jennifer hard in the face. "Something happened up at the lake. You've folded up on me like a cheap umbrella."

Jennifer sighed so deeply the air caught in her damaged lungs and came out on a dry whispering cough. "Josh . . . Stephen said . . ." She ran out of air and sat for a moment without speaking. With an effort she sucked in a lungful and began again, the words coming quickly. "Stephen said everybody thinks Josh lit the fire—this fire—on purpose." She looked up at Anna, waiting for her to say it wasn't true.

Anna floundered around for a serviceable lie but she was tired and didn't come up with one quickly enough.

Jennifer crumpled, resembling a rag doll whose stuffing has all leaked away. "Being he's gone they can say anything. Pin it on him. Like it doesn't matter. Like he won't care that what he'll be remembered for won't be any of the good things he did but for burning down California." No tears stood in her eyes, they were dry and rimmed with red, but her voice was choked with them and for a minute she was unable to go on.

Anna cast about for something comforting to say. "Not everybody says arson," she tried. "Some figure he just let the campfire get away from him—"

"That's crap!" Jennifer snapped, and Anna was silenced. "Josh wasn't stupid and he knew all that

Woodsy Owl shit. Jesus! People think a gay man can't rub two sticks together and make a fire. Give me a break." Anger gusted and was gone, leaving Jennifer once again empty. "Josh didn't let his fire get away. That's crap," she finished softly.

To Anna it seemed a little thing, but in grief people latched onto minutia. At least it was graspable and, with luck or hard work, sometimes even reparable. Time and again she'd seen people who'd lost a child or spouse to accident or disease dedicate the remainder of their lives to a crusade against whatever had taken them.

It was something to do, Anna supposed. It provided direction and a reason to get out of bed mornings. Maybe it made them feel closer to those they'd lost.

"If he didn't do it, maybe somebody else did," Anna suggested. "When we get out of here, I'll talk to the Forest Service; see if we can go over the arson investigation reports."

"Don't. It's crap."

For the moment Anna let it go. Her bag of tricks was empty. "So." She leaned back against the boulder and pounded her heels gently in the sand to work some blood back into her posterior. "Paula said she saw Neil get out of his shelter after the fire?"

Jennifer nodded.

"Neil said the same thing so I guess we'll call it true. What the hell, I'm feeling magnanimous."

Jennifer didn't so much as smile.

"I saw Howard, so did John. That's two down."

"Three," Jennifer said. "I was there when Stephen unwrapped himself."

Anna felt a mild sense of relief. "Good. Neil, Howard, Stephen. Anybody see you?" she asked hopefully.

"Nobody." Though she had to know why Anna was asking, Jennifer didn't seem to care.

Conversation stopped as Paula Boggins pulled aside the shelter serving as a partial doorway and crept in. Her movements were stiff and careful. The second-degree burns would be hurting her. Probably worse than Howard's were hurting him.

Ignoring the other women, she crawled over by Black Elk and felt of his brow and cheeks. "He's hot," she said accusingly, and Anna felt she'd failed in her duties. "Maybe I should put some wet cloths on him, cool him down like you do little kids?"

Anna wished she knew more of medicine. Conserving heat was important but the man was feverish. Either way Black Elk's energies were being spent and he needed all the strength he could get. "Not cold," Anna suggested. "Dip a cloth in warmish water and wring it out good before you wipe his face. Watch him close. See if it seems to be helping any."

Paula turned to the task with the grace of a natural-born nurse.

"You're good at that," Anna said. "What do you do for a living?"

"I got a kid," Paula said as if that was an answer. Maybe it was.

"No job?"

Paula gave Anna a dirty look and for a minute Anna thought she wasn't going to get any more out of her but Boggins wasn't the type to suffer in silence.

"You think everybody's got to get all got up in some kind of uniform and march around like a man or they ain't working? You got your head up your ass, lady."

Anna whistled to prove it wasn't so and it amused Paula. Anger dissipated. Grudgingly, she said: "I work out of my home."

The phrase sounded rehearsed, the words not those Paula would have strung together herself.

"What do you do?" Anna pressed.

"Different things." Paula wrung black water from a black neckerchief then tenderly wiped it across Black Elk's face. "Mostly I sell my pictures. I'm an artist, you know." She tossed her matted hair and Anna knew she was lying but it was a lie she was in love with and Anna knew better than to challenge it.

"Cool," she said, and busied herself stirring the dying coals in the fire pit. "Paula, why did you scratch Leonard Nims's face?" she demanded suddenly.

Paula twitched as if Anna had struck her and for a moment it looked as if she would bolt, but she held her ground. Sullenness settled over her features, robbing her of years till she looked no more than sixteen. "He was messing with me," she said. "Not that it's any of your business."

Anna'd figured that but she wanted Paula to say it in so many words. "Did he get fresh?"

Paula smirked and Anna realized how naive and old-fashioned "fresh" must sound to the young woman.

"Fresh as milk straight from the cow," Paula said, the smirk still in place.

"There was more to it than that," Anna said. "You can talk to me about it now or the incident commander when we get out of here." For an instant it looked as if the threat was going to bear fruit, then Paula's sense of self-preservation kicked in.

"I don't *gotta* talk to nobody," she said. "I know

my rights." She dipped the filthy rag again and bathed Howard's temples.

She was right. Anna had no leverage, nothing to barter with or hold over her. "I've got to go up to the ridge to call Base," she said. "Coming, Jen?"

Jennifer shook her head.

"Come on," Anna urged. "I need you there."

"No. You don't."

Anna had lost her. The tentative hold she'd had on Jennifer's attention had been broken and Short was slipping away again.

"The weather will break soon," Anna said. "It's got to."

Neither of the women replied.

Steeped as it was in pain and hopelessness, the interior of the tent suddenly became intolerable. The gestalt of suffering threatened to topple Anna's carefully maintained defenses and she had to escape. Pushing herself to her feet, she stumbled out with what she knew was unseemly haste. Once in the open, she gulped down air like a woman nearly suffocated.

Jennifer's relapse had shaken her more than she could have predicted. Until then she'd not known how lonely this ridge was, how isolated she was from her fellows. In times of disaster people bonded, took comfort from one another, drew strength. Len's murderer had robbed them of that. Warranted or not, Anna had put her trust in Jennifer and in return she'd found courage. Without trust very little that was good in humans could survive.

People were bizarre, she thought, remembering how when monsters rustled in the closet she and Molly would find each other and so the courage to face any imagined villains. As if two little girls were significantly more daunting to your average axe murderer than one.

Safety in numbers was imprinted on the genetic code. With adulthood and its attendant disillusionment, Anna thought she'd eschewed that particular maxim. Evidently not.

"Jen, come with me," she hollered back toward the boulder. Silence was her answer and she turned away.

Shapes were shifting. Blackened snags were being eaten away by encroaching hoarfrost. Snow was patterned by booted feet. Only the sky remained unchanged and unchanging: still, breathless, dead gray-white—the color of fish bellies.

Anna stood in the ice-fog trying to remember what it was she was doing, where she'd been going when she'd exited the tent so precipitously. Frederick Stanton, she thought, and was immoderately cheered.

In all of Len's horrid little life Anna'd yet to find one worthwhile thing he'd accomplished. In his sordid little death she'd been given a reason to call Stanton every three hours. For that she was grateful to the deceased. "Moderately Useful Dead"; picturing that on Nims's tombstone cheered her further and she attacked the climb to the ridge with something approximating enthusiasm.

Just below the heli-spot she met with John and Hugh. Pepperdine was doing the talking. About what, Anna couldn't hear, but he moved his lips earnestly and shook a finger in the air just often enough one wanted to snap it off. LeFleur had the look of a man not listening but to whom the effort did not come cheap.

"They haven't done anything," Hugh called down

before Anna had a chance to ask what the news was from Base.

LeFleur tried to silence him with a look but Pepperdine was immune to subtlety.

"Not a mother-frigging thing."

Apparently after the "dude" episode Hugh'd lost his nerve for colorful language. Anna looked to John. He pawed his pocket. Still no smokes.

"They're working on it," he said wearily. "Six sawyers and a D-8 Cat. It's a bitch of a job. Treadwell says they've cleared over three-quarters of a mile. Given they've only been at it six hours, that's damn good."

The speech was to educate Pepperdine. If it registered, he didn't show it. "We could be here a couple more days," he said. "That's bullshit. This is the 1990s."

"The weather'll break," John and Anna said almost in unison. Even in stereo it sounded hollow.

"They won't risk a chopper after dark," John said. "Unless this stuff lifts in the next hour or so, we'll be here at least one more night."

To Anna, to all of them, that seemed a long time. Black Elk very possibly would not survive it. Jennifer would have to be watched, made to drink, to stay warm, to eat if any more food presented itself. Paula, surprisingly, was doing well. Maybe she could pull Howard through. There was enough fight in her to withstand nearly anything, Anna guessed.

At heart Jennifer Short had that kind of strength. Anna had seen it. Joshua was her Achilles' heel. Everybody had one. It was just bad luck Jennifer's had been hit at this point in time.

"Where are you headed?" John asked. "Up to the ridge for secret squirrel stuff?"

"Calling Stanton." Anna felt self-conscious admitting it on two counts: the investigation with its surrounding secrecy that further alienated her from the group and each from the other, and because she was afraid her personal agenda stuck out like a sore thumb.

"He the boyfriend?" John asked.

Trust your paranoia, Anna thought. A quick denial leapt to the tip of her tongue but she shook it off. "More or less," she said shyly. Better they think her a fool than a threat.

"Sir Lawrencelot's going to be jealous," Hugh said.

Anna stared, started to count, then gave it up as a lost cause. "If you get a minute later, John, could you kill Hugh for me?"

"Sure thing. Give the Feds my best." LeFleur started down the hill. Anna didn't envy him the news he carried. Though the others knew what to expect, hope—and so disappointment—springeth eternal.

She took half a dozen steps up the trail. Hugh followed. She stopped and turned.

"I'm going with you to make the call," he said before she'd had time to challenge him. "I'm law enforcement. You're working without backup. That's against policy."

Anna eyed him. Hugh's arms were folded across his chest, his jaw set in what, on his peevish countenance, passed for determination. She'd never been adept at reading body language but Pepperdine's was loud and clear. If he'd had four legs he would have been a mule.

Rational argument was jettisoned. "I'm calling my boyfriend. Don't bother me."

"That's a crock."

"Either I'm a murder investigator or a prick

tease," Anna growled. "You can't have it both ways."

"Females can though?"

Anna gave up. "Go away." She took two steps more. He took two. She stopped. He stopped. This could easily degenerate into a "did-too-did-not, your-mother-wears-army-boots," childish squabble. Anna'd never been good with children. Except for Alison and Bella, the daughters of women at Isle Royale and Mesa Verde, she didn't even know any. And Ally and Bella were more close personal friends than children.

Going back to basics, Anna decided telling Mom was the best course. "If you don't quit I'm going to call John and have him drag you kicking and screaming back down the hill."

Pepperdine took a belligerent stance, his hand on the stolen knife. Seconds ticked by. Anna was betting he didn't have the nerve to face John LeFleur. She won.

"I wouldn't dream of interfering with your love life," Pepperdine sneered, and turned toward camp. Anna watched until he was out of sight below the brow of the hill.

"Frederick," Anna said. His voice mellowed her and she snuggled back against the truck with a feeling akin to comfort.

"How are you doing, Anna?"

He sounded so genuinely concerned she felt that weak and weepy sensation building up. "Howard's going downhill," she said to get the subject on neutral ground. "But the rest of us are holding up fairly well. I don't suppose you've got any good news for me?"

"These guys are moving mountains down here but they've got more to move. No good news. The front is moving slowly. It'll probably clear before we get the road open if that makes you feel any better."

It didn't, but to keep her credit good, Anna said she was glad to hear it.

Crunching caught her ear and she stopped breathing. "Stand by," she whispered into the mike, her attention on listening.

Snow falling off a branch. Except there were few branches left and the snow had been cemented on by the lingering frost. Silence reassured her.

"I've got some homework for you if you're ready to copy," she said.

"Go ahead."

Anna could picture Frederick surrounded by lists, pen in hand, his dark head bent, the stick-straight hair falling over his forehead. The picture brought a smile to her lips. She told him of Lawrence Gonzales's accusation. "Check out Len's reputation in Susanville," she said. "And Paula Boggins's run-in with Nims as well as her invisible income." Anna outlined her suspicions briefly.

Then she told him of Jennifer Short's tumble back into depression. "If you could dig up something that cleared Josh of the arson charge, it might help. Even if it only seemed to," Anna added, giving him tacit permission to, if not lie, then put the most favorable twist on the facts.

Frederick responded to this last assignment with a warmth that at first pleased Anna, then became irksome. Had an inquisitor put her in thumbscrews she would have been forced to admit that Stanton's obvious concern for Jennifer was making her a wee bit jealous. Since there wasn't a thumbscrew for a thousand miles, she shrugged it off.

"Can I get anything else for you?" Stanton asked when she'd finished.

"A large pepperoni, extra cheese, extra onions."

Behind her, hidden from view by the truck, Anna heard the same sound that had alarmed her earlier. It was closer.

Quietly she pushed herself to her knees and looked over the hood. Black-and-white landscape camouflaged hummocks, piled snags, hollows. Hiding would be easy. A rustling so tiny it seemed only a tickle in her inner ear held her attention.

"John?" she tried her radio. No answer. LeFleur had his radio off, conserving the battery. Base was helpless to interfere, still she needed to let someone know what was going on. "Frederick?"

"I'm here."

"I've got company, please monitor."

"Anna?" Stanton sounded worried and it pleased her.

"Stand by," she said, and switched the Motorola off.

21

Senses honed to an uncomfortable edge by the furtive sounds, Anna listened. From her stomach she heard the badger growl for company; breath rasped in her ears—the body clamoring for the necessities of life. Consciously she slowed her breathing, forced air deep into her lungs.

With oxygen came a semblance of calm. The ridge was bathed in a silence so deep as to be unnatural. From her years in the back-country, Anna knew she could settle into that silence, wait it out. Few people could, and it put time on her side. Leaning against the remaining fender, she made herself comfortable and focused on seeing, hearing, breathing, staying alert and in the moment.

The wait wasn't prolonged. Humanity hates a silence the way nature abhors a vacuum. To her left she heard movement. Ice had made the snow as brittle as ground glass. Every footstep reverberated.

On impulse, Anna shouted: "Hugh!"

The only response was a crunching rearrangement of body parts on snow. Noise pinpointed location: a pile of downed snags twenty feet from where she stood. Since it had neither color nor shadow, she'd not realized it was big enough to hide anyone. "Come out from behind that deadfall," she called. "You've got to be getting cold hunkered down like that. Don't be such an ass."

The insult gouged Pepperdine out of hiding. A yellow hunchback materialized above the snags—Hugh's back with its yellow pack strapped firmly in place—then his face as he pushed himself up.

They stared at each other across a field of white. Anna was at a loss for words. Those that came to mind were of the four-letter variety and inherently unproductive. What was passing through Pepperdine's mind, she could only guess at. Embarrassment had flitted across his face, anger chasing it quickly away. His brain was in overdrive, she suspected, spinning desperately in an attempt to turn the situation around to where he wasn't the idiot.

"I need your radio," Hugh said, as if that was what he'd come for.

"Why? You seem fairly adept at sneaking and eavesdropping. No sense in carrying the extra weight."

"I suppose you were planning on keeping the fact that Sir Lawrencelot is an arsonist under wraps." Hugh changed tactics. "Did it ever cross your so-called mind that he killed Len to keep him from telling? Or is the mama lion protecting her mate?"

Words were to Pepperdine what whiskey was to some men. Anna could see him getting drunk on his own verbiage. With it, he found the courage to step out from behind the screen of burned logs. His eyes locked on hers in an unwinking stare and she recalled one of her instructors saying when you saw that look, get ready to fight or make love.

Casually, she rebalanced herself, got her fanny off the fender, moved her weight to the balls of her feet. "We only protect our young," she said. "I don't know where you're getting all this stuff from but it's growing a bit thin."

Hugh snorted. "You've been sniffing around Lawrence since day one. If you'd seen him facedown in the dirt whimpering like a girl, maybe you'd lose your taste for Mexican."

More words, more courage. Anna didn't like it. Pepperdine had a screw loose somewhere and she felt inadequate to handle him. "What put a burr under your saddle about me and Lawrence? I hardly know the guy. I'm old enough to be his mother," she threw in for good measure.

"I saw you and sonny boy at that hot springs lake . . . *Mom*." The coup de grace delivered, Hugh took several steps toward her. "I'll be taking that radio from now on."

"I'll tell you what," Anna said. "Howard's feeling so bad I doubt he'd miss his. When we get back down the hill, let's ask him."

"The battery's dead in Howard's."

Anna had switched hers out with Howard. He needed the comfort; she needed the communication. Evidently Pepperdine had already taken the liberty of "confiscating" Black Elk's radio a second time.

Hugh advanced a couple more steps. "I'll be taking that radio."

"You and whose army?" Anna meant it as a joke, a way of lightening the mood and underlining the absurdity of the situation. Pepperdine took it as a challenge. He pushed his brush jacket back like a TV gunslinger and began fingering the hilt of Black Elk's Buck knife.

"Stop playing with that damn knife," Anna snapped. "You're making me crazy."

"This knife?" Hugh said innocently, and pulled the thing from its sheath. He turned the blade this way and that as if catching the light. "This knife scares you, doesn't it?"

Anna said nothing. She was racking her brain for any kernels of information her sister might have let fall when discussing her psychiatric practice on the handling of dangerous lunatics.

Pepperdine made a feint toward her and when she flinched, he laughed.

"Give me the knife," she said evenly.

"Give me the radio."

Anna could see no harm in that. Back in camp, when she had help, she could always get it back. Hugh could do less damage with a Motorola than with a weapon. "Sure." She pulled it from its leather holster.

Hugh's face took on a crafty look, taking her easy capitulation as a sign of his power. "No deal," he said.

Anna raised the radio to her lips and thumbed down the mike button. "Frederick, are you still standing by?"

Hugh rushed her.

Instinct told her to run. Her legs quivered with the need to comply. But something warned her flight would further excite Pepperdine. She'd seen small dogs in hot pursuit; the moment the cat stopped the little beasts invariably backed off.

Hugh wasn't grasping the knife like he knew how to use it. The hilt was in his palm and his index finger extended along the blade, the way children are taught to hold a knife when cutting their food. His arms were in front of him, close together as if he intended to tackle rather than slash her.

These things were noted in the seconds it took him to close the distance between them. The observations were mildly reassuring but the look on Pepperdine's face was not. Committed to an insane act, he was intent on carrying it through.

At Anna's back was the truck. She'd effectively limited her escape routes. Dodging left or right was likely to result in some portion of her person getting pinned between the iron and Hugh's bulk.

Reflexes superseded thought; she threw herself up and back, her butt landing on the hood. Crablike, she scrabbled across the ice-slicked surface.

Hugh dove after. The knife collided with Anna's left ankle, cutting into her boot leather. Black Elk kept his equipment honed and in good condition. Anna didn't thank him for it.

Kicking out, she connected with Hugh's shoulder. Recoil sent her off the far side of the hood. Breath was knocked out on impact but there was no time to give in to the shock. Overcoming the panic of airlessness, she pushed herself to her feet.

Hugh was stretched across the hood like a stag brought home from the hunt. He'd be on top of her in a heartbeat. With the knife clutched now more in the fashion of a weapon than a butter knife, he clawed at the hood, trying for purchase.

The Motorola was still in Anna's grasp. With all the strength she could muster, she brought it down on Pepperdine's wrist. He screamed and his fingers flew open, the knife skittering down the hood and into the snow.

Anna dropped the radio and grabbed Pepperdine by the hair and the back of his collar. Using her weight she pulled. Ice helped and Hugh's two hundred pounds slid across the hood, shot out and fell; a belly flop into the frozen snow.

Before he could recover, Anna jumped on his back, one knee in his sacrum, the other on the small vertebrae of his neck. With both hands, she grabbed one of his and twisted it up behind his back.

Writhing, Hugh tried to buck her off.

Anna cranked down on his arm. "Lay still or I'll bust it. Swear to God, I will."

Pain did what logic could not and Hugh stopped struggling.

Both of them were breathing hard. Seconds ticked by. Anna was trying to figure out what to do next. He was too big to control, too crazy to let go.

"Okay," he panted. "Let me up. Come on, Anna, don't be a bitch."

A laugh barked out of Anna's lungs. Hugh was whining, apparently totally oblivious to what had just transpired. "You've got to be kidding. You just attacked me with an eight-inch Buck knife. I'm never going to let you up. If you move, I'll break your arm." She tweaked it to prove she could. "If you move twice I'll break your neck." She shifted to the knee on his vertebrae to lend weight to her threat. "It might not kill you but as a quadraplegic, maybe you won't be such a pain in the ass."

"The snow is burning me. I'm getting frostbitten. You can't leave me here with my face on the ground."

Face on the ground. The phrase jogged something in Anna's mind and she stared into the nothing that was the sky trying to lure the memory out.

"If you'd seen him facedown in the dirt whimpering like a girl . . ." Hugh had said that of Gonzales. Anna could only think of one circumstance where Pepperdine might have witnessed a scene like that. After the blowup they'd all been facedown in the sand and, she was willing to bet, even the bravest among them had let a whimper or two escape.

"You saw Lawrence get out of his shelter," she said with certainty. "Admit it or I'll break your arm."

"Duress. Won't hold up in court," Hugh gasped through the pain.

"I don't care. I just want to hurt you." To prove it, she did.

Hugh shrieked.

"It wasn't that bad," she said, annoyed. "I hardly even twisted it. As Mom used to say, 'Quit crying or I'll give you something to cry about.' Lawrence. The shelter," she prompted, putting enough pressure on Pepperdine's arm to make a fracture seem like a distinct possibility.

"Okay! I saw!" he yelped. "You're going to break my frigging arm!"

"Fucking arm, Hugh. I'm going to break your fucking arm. So you helped Lawrence out of his shelter. Good. Now, you knew Nims was dead. None of us did. How come? Did you kill him, Barney?" At the sound of the hated nickname, Anna realized what she was doing was cruel. Later she would probably feel guilty. At the moment she just didn't give a damn.

"No. I just guessed. We'd been through a frigging fire!"

"Fucking fire," Anna corrected, and tweaked his arm. "You knew. You killed him."

"He wanted to get in my shelter," Hugh blurted out.

Meanness went out of Anna, taking her strength with it. The firestorm roaring down the mountain, Nims without a shelter, begging to be let in, begging for his life. Pepperdine, a bigger man, stronger, pushing him away, condemning him to be burned alive. Hugh was guilty, not of sticking a knife in a man's ribs, but of craven cowardice. In many ways it was worse and Anna's contempt was tempered with pity.

She still knelt on Hugh and he lay compliant, afraid she'd carry out her bone-crushing threats, but the time had passed.

"If I let you up, what are you going to do?" she asked wearily.

"Nothing, I promise. Just let me up. My face is frozen."

"Don't get up till I say, okay?"

"Okay. Just get off me."

"Stay," Anna ordered. She backed away from him, retrieved the radio and the knife, then moved around to the far side of the truck. "You can get up now."

Hugh pushed himself to his knees, then struggled to his feet and brushed the snow from his jacket and trousers. "I suppose you're going to rush back and blab everything," he said bitterly.

"Not unless you annoy me in some small way."

He stood, shifting his weight from foot to foot, his eyes not meeting hers, and Anna wondered what he was up to. "Can I have my knife back?" he said finally.

"Nope."

"Anna, do you read? Anna, come in please." It was Frederick on her radio.

Hugh sneered as best he could and walked toward the trail leading back to camp. Ten yards from her he stopped and turned.

"You can tell your boyfriend he doesn't need to track down how Paula makes her living. She's a whore. A hooker. She's been working the camp. Everybody knew it. Everybody but you. A trained observer—you should get into another line of work."

Anna had guessed but she'd been so slow on the uptake she didn't feel like defending herself.

"You're Mr. FLETC, why didn't you report it?" Anna returned, but she knew the answer. He wanted to be one of the guys.

Hugh turned his back on her and she keyed the mike.

"Anna here."

"Jeeminie! Don't you ever do that to me again," Frederick exploded over the airwaves. "What's going on up there?"

"It was nothing. Snow falling or something." Anna's back ached from wrestling with Pepperdine and she was in a foul mood. "Forget about Boggins. Just follow up on the Joshua Short thing for me."

"I will. And you call me at eight. You. Call me. Got that?"

"No problem."

"We're going to get you down off that ridge."

"I know you are. I'm turning my radio off now."

"Ten-four. Eight o'clock, Anna. Don't leave me standing at the altar."

Anna laughed. "Eight o'clock." She turned off the radio and leaned her elbows on the truck in an attempt to ease her back.

Black Elk, Lindstrom, Gonzales, Page and Pepperdine were off the hook. That left only LeFleur, who hated Nims and wanted him out of the way professionally; Joseph Hayhurst, removing Nims to stop the oil lease; and Boggins. Paula was hooking. Black Elk's words now made sense: Nims should have paid like everybody else. Len had "messed" with

Paula. Since injured virtue wasn't an issue, attempted rape or blackmail very possibly was. Getting thrown out of camp would cost Paula a bundle in unearned revenues. And she would be blackballed from any fire camp in the future.

LeFleur, Hayhurst, Boggins.

And Short. The time for trusting her fellow men—if there ever had been a time—was gone. No one had seen Jennifer leave her shelter. Blood stained her left glove. Anna knew of no motive, no previous connection between Short and Nims, but it was turning out there were a whole hell of a lot of things she didn't know.

22

Stanton held the portable radio between his knees. Anna hadn't told him the truth, he knew it. While he'd been helplessly "standing by" something had happened. He was worried and hurt, he admitted. Getting to know Anna Pigeon wasn't going to be easy. She'd been alone too many years; come to rely on herself too much. Life was a team sport.

Aloneness, loneliness, had knocked on Frederick's door like the proverbial wolf more than once in the dozen years since his last divorce, but his children—Candice mostly—had kept the wolf at bay. She needed him and, therefore, he needed her. The littles of his life could make her laugh, understand; they could comfort and sometimes even educate. So he told them.

Candice, as yet, had no fear of intimacy and she shared her stories with him: boyfriends, classes, concerts. In turn he was amused, comforted, educated.

Anna had had a husband, Frederick knew. He'd died. Dead was not good. Dead was a tough act to follow. Women got addicted to widow's weeds. Anna guarded her loneliness like a treasure she hoarded as a gift for dead what's-his-name. Frederick doubted he could compete and he was wondering if he wanted to.

He looked at the knot of white pine he'd found and the pattern came clear. The monkeys were not tied together by telephone line. They weren't tied together by anything. They were seated back to back, each oblivious to his companion, anxiously scanning the horizon for some sign of the other. Frederick fixed the image in his mind though he knew he needn't bother. Every time he looked at the wood he would see it in the grain.

He put the radio back in its charger and pulled the notebook with his lists close enough he could read it.

"Boggins/Livelihood" was crossed out, "Josh/Arson" underlined. Duncan Foley, the retired BLM timber coordinator from Susanville, had returned his call regarding Nims. Foley hadn't been too specific. It sounded as if senility rather than reticence slowed his tongue, but Frederick had been left with the impression Anna's suspicions were correct: Nims had some shady deal with the lumber barons that couldn't be proven and it had been deemed in everyone's best interests that he move on quietly.

Frederick had yet to reach anyone at Aztec, Pepperdine's home park.

Putting his hands over his eyes, he began constructing a mental chart that would be the basis of his investigation into the arson and the subsequent death of Joshua Short.

The known: The Jackknife fire had been started near Pinson Lake in the immediate vicinity of Mr. Short's camp. Mr. Short and his dog had perished in the blaze. Mr. Short was camping at Pinson Lake preparatory to staging some kind of protest against a local lumber company to stop cutting in what was believed by some to be an environmentally sensitive area. Mr. Short was an experienced outdoorsman and an environmental activist.

Frederick had seen no official paperwork on the incident but the accepted explanation seemed to be that Short had either set the fire intentionally or had inadvertently let his campfire burn out of control.

Other than that, Stanton hadn't a clue. He needed to see the coroner's report, review the records in the case, talk with the Forest Service's arson investigator and visit the scene of the deaths. This last might prove of little value. Fire, snow and other investigators would have destroyed what physical evidence there was.

Working as a private citizen Frederick had already pushed the limits of not only ethics but legality. His first phone call was to his boss's home on the outskirts of Chicago.

"Jack's laying down," Mrs. McGinnis said disapprovingly. Frederick had met Jack McGinnis's wife several times on social occasions and knew her to be a friendly, charming woman. The disapproval stemmed from thirty years of having her husband's leisure time co-opted by the Bureau.

"I'm awful sorry, Mrs. McGinnis, but this is important."

"It's always important," she said tartly. The phone receiver clattered against wood and Frederick knew she was going to wake Jack.

"Yeah. Stanton. What's up?" Jack McGinnis had the gravel voice of a man who has abused whiskey and cigarettes most of his life and the jowly face to match but as far as Frederick knew he was a teetotaler with no vices except working too hard and drinking too much coffee.

Frederick explained the situation on the Jackknife with the murder and the suspected arson. "Both crimes were committed on federal lands," he said. "We've got jurisdiction."

"I don't recall the Forest Service clamoring for our invaluable assistance," Jack said dryly.

Frederick kept quiet. Jack McGinnis was seldom talked into anything. He was a crusty, dissipated-looking computer. Facts were fed in. He processed them and produced a result. Ninety-nine times out of a hundred he was right. Or closer to right than anyone else.

"I got somebody I can call and lean on. I'll see if they'll invite you to the party. You're on the clock but no overtime. Don't even put in for it. And no travel. Where are you at?"

Frederick gave him the number and listened as he read it back. "Hang on," McGinnis said. "I'll get back to you."

Less than ten minutes later the phone rang. "You're official," Jack said. "The forest supervisor said to call Chris Landis. He's the law enforcement officer for the Forest Service in Chester. He'll bring you up to speed." Jack hung up without saying goodbye but Frederick was unoffended. Over his years in the Bureau he'd come to value time saved above just about anything but life saved. Both were irreplaceable.

Frederick dialed the number he'd been given and within twenty minutes he was on the road to Chester in a borrowed government pickup truck. The Jackknife was news and, as he threaded his way through the press vans and camera setups on his way out of camp, he blessed Burwell for placing the Communications tent out of bounds.

Chris Landis was in his early fifties, a square-headed block of a man with thinning hair combed and sprayed till a moderately believable hair hat had been constructed over his bald pate. A pipe, evidently a permanent fixture, smoked in his right hand.

"The case isn't closed," he said, and Frederick noticed traces of a Maine accent. "You're welcome to what we've got." He pushed a file folder across the blotter of his battered wooden desk. Frederick picked it up but didn't open it. "Find yourself a comfortable spot and give it a read," Landis said. "Then, if you like, we'll take a wander up to Pinson Lake. Snow'll cover up most of it but you can get the lay of the land."

"Thanks a heap." Frederick smiled engagingly in hopes of dissipating any sting FBI interference may have caused. The folder clamped under his arm, he left Landis to his pipe and sought out a quiet corner.

Happily ensconced in a storage closet pressed into service as an employee break room, Frederick sipped instant cocoa and perused the official history of Joshua Paul Short's life and death.

Thirty-three years old, Short was employed part-time as a computer programmer for Harrah's Club in Reno, Nevada. He'd moved to the west from Memphis, Tennessee, four years prior to his death. Short had been arrested three times, all misdemeanor charges, 1991 and 1993 for trespassing and interfering with agency functions in Plumas and Lassen counties in northern California, and in 1989 in San Francisco. The charges boiled down to civil disobedience. The Plumas and Lassen arrests occurred in protest activities to save the spotted owl. The San Francisco arrest was during a gay rights march. Short had never served jail time.

According to the information in the file, for two weeks prior to his death, Short had been camped at Pinson Lake in an ongoing wrestling match with the Timberlake Lumber Company. The Forest Service had leased them that tract of timber for harvest and the company intended to log the area.

An Environmental Impact Statement from the Forest Service was included, either in the interest of justice or in a CYA—cover your ass—capacity, stating that there was no hard evidence of spotted owl activity in that tract of forest land.

On September eighteenth, four days after the Jackknife had been midwifed, the corpses were discovered in the ashes of the burn. On September twenty-eighth the bodies were identified as Joshua Short and dog. As Short had not died under a doctor's care, an autopsy had been performed.

The immediate area of the camp was covered in flash fuels. From past conversations with Burwell, Frederick knew flash fuels were light, dry, tindery materials such as twigs and grasses that burned fast and hot. Due to the nature of the fuels, Short's body had not been completely consumed but his face, hands, chest, belly and the front of both legs were badly burned. Although much of the remaining flesh had been eaten away by scavengers, enough of the internal organs remained intact to reveal in the autopsy that Short had not died of smoke inhalation, as was common in fires, but had burned to death. The only other indication of injury was a hairline basal fracture behind his right ear.

Frederick thumbed through the Environmental

Impact Statement with little interest and moved on to the report written by the first ranger on the scene. The burn had originated from the fire ring in Joshua Short's camp. Best guess, working backward from the time the fire was spotted by the lookout, was that it had been ignited between one and five P.M. on September fourteenth. A mangled Peak I camping stove was found near the fire ring and there were traces of kerosene on the stones surrounding the shallow pit as well as on an unburned portion of Short's left hiking boot.

Stringing together the evidence, the ranger had drawn up a possible sequence of events:

While in use, the camping stove had either fallen into the campfire or malfunctioned. The resultant explosion splattered kerosene on nearby grass and needles. Burned or blinded by the explosion, Joshua Short had fallen, struck his head and lost consciousness. Dry fuels ignited quickly and burned at high temperatures. Before Short regained consciousness, the flames killed him.

Never having been camping, Frederick had no experience with portable stoves, but the sketch seemed plausible enough.

He removed an envelope of photographs taken at the scene. Fire had left the site clean. Ash, swept smooth by the wind, coated the earth, the fire pit, the remnants of the stove, Joshua's pack and the tent he'd been staying in. A few feet from the fire pit a four-legged corpse marked the last moments of the dog's life. About thirty feet away, in the direction the fire had taken, was the body of Joshua Short. Animals had tracked up the ground around the carcasses and, judging from the photos, dined rather well. Other than that, there were no marks in the ash. A refreshingly untainted scene. Whoever had found them was to be commended for resisting the urge to charge in and flail about.

Frederick laid the photographs out in a cross that resembled the pattern used by readers of tarot cards. The table in the tiny break room was round and less than three feet across. Photos used up all available space. Knees pinched together in a maidenly manner, Stanton held the folder in his lap while he stared down at the grisly collection.

Smooth gray ash, polished by the wind, two corpses, pack, tent and twisted chunks of the stove. The trackless space between the disparate pieces in this tragic puzzle niggled at Frederick's mind. Maybe it was just that he was unused to viewing scenes of wildland fire. But it felt like more than that.

Slurping his cocoa, he kept staring. To find out what was missing, he began piecing together what was there, hoping then he would see the holes. The fire had been started between one and five P.M. by a stove accident. Perhaps Joshua had been making himself lunch or a cup of coffee and either the stove malfunctioned and exploded or fell in the fire and exploded.

Smooth polished gray.

"No utensils," Frederick murmured into his cocoa. "You cook with utensils." In the unbroken field of ash there was no sign of pans or cups or plates; no spoons—nothing.

Joshua Short was not cooking, not even boiling water. And he wouldn't use the stove for heat; he had a fire.

Frederick adjusted his storyline. Short takes out his stove to prepare something and discovers it's broken. While he's attempting to fix it, the stove explodes or tumbles into the fire and explodes. Stanton scribbled a note on the fire folder to ask if any tools had been found at the scene. Something small—a wrench or a file—could be completely concealed by the covering ash.

Field repairs ending in a tragic accident. That made sense. The stove blows up, Short is knocked on his keister—or in this case the back of his head—and loses consciousness.

Better, Frederick thought, but not yet complete. There were still holes in the plot. The dog for one. Also knocked senseless by the explosion? Not terribly likely but explosions were unpredictable. Shrapnel from the body of the Peak I or shards of stone blasted from the rocks surrounding the fire pit could have taken out the dog, killed him outright or stunned him enough the fire got him. Too bad no one had thought to autopsy the pooch.

Frederick returned his attention to the ex-Mr. Short. Thirty feet from the fire ring, the report read. That looked about right. The body was facedown, feet toward the fire pit.

Stanton wrote a second note on Landis's file folder. "Ballistics: how far could two cups of kerosene under pressure throw a grown man?" Frederick doubted it would be thirty feet, not leaving all of his body parts still attached.

Facing away from the fire ring, almost as if he were fleeing. That might account for both the distance and the positioning. The stove falls in the fire, Joshua figures it's going to explode and begins to run. Boom. Down he goes, cracks his head.

Frederick liked that scenario. It was both tidy and rational. Only with reluctance did he abandon it. The basal fracture was at the back of Short's skull. Being knocked face forward wouldn't account for it.

Shrapnel got both the dog and his master.

Unlikely, Stanton thought, but dutifully added

"Cuts to the back of skull?" to his list. No chunk large enough to strike a man senseless was visible in the photos. Anything smaller, delivered with body-stopping force, would have broken the skin.

Again Frederick rewrote Short's story. During repairs the stove falls in the fire. Short flees. In haste he trips and cracks his head. Disoriented, he staggers a ways and collapses facedown. Fire overtakes him.

Do-able, Frederick conceded. Not graceful or poetic, but definitely possible.

Smooth ash, polished.

"Hit his head on what?" Frederick mumbled. The campsite was flat, no stones, no logs. "Look under ash" he added to the end of his list. A flat rock could be concealed, one large enough a man could fracture his skull against it were he so inclined.

The same fog that held Anna and the San Juans captive on the ridge smothered Pinson Lake. The water was as flat as glass and the color of lead. Frederick was used to the cold. He liked it. It helped his mind work. Snuggling his hands into the pockets of his down jacket, he whistled "California Dreaming" under his breath while his eyes roamed the unbroken expanse of white.

An inch of snow had taken the place of ash and the scene was amazingly unchanged from what Stanton had seen in the pictures. Joshua was gone as was the dog, the tent and the pack, but the fire ring remained.

Chris Landis, shivering in Forest Service green, stood beside him, bareheaded, his coiffure too fragile to support a hat, his pipe clamped in his teeth. Between the fog and the snow his smoke was invisible but Frederick could smell the pleasant aroma of tobacco.

"This investigation drew the short straw, I'm afraid. The Jackknife's been taking up our time and attention for the last little while." Landis puffed on his pipe as it threatened to go out. When he'd produced a good head of steam, he said: "Day's not getting any younger. We may as well get to it."

They unloaded two rakes from the back of his Land Rover. Frederick started several yards above where Short had fallen. Landis began at the fire pit. In less than an hour they'd raked the area. No stones. No tools.

Landis puffed. Frederick leaned on his rake handle and thought.

"He could've hit his head on one of the rocks in the fire ring," Landis suggested. They looked at the small, charred stones. Neither was sold on the idea. The physics of the scene didn't fit. The rocks were too small, the location wrong, the injury wrong.

Whatever struck down Joshua Short had come from behind and been removed from the scene before the area burned. Short may have started the fire but someone else made sure he stayed to enjoy it.

"Looks like we've come across a bit of a snarl," Landis said.

23

No good news; call at eight. They were going to spend another night on the mountain. Tears of self-pity wormed their way through the muck on Anna's face. Lest they leave evidence of weakness the others might read, she smeared them away. Mountain fogs never lasted, she lied to herself with feeling, not like valley fogs. She'd look at it like Christmas Eve. A long night waiting for a morning that would produce treats hitherto only dreamed of. Come morning Santa would have brought clear skies and helicopters and food.

You're just tired, she excused herself. And hungry. Hungry enough to eat a badger. Again. She smiled at the rustic image of the nine of them chowing down on charred rodent. LeFleur had saved the pelt. Somewhere along the line he'd picked up the art of tanning and was going to tan the hide for Lawrence. *How to Win Friends and Influence People;* badger breakfasts deserved a chapter in any new editions.

Using the bumper for leverage, she pulled herself to her feet. Joints cracked in protest. Muscles strained while frolicking with Mr. Pepperdine had stiffened from sitting so long. Movement pried them apart and aches were renewed with a vengeance. Viewed from the vantage of a warm house and civilized pursuits, forty wasn't old. On a mountain in the snow every year gone by made itself felt. Gonzales and even the lumpy Pepperdine still possessed reserves of energy.

On principle, Anna cursed everyone under thirty.

Walking back to camp, she went over what she needed to do.

She missed Stanton and his ubiquitous lists. Her brain kept short-circuiting and it was hard to keep her metaphorical ducks in a row.

Whatever had been removed from Nims's corpse troubled her, though she had little hope of solving that particular mystery. Since she'd not seen fit to search the body when they'd first discovered it, whoever had taken the missing item could be wearing it around their neck for all she knew.

With Page and Pepperdine off the suspect list some of the fun had gone from the investigation. Personally, Anna rather liked all of her remaining suspects. Even Paula Boggins had begun to grow on her. The girl was a bit on the obvious side, a tad snippy, but Anna admired her fighting spirit and the gentle way in which she nursed Howard Black Elk.

Still, Paula Boggins needed talking to. At present she was a promising candidate for the position of murderer. She had the means—as they all did—a functional left arm and Len's knife ready at hand. The opportunity: she'd been through the firestorm in a shelter no one had seen her get out of. And, now, a motive: attempted rape or blackmail.

Joseph Hayhurst was next with all of the above.

His motive was more highbrow but sufficient—the saving of an historic site.

LeFleur was still in the running but Anna wasn't putting her money on him. His motive was weak. John had knocked around government service long enough to know how the system worked. The line of promotion was indistinct. The Office of Personnel Management was an unpredictable beast with a heavy political agenda that, in the present social climate, did not include white males.

Jennifer Short had means and opportunity but, as far as Anna could see, no motive.

By the time she reached the wash, daylight was fading from the sky as if the sun was on a slowly dimming rheostat. She had more of a sense of going blind than of coming night.

Everybody but Neil and Joseph were crowded into the shelter. Howard was propped up on the packs, his breathing shallow and wet. His eyes were open but he didn't look as if he saw. Paula sat near him singing a lullaby in a voice just above a whisper. Anna recognized the tune, a song from childhood: "The Bear Went Over the Mountain." Paula sang it in Spanish, the way Anna remembered learning it in Mrs. White's first-grade class.

Jennifer was curled up in the fetal position, her head resting on John LeFleur's thigh. Both had their eyes closed. Anna hoped Jen was sleeping. Lawrence and Stephen sat side by side, their backs against the rock, their feet stretched toward the fire pit, newly heaped with coals. Lawrence pretended to be absorbed in cleaning his fingernails with a pocketknife.

Pepperdine was squashed in a corner with only the thin shelter at his back instead of stone. Tension clogged the air, Lawrence's face was crimped in irritation and Anna suspected LeFleur's sleep was feigned. On close examination she saw a faint tic high on his cheek under his left eye.

Hugh had been sniping, she guessed. Indulging himself in words in an attempt to shore up a damaged ego. She'd rather thought his recent comeuppance would have left him subdued. But a man of Hugh's habits must get brought up short at fairly regular intervals. Clearly his response hadn't been deep introspection followed by the turning over of new leaves. With each failure he dug in deeper, till he'd entrenched himself behind a wall of self-justification years thick. For an educated man, Pepperdine was apparently not a quick learner. Anna was glad they worked in different parks. He struck her as the type who would find ways—small miserable ways—of getting back at those who crossed him.

Hugh's pack was tucked under his arm like a security blanket. With a flash of anger so vicious it scared her, Anna wondered if he still had food.

"I gotta pee," Paula announced suddenly.

"Thank you for sharing," Lindstrom said.

Paula laughed and cuffed him on the head as, stoop-shouldered, she threaded her way through the tangle of legs.

"I'll go with you." Anna creaked to her feet.

"What is it with women?" she heard Lindstrom asking the general public as she followed Paula out. "Urinating is not a spectator sport."

A smear of gray silhouetted the blackened horizon to the west but the rest of the world was cloaked in lightless, heatless, featureless night.

Headlamp in hand, Boggins stumped up the creek bed. Since she hadn't made any rude comments, Anna guessed she was welcome to tag along. Muffled, fog-shrouded, the gully was creepy during the day; at night it was enough to give a vampire bat the heebie-jeebies.

Watching Paula's dim outline and the yellowing light that led the way, Anna wondered how to broach the subject of blackmail and murder while they relieved themselves.

Cold had soaked so deep into Anna's bones, she felt it more as an abiding fatigue than a physical sensation. Both mind and body were benumbed. Even the aches and bruises from her flight from the Jackknife and her fight with Hugh had melded into a general feeling of ennui. She could easily understand the temptation to lie down in the snow and let the last vestiges of heat peacefully leave the body in the fashion that purportedly seduced victims of hypothermia. It would be so good simply to rest for all eternity. To sleep. Perchance to dream . . .

Always, there was the rub.

Boggins stopped. "You hold the light," she said, handing Anna the headlamp. "I'm going to squat over there. Hang my fanny over a cold rock. Yippee, skippy. This may take a while. It feels like I got a baby bear sticking its nose out my ass."

"Sheer poetry," Anna commented as she took the light.

"Yeah. Well. I dropped out of finishing school early on." Paula retreated to her chosen spot. Anna fiddled with the light listening to the sound of a buckle being unbuckled, a zipper unzipped.

Now was as good a time as any. Anna still had Howard's Buck knife and Boggins's trousers were down around her ankles. Danger was at a low ebb.

"Nims knew you were working the camp, hooking, didn't he?" Anna asked. She tried to make it sound as if she'd known about the prostitution all along in hopes it would be less threatening that way.

"I'm busy over here," Paula said irritably. "Can't you shut the fuck up for one cotton pickin' minute?"

"You said he was messing with you. What did he do, threaten you with exposure?"

No answer.

Anna upped the stakes. "The way I figure it, Nims tried to get a piece of the action, said he'd report you if you didn't cut him in and you clawed his face. Am I close?"

Paula grunted. "He wanted a piece of something all right. A piece of my ass."

Anna played the light over the snow. All vestiges of beauty had been crushed by blackened fire boots and her own rotten attitude. "Was that the deal; you give him sex and he keeps his mouth shut?"

"There's one in every camp," Paula said. Boggins sounded more like a jaded businesswoman than a murderess. Still, Anna pressed on. It was something to do. At times she felt more like an addict than an investigator. The reasons had grown muddled with the cold, the dark, the general weirdness of the world in which they'd found themselves. Now she just had to know because she had to know.

"How much money did you get?" she asked.

"Jesus, girl, can't you even let me take a dump in peace?"

Anna shined the light in Paula's face. Boggins didn't look guilty or scared, just annoyed.

"Move the light, Ms. Gestapo, unless that's how you get your kicks. Kinky shit's extra. You can't afford me."

"How much?" Anna repeated, but she moved the light.

"Eighty bucks a trick," Paula said, and there was pride in her voice. "Why? You thinking of going into business for yourself? Forget it. You're too old. You couldn't get forty." Paula laughed while Anna did mental arithmetic.

Five to eight hundred dollars a night for twenty nights. "Not a bad piece of change," she said aloud. "There's a lot of people who would kill for that kind of money."

"I'd kill for some toilet paper," Boggins said. "I got a world-class case of flaming asshole."

Anna forbore comment. "Did you kill Nims to keep him from reporting you?"

"Like I didn't know that's what you were getting at? Big surprise. Duh. If I stuck a knife in everybody put the squeeze on me half the cops in northern California'd be dead. Nims pissed me off so I scratched him. If'n he'd of kept at it, I'd've screwed him. Shoot, he's only got a twenty-one-day dispatch, eight of it gone. The old fart probably couldn't get it up often enough to cut into a day's take. Now will you shut up and let me do my business?"

"Sure. Page pimping for you?"

"Yeah. Neil pimps. Shut up."

"I'm shut." Anna made designs in the still-white snow of the creek bank with her light. The beam was turning a dirty brown. "I'm turning off the light to save the battery," she warned Paula as she flicked it off.

"Fine."

In the frigid dark, Anna tried to think. Paula could be lying but she doubted it. Two arrests as a juvenile; Boggins had probably been hooking most of her short life. Prostitution was vulnerable to bribes, blackmail, payoffs. The price of doing business. Murder tended to scare off the clientele.

"What did you take off Leonard's body?" Anna demanded just to see what kind of a reaction she'd get.

"You're out of your fucking mind, you know that?" Paula said.

The obscenity had the ring of innocence to it. With Boggins out of the picture, if not with an iron-clad alibi, at least as far as Anna was concerned, that left LeFleur, Hayhurst and Short. LeFleur was a long shot. Hayhurst and Short then. Anna sighed. She was not having fun.

"You know what I'd like?" she said.

"What?" Boggins sounded wary and Anna smiled. Paula was probably used to bizarre requests from all manner of folk.

"I'd like to watch TV. Hours of mindless TV with a loud obnoxious soundtrack. I'd sit in a warm room and guzzle hot tea and just watch." Wine would have been her first choice but it seemed better not even to think about that.

"Why don't you wish for a million dollars while you're at it?" There was a sound of movement and zipping. "And a roll of toilet paper." Boggins emerged from the greater darkness of her wilderness privy. "You gotta go? I'll stay if you want. Keep you company."

Anna took her up on her kind offer.

24

Pinson Lake lay dead at their backs, the raked snow ripped away from their feet to beyond where Short's body had been found. Frederick leaned on his rake handle and stared at the empty clearing.

"Who'd want Short dead?" he asked.

"Nobody I know of," Chris Landis puffed out on a cloud of aromatic smoke.

"How about the lumber company? They'd want him out of the way, wouldn't they?"

"Sure they would. But killing him would be more trouble than it's worth. Short was a pest, a gadfly. California's got more protesters and bleeding hearts than we've got med flies. We don't kill 'em, we shoo 'em away."

"Murder's not as handy as it looks," Frederick agreed.

"Anyway, Timberlake wouldn't want the trees burned," Landis added. "It's money out of their pocket."

"Insurance?"

He shook his head. "Public land. Uncle Sam absorbs the losses."

"Mind if I talk to them anyway?" Frederick asked only as a courtesy.

Chris Landis knew the game and appreciated the consideration. "I'll drive you down."

Landis radioed ahead and his secretary set up the appointment. By the time they arrived at the Timberlake Lumber Company on the edge of Chester it was quarter past five. Quittin' time and then some. The foreman, Pete Hollis, was not in a receptive mood. He had his coat on and sat with one haunch on the desk and one eye on the clock. Hollis was in his mid-thirties, bigboned, with the look of a man who keeps a little woman at home and expects dinner on the table when he gets there.

Frederick took a chair just as if he'd been offered one and ostentatiously made himself comfortable, settling in for a good long chat.

Hollis sighed, fidgeted, looked at his watch. Frederick hoped he'd want to get the interview over with badly enough he'd tell the truth right up front just to save time.

"Are you familiar with the name Joshua Short?" he asked.

Hollis shook his head. "No. But this is a big operation. I don't know the names of a lot of the guys that work for us."

"Were you involved with the planned harvest of that forest land to the northwest of Pinson Lake?" Landis asked. Landis had pulled the pipe from his jaws and scraped the bowl with a little silver tool made for that purpose. His hands were busy, and his eyes had someplace neutral to go when he chose not to look at the interview subject. A pipe might be a good prop, Frederick thought. It gave off such an air of homey trustworthiness.

"Yeah," Pete replied. "That tract was on hold . . ." The sentence dribbled to an end. "Short. That was the guy died up there in the fire, wasn't it? Burnt himself and half of California in the bargain?"

"Joshua Short," Frederick said. "He was also the one who had the logging on hold."

Hollis had a pained look on his face but Frederick wasn't at all sure it was because he had something to hide. Stanton was FBI, he'd flashed his badge, now he was asking questions about a dead man. He would have been put on his guard by anybody who didn't squirm a little.

"I'm just the foreman here," Pete said carefully. "I think you'd better ask the boss. Things in that area are pretty sensitive. We've got loggers burning spotted owls in effigy and we've got do-gooders from far away as New York City out here getting lost and mosquito bit and thinking they're striking a blow for the Amazon rain forest. All I'll get stirring in this mess is a thick finger."

Frederick laughed. "You're a wise man, Mr. Hollis. Thanks for your time." He leapt up and pumped the foreman's hand. "Chris and I won't keep you from your supper any longer."

Landis had repacked his pipe and puffed it back to life as he followed Stanton out.

"Who was handling the Short/spotted owl situation?" Frederick asked while Hollis locked the office door behind them.

"Martha Pitt, our bookkeeper. She handles the newspapers when it's got to be done. James Beldon owns the company. He hires jobs out. Anybody works here is too hot under the collar when it comes to owls so he leaves us out of it." Hollis clipped his keys back on his belt and led the way through a lighted yard stacked with lumber already resembling the buildings it was destined for.

"Who did he hire this time?" Frederick asked when they'd stopped so Hollis could lock the gates to the yard.

There'd been too many questions and the foreman was done talking. "I think you'd better ask Mr. Beldon," he said.

Landis drove. Frederick slumped down in the passenger seat. Joshua Short had been murdered. The Jackknife fire had been set either for the usual reasons—fun or profit—or to cover up the tracks of the murderer. Arson, homicide, happened all the time. A look at the statistics or the six o'clock news attested to that. It was not inconceivable that, but for an accident of geography, Joshua Short, Len Nims and Newt Hamlin's deaths were unrelated.

Ruling out Hamlin's death as strictly a casualty of the fire, Frederick tried to think who might have had reason to murder two such different men: a gay environmentalist and a redneck bureaucrat. He drew a blank. Joshua Short and Nims apparently didn't know one another. Several of the San Juans knew both Joshua and Nims—Jennifer, Stephen Lindstrom and possibly Lawrence Gonzales simply because he'd once lived in northern California. Jennifer and Stephen might have had reason to kill Nims but surely not Joshua. Gonzales might have wanted Short dead for some obscure reason but Anna'd said he was alibied for the death of Nims.

Detecting piecemeal and by remote control—if anyone could be said to control Anna Pigeon—was an exercise in frustration. Frederick felt as he had as a kid when the carnies lured him into fishing for surprise packages using a mirror and a pair of awkward mechanical pincers in the place of hands.

Landis muscled the Rover onto the main street cutting through Chester. Pine trees and one-story buildings lined the road. Night had crept down through the fog. A lighted digital clock on the dash read seven-forty-nine. Frederick wouldn't be there when Anna radioed in.

"Is there a phone anywhere handy?" he asked. "I've got a call to make."

Landis pointed ahead and Frederick recognized the long low roof of the Forest Service headquarters.

"Take your pick," Chris said as he switched on the office lights.

By the time he got through to Gene Burwell it was three minutes of eight. Frederick had the breathless sense of skidding in just under the wire though he wasn't sure if the information he had would prove of any value to Anna. Mostly he wanted contact, even vicarious contact, with the elusive Ms. Pigeon. It even crossed his mind to ask Burwell if there was some way, *any way*, to patch his call through. Common sense and a healthy dislike of looking the fool saved him from putting voice to his thoughts.

Burwell took down his information and Frederick stifled an urge to ask the incident commander to read the message back so he could check it for accuracy.

When the conversation reached its logical conclusion Frederick found himself loath to hang up the phone. He wanted to be there, even second hand, when Anna called in. Puppy love was unbecoming in a man of his middling years, he thought.

With bulldozers and media hounds roaring, lives and careers at stake, Burwell did not take the time to tell him what Anna had said in her radio transmission, not even the gist of it, and Stanton was hungry for every detail.

"Have you got a place to stay tonight?" Landis dragged Frederick out of his brown study. "We've got two spare rooms—the boys are away at college—and Mrs. Landis orders a mean pizza."

"I'm fine," Frederick said. He was tired and slightly depressed. "But thanks." The offer of a bed and hot food hadn't tempted him for even a second. His first thought had been of Anna. He enjoyed a moment of feeling noble. It was short-lived. He could do no more for her from a sleeping bag on the cold ground than from a soft warm bed. It was for himself he needed to be close, if not to her, then to the radio.

25

Out of habit, Anna sat by the wreck of Paula Boggins's truck. On the desolate ridge its junked chassis was perversely comforting, garbage ever a reminder of civilization.

Night had mixed with fog and settled ink-black around her. Anna experimented with palms and fingers. Truly, she could not see her hand in front of her face. She pulled off her glove with her teeth, grimacing to keep lips and tongue off the filthy leather. Squeezing the tiny silver buttons on her watch, she squinted at the numbers. Eight-oh-two. That was fashionably late enough.

Thumbing down the mike button, she called Stanton. The incident commander responded and only twenty years of consuming Emily Post with her breakfast cereal kept Anna from demanding Frederick. When Gene Burwell told her Stanton was in Chester, Anna found her mind echoing the childish refrain "but he *promised* . . ."

Pride mixed with exhaustion in Burwell's voice as he told her two and a half miles of road had been cleared of deadfall. Anna was impressed. She'd cut and swamped enough timber to know in their efforts to reach the San Juans they had managed something close to a miracle. Girding up the loins, she culled every bit of weariness and disappointment from her voice and heaped on the well-deserved praise.

"God willing and the river don't rise, we'll get to you sometime late tomorrow," Burwell promised.

"We'll be here with bells on." Anna's radio was indulging in the staccato static of a dying battery. John's was in no better shape and the one Howard used for a security blanket was dead as the proverbial doornail. "My radio's going," she said. "Anything else?" She knew she sounded abrupt and she knew Burwell wouldn't hold it against her.

"Yes. I'll make it quick. You've got a message from Frederick Stanton."

Anna's heart lurched like a girl with her first valentine. "Shoot," she said evenly.

Burwell related the findings of the arson investigation. When he'd finished, Anna said: "I'm going to save what juice I can. I won't call unless something comes up. Are you okay with that?"

"I guess I'll have to be," Burwell said, and: "Hang in there."

In its wake, the conversation left a silence so deep Anna's ears rang with it. Seldom in wilderness did one experience dead quiet. Life in all its minute rustlings, pipings and exhalations created a cushion of sound as comforting as the murmuring of a brook. Dead quiet was reserved for abandoned buildings, alleys, vacant lots. Without light, total absence of sound was disorienting. Time and space became as relative as the physicists always insisted they were.

For a second Anna felt as if she were falling and her finger twitched near the headlamp's power switch. Then the soaking cold and a nagging ache in the small of her back reassured her she was still in the world. Rescued by life's ubiquitous slings and arrows, she left the headlamp dark.

This suffocating night lacked the comforting touches of many backcounty nights she'd enjoyed but Anna knew there was safety in its squid-ink cloaking. No one could find her, not without giving their own location away. After being spied on by Pepperdine, her natural wariness had blossomed into healthy paranoia. Hugh was a tenderfoot, an oaf, yet she'd not heard him tracking her to the hot-springs lake. Somebody with more guts and experience could have killed her at any time.

If Burwell was correct in his estimate, within twenty-four hours rescue would reach them; rescue with all its modern technology and color of law. Anna'd been nosing around, asking questions. No one knew how much or how little she knew, how much or how little she'd shared with Frederick Stanton. She couldn't avoid the possibility that whoever had killed Nims and possibly Jennifer's brother wouldn't want her to be among those carried off the mountain.

Joshua Short murdered. Anna thought about that awhile. The news had come as a shock. Usually she was quick to suspect accidental deaths but the Jackknife had proved such an indiscriminate adversary she'd accepted that first life taken as had everyone else. Nature was a killer that had always been with mankind. Her choices went unquestioned, acts of God.

Josh's murder cast a new light on Nims's death without illuminating anything. The murders could be unrelated. Of those with no alibi for the time of Nims's death—John, Jennifer and Joseph—Anna could think of no one who would want Joshua Short dead. Clearly not Jennifer. She'd loved her brother. Besides, she and Anna worked together at Mesa Verde; Anna knew Jen had been nowhere near California at the time Joshua had died. Joseph and John she couldn't vouch for but she had no reason to believe either one of them had even been acquainted with Josh.

Joseph Hayhurst was an activist, if not for the environment, then for the rights of Native Americans to preserve their cultural heritage. It was not inconceivable Josh and Joseph's paths had crossed before. The information Frederick had unearthed about Hayhurst fighting the oil leases provided a motive for Nims's murder. Much as she didn't like it, so far Joseph was the only one who filled all three requirements for a self-respecting murderer: means, motive and opportunity.

Light marred the soupy darkness on the far side of the ridge and Anna tensed. The yellowing beam of a headlamp moved across the snow.

"Anna!"

The shout came in Joseph Hayhurst's voice. Speak of the devil, Anna thought, considering whether or not to answer. The loneliness of the place was suddenly threatening.

"Anna, where are you?" The beam poked here and there, a dirty finger trying to scrape her from hiding. "By the truck," she said, and flashed her light once. Joseph might be a murderer but at least, this way, Anna would know where he was during the long walk back to camp.

Footsteps crunched over the snow as she got to her feet, reassured herself she still carried Howard's Buck knife and could get to it easily if she had to.

"Got your radio off?" Joseph asked as his headlamp picked a path to her.

"Battery," Anna said.

"John's is almost dead." He was beside her now and Anna rocked on the balls of her feet, waiting to see what came next.

"The crowds got to me. All of us packed in like sardines, that shelter's beginning to smell like a locker room. John sent me up the hill to see what Base had to say."

Anna couldn't see his face but his voice was relaxed, conversational. Her defenses dropped a notch, the clutch in her belly loosened.

"Good news. Tomorrow—late but still tomorrow—they should get to us. They cleared over two miles of road today."

"It could be better," Joseph said. "We could be sitting in front of a fireplace somewhere entertaining our friends with tales of our harrowing adventure, but I'll take it. This has been a long couple of days."

For a minute neither of them spoke. Fatigue was pooling in Anna's joints, filling her lungs like poison.

Joseph laughed suddenly and it scared her. "What?" she demanded.

"Everybody is flipping out," he said. "Neil's reliving his glory days in high school football, Lawrence is waxing erotic over his mother's enchiladas, and John's ready to kill for a cigarette."

And Paula was ready to kill for a roll of toilet paper. A hot bath might motivate Anna to murder, if not today then tomorrow. People said they'd kill for one thing or another all the time. Mostly it was just a figure of speech but now and then a child was beaten to death for his sneakers, a baby smothered because it cried, a man killed for an empty wallet.

Society maintained the illusion that human life

was of great value but more often than not it was taken cheap; a matter of convenience or whim. Len or Josh could have been killed for toilet paper or cigarettes. Digging for deeper reasons and complex motives was a sign of respect for one's fellow man, elevating even a murderer to a plane where life was too precious to snuff out casually.

Suddenly it took all of Anna's strength just to keep on standing. She must have sighed or, worse, whimpered, because Joseph said: "Worn out?"

"Plumb tuckered. You?" she asked, to return the favor. If he said anything but yes she wouldn't believe him.

"Fresh as a daisy. Shall we head down?"

Anna slipped the elastic band of her headlamp around her forehead where it was designed to be worn so her hands would be free. "You go first. My lamp's burned out," she lied. She didn't relish the idea of him walking behind her. He led off and she followed at a discreet distance. She was so tired she was stumbling. Christmas Eve, she thought. They only had to hold things together one more day then Santa was coming with the cavalry.

When they'd passed the heli-spot, gotten close enough to camp Anna calculated if she screamed she'd be heard, she brought up the subject of murder. Or of oil leases. In her mind and possibly Joseph's the two were linked.

Under better circumstances, with plenty of food and rest shoring her up, Anna might have found the energy to employ a little tact. As it was she chose the Bigger Hammer method of investigation.

"The FBI agent down at Incident Base ran a background check on you," she said bluntly. "You were working with the Navajo nation to stop the BLM from granting an oil lease near the Bisti. There're just a handful of us up here. Pretty nearly everybody's got an alibi but you. Once Forensics gets up here it won't take long to sort out who killed Nims." That was not precisely true but Anna thought it sounded convincing. "If you did it to stop that lease, tell me now. I can't promise anything but I'll tell the district attorney what a swell guy you are. It might make the difference between life without parole and life with at least a shot at an early out." She'd said her piece in one breath and found herself faint and shaken at the end of it. She needed food.

Joseph stopped and turned, shining the light in her eyes. Anna sidestepped the beam but she'd already been blinded. "Get the light off me," she barked.

"Sorry." He moved the lamp to the ground at her feet.

"All the way off," Anna said. He clicked it off. The darkness was so absolute even without being night-blind Joseph had thrown away his advantage.

The Buck knife was in Anna's pocket. She eased it from its sheath and let her arm fall to her side.

"You're asking if I killed Mr. Nims?"

Disembodied, Joseph's voice had a sinister ring though there was nothing in his tone to warrant it. That was the problem: there was nothing in his tone, not incredulity, outrage, curiosity, malice, shock, amusement. He spoke almost in a monotone. Because it gave nothing away, it made Anna nervous.

Her hand strayed toward her headlamp but she didn't switch it on. Light would be of little value and it would pinpoint her whereabouts. One step at a time, she eased carefully back up the trail. On the packed snow her boots made little noise. "Leonard Nims was the one who would say yea or nay to the lease application," she said to cover any sound she made.

"No," Joseph replied. "Nims was the one who would say *yes* to the lease." Color returned to his voice, bitterness from the sound of it.

"It was a done deal?" Anna asked. Frederick had assured her it was pending. She was fishing for a lie. Lies, when one knew they were lies, could reveal more than the truth.

"In a sense," he replied. "Len was taking bribes from the oil and gas companies. In return he marked the Environmental Impact Statements 'No Significant Impact,' letting them drill wherever they wanted to."

Anna waited for the rest of the story but Joseph had done talking. Silence stretched, thickened. Anna's nerves stretched, grew thin. Finally she could stand it no longer. She reached up and turned on her headlamp and screamed.

Joseph Hayhurst had moved soundlessly up the trail and stood less than two feet from her.

"Old Indian trick," he said. "I learned it in Boy Scouts."

Anna stepped back and pulled the radio from her belt. "John, come up toward the heli-spot. Now."

"John's radio's off. Saving batteries, remember?"

Anna remembered. She was hoping he hadn't. "Okay," she said reasonably. "We're alone, no radio contact, I'm accusing you of murder and you're sneaking around scaring the pants off me. Before I start screaming my head off just to get some company up here, do you want to level with me?"

"Isn't this where they say 'I'm not talking without my lawyer'?"

"No. They say that in warm comfortable interrogation rooms." Anna began walking backward, careful not to trip. "I'm putting distance between us. It's all I've got—"

"Besides Howard's knife."

"—besides Howard's knife. Respect it please. I'm too tired and this is all too creepy for you to play any more games with me."

"No more games," Joseph said. "Someone could get hurt. Maybe even me." He smiled his Mona Lisa smile.

Anna didn't smile back. She was remembering his quickness and his strength. She kept her light trained on his face. He stood perfectly still and made no attempt to dodge the glare. Apparently he'd grasped the fact that her fear made her dangerous despite the fact that he was younger and stronger than she.

"If Len was taking kickbacks, why didn't you report him?" Joseph laughed without humor. "You don't think the BLM had figured it out? Why do you think Nims got bumped out of his last job? Kickbacks for timber leases. The government had no proof and, if you ask me, no white-hot desire to find any. Scandal, don't you know. A lot of career bureaucrats might look the fool, land on the wrong side of the party line. Our guess was they intended to handle the oil lease problem in the tried and true method. John might wonder why they were so anxious to promote Len into that fire management slot but I don't. They want him out of temptation's way."

"You knifed him to stop the lease," Anna said.

"Au contraire. I wish Len was alive and well. True, the lease will be on hold briefly, but then a new cog will be put in the machinery and we'll have to start all over. Find out if he can be bought and by whom, if he's ambitious, if he has any sense of responsibility toward the land. By the time that's untangled some antsy supervisor will have knuckled under to the considerable public pressure to okay the lease and the drills will roll in.

"We had nearly enough to hang Mr. Nims. In court, in public, in the media. Nims dead is a bad thing. We needed Nims."

Anna studied him. It sounded plausible and it would be easy to check. For tonight she'd let it go. As if she had much choice.

"Why did you sneak up and scare me half to death?" she growled.

"Why do children play with scorpions?"

For once everyone was present and accounted for, and the shelter was crammed with bodies. The fire pit was gone, raked over to make more space. Morale was low. When Anna and Joseph squeezed themselves in nobody even bothered to speak.

"Tomorrow, Base said," Anna told the others. "We've only got to get through tonight."

"Everybody cuddle up," LeFleur told his crew. "I don't want anybody freezing to death."

Anna squashed herself between Stephen and Lawrence as the lesser of the bundling evils and felt some small warmth from their closeness.

Headlamp on and pushed down in the sand so it shined upward casting a faint and shadow-filled light over the group, Hugh Pepperdine was wasting batteries. No one remarked on it. They only had to survive one more night and they were all glad of the light. By its feeble glow Anna studied her companions.

Lindstrom had his gloves off and was sucking on the little finger of his left hand where rough leather had worn it raw. Lawrence had his hands and arms pulled inside his brush jacket and the sleeves tucked behind his back in the classic style of a straight jacket. Jennifer had set herself slightly apart. Knees hugged tightly against her chest and her face buried in her folded arms, she sat near the shelter's opening.

"Jen, it's too cold where you are. Move in." Anna sounded harsh but there wasn't anything she could do about it.

"I'm fine," Jennifer mumbled against the fabric of her sleeve.

"John?" Anna pleaded.

LeFleur was seated between Joseph Hayhurst and Neil Page, his legs stretched over the cold fire pit. "Shove over," he said to Joseph. Half crouching, he reached out, grabbed Jennifer by the upper arm and pulled her across the Apache's lap, stuffing her into the space between them.

"They want your body," Lindstrom said.

Jennifer made no reply but allowed herself to be arranged in the relative warmth between the two men.

To Anna's left was Stephen, then an open space, then Howard Black Elk propped against the yellow packs. On his far side, against the thin fabric of one of the fire shelters that made up the tent, was Paula Boggins. Shivering in an oversized NoMex shirt, she squeezed her hands between her thighs for warmth. Pepperdine sat apart, like a leper.

Boggins was somehow changed and it took Anna's tired mind a moment to figure out what was out of place. The brush jacket: Paula had taken it off and spread it over Howard's legs.

"Put your coat back on," Anna ordered sharply.

"And move over here between Stephen and Howard."

"Howard'll get the draft," Paula protested as she struggled into the jacket.

"No he won't," Anna said. "Hugh, move up beside Howard, between him and the shelter wall."

"Why can't Paula stay where she's at?" Pepperdine asked sullenly.

"Because she's little and hurt and you're big and fat," Anna snapped. "You'll block more draft."

Hugh opened his mouth, noted the eyes on him from the others, closed it and moved. As if for spite, he turned out his lamp.

"Snug as bugs in rugs," Stephen said when they'd all done stirring. His words were light but the fun had gone out of him. It had gone out of all of them, Anna guessed.

Tucking her hands in her armpits for warmth, she leaned her head back against the boulder and closed her eyes. Bodies were piled together like puppies in a basket. One would have thought that would engender a sense of safety. Not in Anna. The dark was absolute, fatigue clouded everyone's mind. No one was farther than an arm's reach away. Black Elk was unconscious, Jennifer half comatose with grief. A knife, sudden and well placed, a heart stopped, who would be witness to it? Likely not even the victim.

Someone began to snore. Not the rip-snorting variety that destroys marriages and sets dormitories to warring, but the soft purring snore of a contented child. Out of deference to her sex, Anna guessed it was Paula or Jennifer but it could have been anyone.

The purr was soporific and Anna could feel a welcome sea of sleep lapping at the shores of her mind. Lest she give in to it, she marshaled her thoughts, laid out what facts she had.

Nims had been killed during the burnover. Eight shelters, nine survivors; the man or woman who didn't have one at the firestorm's end had shared with Nims. Paula had seen Page with his, Pepperdine had seen Lawrence, she and John could vouch for Howard, Jennifer saw Stephen. That left John, Joseph, Paula, Hugh and Jennifer.

Hugh's cowardice cleared him in Anna's mind. He'd turned Len out to die. The only motive Paula had, viewed from the perspective of business economics, ceased to make much sense. Joseph needed Nims alive so he could hang him later.

That left only John LeFleur and Jennifer Short and neither one of them had a motive that amounted to anything.

Threads of thought began unraveling. Anna let her mind drift. Dimly she was aware of the rock, unrelenting against the back of her head, the earth icy beneath her rear end, the faint warmth of the men at thigh and shoulder.

Nims: why had he needed killing? He blackmailed a young woman for sex and tried to blackmail a high-school boy into committing arson. He took kickbacks for oil and lumber leases, abandoned Hamlin to the Jackknife. The warden in Anna's mind was quick to remind her they had all abandoned Newt and she amended the thought; Nims had been quick to abandon the boy. The rest of them had dithered humanely for a moment or two.

Nims was divorced. He'd left a wife and half a dozen kids in Susanville. Single mom to six? Maybe the ex-Mrs. had a reason to do in Leonard.

Without Mrs. Nims at hand, Anna was inexorably brought back to Short and LeFleur. LeFleur and Short. Short and LeFleur. Despite her best efforts, sleep crept up, not in a slow drift but in a sudden fall, as if she had been pushed off a cliff.

26

Anna wasn't sure what woke her. In the impossible dark beneath the shelters, down in the wash, under the fog, it was difficult to be sure that she wasn't still sleeping or, better yet, dead. Cramping in her legs penetrated the swamp of dreams. She was awake and alive. However short her nap, her body was somewhat revived. Her brain remained a questionable resource. Too long without light or food, dreams tangled unpleasantly with reality and she doubted the reliability of its workings.

Butt and heels were numb with cold and her knees ached from being too long straight. Sandwiched as she was between Lawrence and Stephen, movement was almost impossible. Breathing enveloped her, the deep even breaths of Gonzales's young healthy lungs, the uneven exhalations from Stephen's uneasy slumber, rasping from Black Elk.

The purring snore had stopped. In its place was a faint whispering, gentle and all-encompassing, the sound of feathers sweeping powdered snow. Wind, she realized with a rush of gratitude, high distant wind. The weather was breaking. Fog would be blown from the canyons and they could go home. Better than reindeer stamping on the roof.

Furtive sounds, then something nudged her boot. Feet and legs were so numb it felt as if someone had kicked a block of wood on which she stood. It was touch that had pulled her from her dreams. Not because it was violent or unexpected, but because a woman waiting to be knifed is sensitive to these things.

The bump triggered the uneasy musings that had preceded sleep and a spurt of adrenaline was loosed in Anna's bowels. Resuming her rest became out of the question. Were she not called upon to defend her life, she would still have to crawl outside to go to the bathroom—euphemistically speaking: no room, no bath.

To prepare for either event, she began wiggling her toes in an attempt to wake them. Excruciating tickles from toe to hip rewarded her as nerves practiced their signals.

Another stealthy sound; Anna stopped the toe action the better to listen. She thought to unsheathe Howard's Buck knife but in the dark and crowded confines of their bivouac an accident was practically guaranteed. Finding herself to be the dreaded night slasher would not be a good joke.

The creepings and sneakings leaked from the darkness to her right. Closing her eyes—as if it made a shred of difference—Anna tried to remember where everyone had been when the lights went out. Right: Lawrence, then John, Jennifer, Joseph and Neil. Anna opened her eyes again and listened till her head swelled with the effort. Or so it felt in the dark. Neil was on the end, nearest the foil tent wall. Unless he moved in instead of out, the noise wouldn't fit. Joseph, like Page, was close to the outside.

Anna's foot was bumped again and someone grumbled, "What the hey . . ." John's voice. Not John then.

"Got to pee." Jennifer Short.

Anna had a strong need to avail herself of the facilities as well and began inching from between Lindstrom and Gonzales, squirming forward one heel at a time till she'd cleared their legs. Lindstrom never stirred and she was saved any commentary on the sociology behind yet another group ladies' room event.

This joint venture was half necessity and half concern. Jennifer was not in any shape to be left alone. Exposure, grief and, Anna had to admit, possibly guilt, had robbed her of much rational thought. The knowledge they were going home might have poured the nearly inexhaustible strength of hope into the veins of the others but that wasn't necessarily true for Jennifer. There was the possibility she had no intention of leaving this spectral forest.

Slithering like something unpleasant from under a rock, Anna left the shelter and pushed herself to hands and knees, allowing the nether parts of her anatomy to come back to life before she attempted to stand. An icy breeze cut across the back of her neck. Miserable as it was, the fog had kept the temperature constant. Clearing skies and wind chill would drop it into the teens or lower.

On a night like this, one little woman could very easily shake off the mortal coil if she so chose. A simple nap in the snow would do the trick. An hour or two and Jennifer would wake up dead. The more prosaic explanation of having to pee was probably the truth but Anna didn't feel lucky enough to gamble on it.

By the sound of her steps Jennifer was headed downstream. The accepted ladies' room was upstream of the boulder. Perhaps Jen required virgin territory. A luxury that could be indulged now that rescue was close at hand.

Having shaken some function back into her lower limbs, Anna limped down the creek bed, following Jennifer's crunching progress. With a little care, she was able to time her footfalls with the other woman's and mask the sound of her own passage.

Though nature and altruism were the vaunted reasons for tailing Jen, Anna didn't use her light. Short was one of two people left on the prime suspect list and it wasn't beyond the realm of possibility that this nocturnal adventure was inspired by ulterior motives.

Jennifer reached the pile of rocks downstream of the bivouac where the creek divided into the north and south forks. She hesitated and Anna stopped as well, wondering what went through her mind: self-destruction? Urination? Humans were a complex jumble of the divine and the ridiculous.

Jennifer began to sway, her light to swing. Sweat pricked in Anna's armpits, trickling down in icy rivulets; the sweat of fear. Jennifer was an inch or so taller than Anna and perhaps ten pounds heavier—but Anna believed, if she had to, she could overpower her. Age had robbed Anna of some physical strength but it had toughened her. Women were taught not to hurt, not to let themselves be hurt. They were taught to give up. Anna wouldn't quit and that sometimes gave her an edge when size and strength failed. She remembered a self-defense instructor saying that maybe in opera it ain't over till the fat lady sings, but in defensive tactics it ain't over till the fat lady's dead.

Insanity was what frightened Anna. Were Jennifer crazy then all bets were off. Actions, reactions, couldn't be anticipated. Jen could give up or bolt or attack. If she attacked she'd fight like a crazy woman. Anna'd seen that once when she was putting in her requisite sixteen hours in the psych ward to get her emergency medical technician's certification. A smallish woman had taken it into her head that the orderlies were IRA out to kill her. She fought like a cat with its tail on fire. Anna didn't relish walking into another buzz saw like that.

Jennifer came to a decision. From the light reflecting back off the snow, Anna could see the silhouette of her head and shoulders as she turned left and started down the south fork, the part of the creek quarantined because of Nims's body.

A path had been trampled to Leonard's temporary resting place but it hadn't had the foot traffic of the other areas and it was difficult to walk without making noise. Anna stayed where she was till Jennifer had gone ahead twenty or thirty feet, then matched the other woman step for step.

The corpse could be her only destination and Anna felt curiosity overcoming fear. Nims had lain in his foil shroud for a day and a half. Only once before had the body been disturbed. Was Jennifer the desecrator of his impromptu grave? Did she go now to take something else, something important that Anna had missed? Or did she go to put something back, either returning what had been stolen or planting an item intended to incriminate?

Or was the visit unrelated to the murder?

Images of the Donner party and of the soccer players stranded in the Andes floated up in Anna's mind and she suppressed a shudder. Not that she didn't believe in munching up one's fellows given they were dead and you were starving. What are friends for? Anna just didn't want to watch. And fourteen or fifteen hours without food hardly constituted starving.

Unless you were crazy.

As a citizen Anna had nothing against crazy. It made for an interesting world and kept her sister in a thriving practice. As a law enforcement officer, she hated it. Winning was hard when your opponent was playing on a different game board.

Absorbed in thought, she took a step out of cadence and the racket of the ice crystals crunching beneath her lug sole cracked so loudly she was surprised it didn't set off colored lights like a Fourth of July sparkler. She froze, waiting for Jennifer to stop and turn the headlamp on her.

Jennifer didn't even break stride. Her trudging steps kept falling with the regularity of a metronome. Either Jen knew she was being followed and intended to lead her shadow farther from the bivouac before she dealt with it, or she was so caught up in whatever mental machinations had dragged her out in freezing temperatures that she was deafened to all else.

Neither explanation soothed Anna's raw nerves. For a second she considered going back to the shelter and rousting Lawrence or Stephen but decided against it. In the time it took her to get help she could easily lose Jennifer.

From now on, Anna decided, she was going to the bathroom all by herself.

The erratic trail Jennifer's headlamp was blazing came to rest on the foil shelter shrouding Len's remains. A circle of gold light eight inches in diameter—the battery could produce no more—crawled slowly down the length of the shroud as if looking for a way in. The aluminum fabric had settled close, frozen in wrinkles and folds. Frost cloaked the shelter where earlier depredations had shaken it free of snow.

For the most part, the corpse had ceased to bother Anna. Not because she'd had the ill luck to see so many she'd become inured to death but because, as an EMT, she had often seen the last of life struggling out of a crushed body that had been its home. Life was precious if it was yours or someone you loved, death awe-inspiring regardless of who died. But the husk that remained behind after these miracles had transpired fit into two categories: revered garbage and evidence. Anna's interest in both quickly became academic.

Jennifer had not yet come to terms with human detritus and, by the wavering of the lamp, Anna guessed her hands shook. With a suddenness that startled, Jennifer dropped the headlamp into the snow and collapsed to her knees. Using both hands as a dog would use its paws to dig out a gopher, Jennifer began worrying at the edge of the cloth covering the body.

Bile rose in Anna's throat and she wanted to look away but the action had her mesmerized. Yellow lamplight caught the side of Jen's face. Strings of soot-blackened hair fell over her jawline. Her lips were parted slightly, her tongue ghoulish and pink against the coal-colored skin. Short's blue eyes were open wide, white showing on three sides of the irises. So macabre was the scene—an image gleaned from late-night horror movies—that Anna found herself more fascinated than frightened. If at some point Short began gnawing hunks of raw meat from the carcass Anna would step in if, indeed, what she was witnessing was a full-blown psychotic episode.

Fabric made a ripping sound as it tore free of the frozen earth, exposing Nims's left side and his face. Even the dirty amber of the dying lamp couldn't invest the dead flesh with color. Crescents of white showed where Nims's eyelids had failed to close completely under Anna's ministrations.

Tiny heartbreaking noises, the kind puppies make when they dream, percolated out of Jennifer. Anna doubted she was even aware she made them. Juxtaposed with the frantic pawing at the dead man, the noises made Anna's scalp crawl. Above the ridge the high whine of wind through the snags sawed at the night and she was put in mind of the Windigo, the flesh-eating spirit that haunted the north woods.

With clutching motions, Short worked her hands up Leonard Nims's body, up the arm stretched above his head then tried to drag it back toward her. Rigor mortis would have passed off but Anna doubted he'd become any more flexible. Temperatures had stayed in the mid-twenties and were dropping. Nims would be frozen stiff.

The sleeve of his yellow brush jacket was stuck hard to the ground. Jennifer swung over, straddling the corpse. With both hands closed around its wrist, she pulled. The puppylike whimpering increased in intensity, the cries closer to human. The fallen headlamp illuminated Short's belly and chest as she tugged, each effort drawing forth a small cry.

Nims's arm came loose with a sickening crack, either ice releasing the sleeve or the ball joint in his shoulder snapping under the strain. Short fell back, her butt landing on the back of the dead man's knees, the rigid arm thrust up between her thighs. Struggling up to a crouch, one knee on either side of the body, Jennifer wrestled with the arm. Awful sounds of dry retching underscored the ghastly chore. She pulled the arm down behind her body where Anna could no longer see it and the fight continued; the quick and the dead in bizarre combat.

With a grunt of triumph more awful in its glee than the previous sounds of suffering, Jennifer achieved her goal. Snatching up the headlamp, she tottered to her feet and stumbled away, farther down the creek bed into the darkness.

Seconds ticked by. Anna fought to control her stomach. Breath, cold and odorless, was sipped in through pinched nostrils as if it carried the stench of the charnel house.

Jen's light winked out. Maybe she'd disappeared behind an outcrop. Maybe she just waited in the dark. Anna stepped over to Nims. Shielding her light with her body, she trained it on the corpse. His hand, the color of ash, two fingers broken during the encounter, lay palm up on the snow, a dead white spider. Jennifer had taken Leonard's glove. Confusion swirled through Anna's brain in a numbing wind. Why on earth steal the glove?

Nims's right hand had lain palm up at rest in front of his face. With his body twisted up it floated there as if warding off a blow. Anna studied it: a plain leather glove with a small "s" in ink stenciled on the wrist. Nothing out of the ordinary. Evidently only the left glove had any value.

Anna turned off her lamp and rocked back on her heels. She needed light, heat, food. She needed a vacation.

Vacation.

Motive.

LeFleur mentioned Len had returned from vacation shortly before they'd been dispatched on the

Jackknife. Nims had been visiting his kids from a prior marriage. Leonard had lived and worked in Susanville, California, for twelve years. Where better to have left a family? Susanville was not more than an hour—two at most—from the south end of Pinson Lake where the fire had started, where Joshua Short had been killed.

Nims took kickbacks from oil and gas lessees; when in California, from lumber lessees. It wasn't a great stretch of the imagination to picture him taking money for other less than legal chores. Like scaring off pesky protesters. If Len had killed Joshua—or if Jennifer believed he had—she had one of the best motives in the world for sticking a knife between his ribs.

"Damn," Anna whispered.

Footsteps retreating brought her back to the present. Jennifer was running now, Anna could hear it. Logically, she should go back to the bivouac and get help, but she couldn't shake the idea that Jennifer was a greater danger to herself than to anyone else. Len's murder had been a crime of passion. Short meant to cover it up but Anna doubted she'd be willing to kill again to do so.

"Want to bet your life on it?" Anna muttered aloud. Then she turned on her lamp and started down the creek in the direction Jennifer had taken.

Sharp pains shooting through ankles stiffened by cold and immobility slowed her to a lumber and she cursed her frailty. Each step made enough noise she could no longer hear Jennifer. Several times Anna started to call her name but thought better of it, afraid it would only increase the woman's panic. Glimpses of Jennifer's light were all Anna had to guide her and it appeared and disappeared out of the unnatural night like swamp gas.

Suddenly that winking golden eye turned and stared back. "Jennifer," Anna called. "It's me. Wait up." The words were so pedestrian they rang in her ears, but her other choices, "Stop, police! Drop that glove!," struck her as absurd.

"Stay back," Jennifer screamed, her voice guttural edges and cutting highs. "I got to pee!" She turned and began scrabbling up the frozen embankment on the northern side of the wash.

Anna plunged after, reaching the bank just as Jennifer's boots disappeared over the edge. Clawing her way up in darkness, her headlamp slung by its elastic band over her wrist, Anna wished she'd had sense enough to wear a hard hat. "Talk to me, Jen," she yelled as she tried to find a grip on the frozen earth. Crusted snow broke off and fell down into her gloves. Her knee banged against something hard. "Talk to me."

Anna reached the top and hauled herself over the lip of the ravine.

As soon as she'd found her feet, she shined the light in a half circle. Jennifer was gone, her tracks leading up the hillside toward the ridge. For an instant Anna listened. Crashing sounds of flight reassured her and she started up the hill following Jen's trail. Every few feet she stopped, listened, heard the footfalls and pushed on.

The way was not particularly steep but it was mined with pits where the Jackknife had burned well below ground level in pursuit of living roots. Snow and frost had conspired to camouflage the holes and the ground was treacherous. Anna had the relative security of following in Jen's footsteps and so made better time. With each stop she could hear the distance between them had shortened.

The last time she paused to listen the rushing retreat was checked by a crash and a cry.

"Jen!" Anna hollered. There was no answer, not even the sound of running. Anna slowed her pursuit, trained the faltering light as far ahead as she could, sweeping it in short arcs, looking for any indication Jen's trail was interrupted or had doubled back. Black post-hole steps led cleanly through the humps of white and spikes of charcoal that gave teeth to the landscape. After fifteen yards or less Anna's vigilance was rewarded by a splash of color, the lemon yellow of a jacket designed to be easily spotted in a search.

Collapsed in a heap, Jennifer Short craned her neck and looked up at Anna's light. A wild and staring look was in her eyes. Straggling hair half hid her face. Muscles along her jaw bunched as she clenched and unclenched her teeth. Any illusion that humans have somehow shed their animal natures was shattered.

Anna stopped where she was and sat on her heels, letting her lamp split the distance between them. "Are you okay, Jen?" she asked conversationally. Jennifer didn't respond. "I heard you leave the bivouac and got scared you'd hurt yourself so I came after."

In the half-light Anna could see the rigid cast of Jennifer's features soften slightly. "And, too, I had to pee," Anna added, and laughed. Short didn't smile but the softening process didn't stop either. "To paraphrase the Queen of England, I expect this is not a time you will look back on with undiluted pleasure." Anna went on talking just to talk, to build a fragile bridge between them. "You've had a rough couple of days. That's why you're feeling nuts. Bad as it is, it'll get better. Cross my heart and hope to die."

Jennifer's face grew slack, her eyes hooded. The transformation from stretched muscle and taut skin was so marked it was alarming. The other at least mimicked life in its energy and violence. This was the face of the comfortably comatose.

"What happened, Jen?" Anna asked gently, and duck-walked a couple steps closer. "Did you step in a stump hole and twist your ankle?"

Short nodded and pointed like a very young child.

"You landed on your right foot?" Anna waddled closer. "Does it hurt?"

A childlike nod.

"Can I look?" Anna didn't get a "no" or a shake so she slipped carefully down the side of the hummock that had tripped Jennifer. A depression several feet deep and five or six feet in diameter held them both like mice in a teacup. Short's left leg was curled under her, her right thrust out. Beneath her left thigh Anna could see the fingers of Len's glove peeking out. The glove was dark brown and stiff as if it had been dipped in chocolate and allowed to harden. Anna was careful not to notice it.

With both headlamps on, shining not on them but on the reflective surface of the snow, Jennifer looked like the heroine in a sepia-toned tragedy.

"When you fell did you hear anything?" Anna asked. "A crack or a snap?"

At first Anna didn't think she was going to reply, then she said, "A snap, I think." Her voice was little, as childish as her movements had been.

"Not good," Anna said. "You may have busted it. I'll go get some of the guys and we'll carry you back to camp and cut the boot off there. May as well leave it on for now. It'll keep your foot warmer and act as a kind of a splint."

Huge tears rolled down Jennifer's face. Their size

and clarity transfixed Anna. These were not shallow tears but flowed from a well of hurt so deep the pressures were nigh unto intolerable.

"Will you be okay alone here for a minute? I'll be as quick as I can," Anna said.

"Don't you want to know what happened?" Jennifer's voice was drowned in tears.

"If you want to tell me."

"Len killed Josh," she said. "He was supposed to scare him off but he hit him too hard and killed him. Then he set the fire. He killed Newt too, with the fire." Tears filled her throat, choking off her words. Anna knew a better woman would take Jen in her arms and hold her. Anna wanted to do it but she didn't know how so she held the broken foot tenderly and waited.

Jennifer must have let Len into her shelter. When the firestorm was upon them he had told her and she'd killed him.

Anna set Jen's foot down gently. Not wanting to focus on Short's grief-ravished face, her eyes came to rest on the big chocolate fingers digging into the snow under Jennifer's leg. Len's glove. It had fallen off his hand, Anna remembered. With some misplaced idea of propriety, she'd threaded it back on the dead fingers. A big glove for so small a hand.

Abruptly Anna clapped her hands close to Jennifer's face, startling her out of her tears.

"Quick," she demanded. "Ten seconds or less: why did you take Leonard's left glove?"

Jennifer just stared, her eyes panicked. Five seconds passed, ten, twenty.

"I cut my hand," she stammered at last. "My blood would be mixed with his."

Anna sighed and shook her head. "That's what I thought."

"DNA tests would show that, wouldn't they?" Jen challenged.

"Yes," Anna replied, and plucked the glove from beneath Jennifer by a finger. "They will."

Jennifer's eyes flashed with sudden understanding. She grabbed at the glove but Anna whisked it out of her reach. "Sorry. Nice try. I'm going for help." Anna heard Jennifer beginning to sob as she walked away but she didn't look back.

27

Back to a sturdy snag, Anna stopped just out of sight of Jennifer's probing light. Before she moved again she needed time to think. Wind was rising, slicing across her face like a razor. Her skin hurt with it, her hands and feet ached with cold. Jennifer's cries found her but she ignored them, her mind churning through the night's revelations.

Len's left glove—a large on his small hand. The right glove, the one not saturated with blood, had an "s" in ink on the wrist, size small. Under the chassis of the truck the first night, over badger, then again with the abrasion on his little finger: Stephen fussing with his left glove. Because it didn't fit. Gloves were so necessary to firefighters that an ill-fitting one would be tolerated only briefly. The bloody left glove belonged to Stephen Lindstrom. It had become soaked with Len's blood not during some awkward contortion of a man with a knife in his heart, but by the blood pouring from the wound beneath the murderer's hand. Stephen had switched gloves, taken the unbloodied glove, but it was way too small.

The rest of Jennifer's story was probably true. Nims was Catholic—though there were cynics who would say, faced with death, we are all Catholics. Searching for absolution he'd chosen the wrong father confessor. Two things Anna hadn't recognized as important at the time became clear. When she'd told Stephen Joshua Short had been killed he said he was a friend. And when Stephen had been arrested in 1989 for obstructing traffic, Josh was arrested that same date in a gay rights protest in San Francisco. Stephen either was or had been Joshua's lover.

For the murder Anna could forgive Lindstrom. Forgive wasn't the right word, the trespass had not been against her. Understand then. The betrayal that she was having trouble accepting was Stephen allowing Jennifer to cover for him. Landing Joshua's only and beloved sister in the slammer for murder jerked the rug out from under any sort of True Love Revenged defense he might be using to rationalize his act.

Anna was furious at Stephen for not being the man she'd come to like and admire and furious at Jennifer for letting herself be used. The womanly virtue of self-sacrifice didn't hold any allure for Anna. Teaching dogs to love their leash.

She glanced over her shoulder in Short's direction and was surprised because she could see. The jaws of night were being pried apart by the dawn. Fog had thinned. Scraping her head back against the charred wood, Anna looked up. One, two . . . seven; seven stars were visible through a rift in the ceiling that had held them down for so long.

Tears welled up in her eyes. Stars. She'd not realized—or hadn't let herself think—how much she had missed them. And the sun. If ever a girl had needed the sun it had been over the last forty-eight hours. She filled her lungs as if it was the first breath she'd drawn since they'd crawled out of their fire shelters.

With oxygen came clarity and Anna knew what she must do. Nothing. The glove was safe in her pocket. It was Stephen's work glove; DNA testing should find plenty to tie him to it and, since Jennifer lied about bleeding on it, nothing to tie her to the murder. She'd get help, carry Jen back to camp and wait. Rescue would reach them sooner than later if the clearing trend continued. Stanton could have the glove. Stanton could have Lindstrom.

Hunching her shoulders, Anna pushed away from the snag. Jennifer had stopped crying or pursued the pastime quietly. Anna thought to check on her but didn't want to start the waterworks again. Mostly she didn't want to see Jennifer till she'd cooled off. She was afraid she would say something unkind. Later, when she'd rested and eaten, empathy might overcome anger. She'd call Molly. Molly would explain away weakness in blame-free psychological jargon. Anna would believe her. Post-traumatic stress disorder: Jennifer could certainly present a case for it.

Feeling kinder already, Anna started back down the slope, following the light from her headlamp and taking courage from the hints of gray brought by the coming day.

Another light joined hers at the same moment as a shout. "Jen! Is that you?"

It was Stephen Lindstrom. There was a murmured exchange then another shout: "Jen!"

Since Lindstrom wasn't alone, Anna shouted back.

"It's Anna. Jen's sprained or busted an ankle. Who've you got with you?"

"Hugh" came with the sound of footsteps on the snow.

Anna's heart dropped, still Hugh was better than nothing, if only marginally.

Even with Pepperdine's irritating but less than murderous bulk to ease the situation, Anna was at a loss. If she sent Hugh for help, she and a crippled Jennifer would be left alone with Stephen. Should she go herself, she'd be leaving a cripple and an incompetent alone with him. If Stephen went, then he'd be out of her sight. Anna was reminded of a story problem in third-grade math involving a fox, a goose, a sack of corn and a rowboat.

They'd all have to go together.

"Think the two of you can carry Jennifer back without hurting her too much?" Anna asked.

"Sounds like you're not planning on doing any of the grunt work," Stephen kidded her, a light punch landing on her arm.

Anna wanted to punch him back hard for preying on Jennifer's grief and love of Joshua but she managed only to flinch away from his touch. In the semidarkness it went unnoticed.

"There are people for that," she said calmly. "Large people with muscles all the way up between their ears."

"What were you guys doing way out here anyway?" Pepperdine asked aggressively. Still trying to make up for the incident with the Buck knife, Anna suspected. She ignored him.

"Jen's up the trail a ways." She gestured up the hill and stepped aside to let them pass.

"Stephen?" Jennifer called. She'd heard their voices.

Anna held her breath. "Don't, Jen, don't do it," she whispered to herself.

"It be me," Lindstrom called back cheerfully.

"She figured it out," Short cried. "Anna knows."

Momentarily the four of them froze in a tableau: Anna, Hugh and Stephen strung out along the trail, Jennifer in her hollow of earth. Hugh broke it first, his head rocking back and forth in a parody of the dolls used to decorate the rear windows of cars. "What? Knows what? What's going on here?" he demanded of all, and got explanations from none.

Anna was concentrating on Lindstrom. With the dawning light, she could just make out his features. They had the closed desperate look of a cornered animal's. Either he'd give up or he'd run. Should somebody try and stop him, he'd fight. Anna had no intention of getting in his way. There wasn't a chance in hell she could stop him without getting badly hurt and probably not even then. Running would only buy him time and not much of that. Once onto his trail, helicopters would track him down before the day's end.

Stephen's face set, his center of gravity dropped, he pivoted and sprang, lunging back down the trail the way they'd come. Anna leaped aside. Hugh wasn't quick enough and got knocked on his butt.

Stephen would head north and east, deeper into the Caribou Wilderness. Even with his strength and wilderness survival experience the helicopter would pick him up. Anna couldn't but admire his courage.

Pepperdine hauled himself to his feet. "Lindstrom killed Len?"

"Looks that way."

"Are you just going to let him go?" Hugh was trembling with relief or excitement. Anna couldn't tell which. "Give me the knife, I'm going after him."

Anna looked at Hugh as if he'd lost his mind. She wasn't altogether sure he hadn't. "They'll catch him later," she said. "He won't be able to get far in the snow without leaving a trail a blind man could follow."

"You'll attack me but won't chase down one of your little pals, is that it?" Hugh said.

Anna let that pass. She wasn't in a mood for setting any records straight. "Leave it alone, Hugh. Let's go get John and the others and get Jennifer back to the shelter."

"Screw that." Hugh wasn't exactly frothing at the mouth but specks of saliva had formed at the meeting of his lips and he sprayed out spittle with his words. "You'll go after him with John or Joseph but not with me. You don't think I have the balls, do you?"

"I have no interest in your balls or lack thereof," Anna said.

That was the wrong answer. Hugh exploded, one meaty fist slamming into the other. Barging down on her like an enraged rhino, he shot past, in hot pursuit of self-respect. And Stephen Lindstrom.

"Damn it, Hugh, come back here," Anna shouted. Either he didn't hear or he didn't care. Were Hugh unlucky enough to catch up with Lindstrom he was bound to get hurt. In the heat of the moment he might even get killed. Nims, a jury might excuse. Nims and Pepperdine, never.

"Doggone it," Anna growled. "I'll be back," she shouted to Jennifer.

Lindstrom had cut back down to the wash, crossed it and headed off at an angle up the far slope. Above the bivouac the new trail pursuer and pursued blazed joined up with the path to the hot springs and the going got easier. Individual tracks became indecipherable and Anna tracked by what was not there; no fresh prints leading off the beaten trail.

Around the thermal area much of the snow had melted and the rest would melt quickly. Stephen was hoping to lose his trail. He was a clever man, but Anna already knew that.

At the top of the low ridge above where Lawrence had killed his badger in what seemed like the good old days, Anna heard yelling. Male and angry, it wafted over the rise separating her from the thermal lake. Evidently Hugh had cornered his quarry. What an idiot.

Anna had been alternately walking and jogging, nursing a stitch in her side. Now she quelled the desire to sprint the last hundred yards. Exhausted, she'd be little use to anyone and a danger to herself. Forcing herself to relax and breathe, she walked through the vale and up onto the next ridge.

Clear light was touching the last of the fog and each particle of moisture caught it. Steam roiling up from the lake, the mud pots, the fumaroles, glowed in opalescent plumes. Bright and shadowless and surreal, the lake muttered and fussed, eerie streams of color moving as if they had plans of their own.

The yelling had stopped. No one was at the lower end of the lake where Lawrence and Anna had enjoyed their public bath. Quickly she scanned the periphery trying to penetrate the moving curtains of mist. Grunting aided her search. Eyes followed sound as a finger of wind plucked at the steam and exposed Hugh and Stephen on the top of the crumbling bluff that rose out of the boiling lake. For twenty feet beneath them gray-white earth, ridged and pitted, steam pouring from hidden vents and runnels of mud hardened over the years, fell in a ragged curtain down to the superheated water.

Like two moose in rutting season, they were locked together, a headless beast that danced two steps forward and two steps back. Suddenly Anna felt desperately tired. She wished she had a cattle prod or a can of pepper spray. Supposedly the stuff worked on animals. This would be a good opportunity to test it out, she thought.

Dropping into an easy jog, she took the long way around, following the ridge to where it joined with the bluff above the lake. Footing in thermal areas was too hazardous to risk unless one had to. Along the high ground trees were sparse so deadfall and stump holes weren't much of a problem and Anna made good time.

The shoving match was still in progress when she got there. From the look of the ground beneath the combatants' feet, it had been going on for several minutes, a phenomenally long time to sustain a fight. The men's breath came in gasps and grunts. Both were too engrossed to take note of her arrival.

Standing back a relatively safe distance, Anna shouted. Neither looked up. Energy could not be spared. Locked in their grunting samba, they were working closer to the edge of the unstable bank.

Annoyance turned to alarm and Anna eased closer. "Give it up, Hugh," she shouted. "You're too close to the edge."

Reason was a thing of the past. Stephen was probably the better fighter but Pepperdine had weight on his side and a score to settle, not with Stephen but with a world that called him Barney and wrote him off.

Huffing like a steamroller, his boots digging up the soft soil, Pepperdine began dozing Lindstrom toward the drop.

"Stop it!" Anna yelled.

Pepperdine started to roar, a low rasping sound that built as he pushed. Stephen was losing ground. His boots scrabbled on the edge. Chunks of bank, riddled with holes from eons of steam percolating through, began to fall away.

"No!" Anna shouted, running across the small clearing. "No, Hugh." Grabbing his arm for leverage, she stomped down hard on the arch of his foot. Most of the blow was absorbed by his heavy boot but she got his attention. Pepperdine's heavy face swung toward her. There was no lessening of hostility when his eyes met hers. Indeed, it was as if he'd been waiting for just such an opportunity. As his fist drew back Anna threw up an arm to protect herself, afraid to dodge lest she lose her footing. His knuckles glanced off her cheekbone. Falling back, hands groping for something to hold onto, she wished she'd been a little nicer to Hugh. Or killed him outright.

Somebody shouted her name. Her right shoulder slammed down with such force the air was knocked from her lungs. Paralyzed, Anna slid downward headfirst. Sulphur fumes burned her eyes and penetrated her skin until she could taste the stuff. Breath returned in a rush and she sucked the stench of this local hell deep into her lungs.

Slowly the sickening slide stopped. She didn't dare move for fear of starting the process over again. Carefully, Anna opened her eyes. Head down, she was mired in mud. A dam of whitish slime had been pushed up by her shoulder and kept her from slipping down farther. Feet and legs were strung out above her. Without moving her head, she could see the tip of her knee. Their weight was trying to push her farther down; she could feel it press on her diaphragm and stomach. One arm was pinned beneath her. The mumble and pop of the lake was nearby, just below where she lay. Ooze, not hot enough to burn but hot enough to remind her what waited below, soaked through the leg of her trouser.

She shifted her arm free, hoping to drive it into the muck to stabilize her position. Even that small movement upset the equilibrium and she slid several more inches before again coming to a stop.

"Anna?"

It was Stephen.

"I'm kind of busy right now. Where's Hugh?"

"He's resting."

"Get me out of here." For a moment she didn't hear anything and a terrible fear that he'd simply walked away welled up in her. "Stephen!"

"I'm here."

Anna couldn't move to look up. "Get me out of here."

"You've got to listen, Anna."

"No kidding."

"Len killed Josh."

"So Jennifer said."

"Not like that. I didn't tell her all of it. Josh wasn't dead. Len knew it but he lit the fire anyway. He was afraid Josh would press charges. Anna, he heard him screaming but didn't go back. That's what he confessed."

"Yeah. Well. Whatever. We've all got our problems. Get a branch. Please. The blood's going to my head. I'm going to pass out, Stephen." Anna heard the note of pleading in her voice and changed the subject. "You set Jen up, Stephen. Josh's little sister. That cancels out your defense." Anna'd not meant to antagonize, she'd just needed to get the taste of begging out of her mouth. Triumph, if there was any, evaporated in the silence that followed. Fear took its place.

"Stephen!" Anna shouted.

"I never set Jen up," Stephen said. Anna felt such a rush of gratitude that he was still there she could have cried had not every sphincter in her body been squeezed tight. "When we came up here to bathe yesterday I told her Len had killed Josh. I thought she had a right to know. Len being dead—I thought it would make her feel better somehow. If I'd known it was going to push her back into a funk I would've kept my mouth shut. I didn't know she was going to try and get me off the hook or I'd've stopped her. I guess she needed to do something for Josh. I wouldn't have let her, Anna, believe me."

"Fine," Anna said sourly, but she believed him. "You're a swell guy. So get me the hell out of here."

"I can't go to jail."

"There were extenuating circumstances," Anna managed. Sulphurous mud crawled in her mouth with every word. "They'll go easy on you."

"Sure. Crazed faggot revenges homo lover. Juries love that. I can't go to jail, Anna. It'd kill me. I can't be locked up. I'm sorry."

From the corner of her eye, Anna noticed the little dam of gray mud that kept her from falling into the lake was cracking, beginning to fall apart.

28

As Anna pried up an eyelid, Hugh Pepperdine flinched away then squawked at the pain the movement caused. "Don't sit up yet," Anna cautioned. He blinked up at her. His eyes had a vague unfocused look.

"What's your name?" Anna asked.

"What happened?"

"Do you know what day it is?" Anna asked, then realized she didn't know what day it was.

"Tuesday." Hugh's eyes were clearing. They roved slowly over Anna's face. "Who are you?"

"You've had a blow to the head," Anna explained. "You're probably concussed. Do you know your name?" she pressed.

"Shit. It's you, Anna." Pepperdine closed his eyes. "What happened to your face?"

Anna reached up and felt of her nose and cheeks. Hair, ears, skin, all were filled with gummy whitish mud. Maybe Hugh wasn't as bad off as she'd feared. She'd scarcely recognize herself.

"Don't you remember?" she asked.

"I remember coming up here after what's-his-name," Hugh said, eyes still closed. "What hit me? My head feels like it's broken."

Anna ran her hands over his skull, touching lightly, looking for any abnormalities. She worked her fingers down the back of his neck feeling for displaced or deformed cervical vertebrae, checked his ears for fluid and behind them for the bruised look of battle signs that sometimes accompanied severe head trauma. "You've got a knot the size of an ostrich egg on the back of your head but I don't think anything's fractured. You'll have a headache for a few days."

Running her hands down his arms and legs, Anna pinched and poked and asked questions till she'd satisfied herself there was no central nervous system damage. Hugh lay still, letting her conduct her secondary survey. "Looks like everything still works," she said when she'd finished, and: "You honestly don't remember a thing after coming up here?"

"I said that," Hugh replied testily. "Is my head injury making you deaf?" Then his tone changed to one of fear. "Why? Does that mean anything?"

"No. No," Anna reassured him hastily. "It's fairly common. You get a hard enough knock on the head, you forget the events immediately prior to the injury. It's not like you forget all your past lives. It's usually just a matter of minutes that get erased."

Hugh seemed determined to sit up at this point so Anna helped him. Groaning, he held his head between his hands in the necessary cliché of a man with head pain. "It feels like my head's the size of a beach ball and made of lead," he complained.

"It'll get better," Anna promised. "Can you walk?"

He started to shake his head then thought better

of it. "Not yet." Carefully, so as not to jar his brain, Hugh lifted his face and looked around. Streaks of blue showed through the fog. The sun was not yet up but the light was strong enough to paint the steam in pale shades of peach.

"Where's Lindstrom? I was chasing Lindstrom. I remember that much."

"You really don't remember?" Anna asked for the third time. He just glared at her. She took it for a "no."

"I got knocked down the bank, almost to the lake. You pulled me out. Lindstrom hit you and you fought. Stephen fell back, into the thermal area. You got knocked down and hit your head."

"Lindstrom?"

"By the time you'd got me up the bank he was gone."

"He sank in that stuff?" Pepperdine had the decency to look appalled.

Anna didn't reply.

Pepperdine worked his head gingerly from side to side testing its limitations. "Hey, I saved your life," he said with sudden realization.

"Yeah," Anna said. "I owe you a beer. Can you walk?"

With help, Hugh got to his feet. Half a dozen times on their slow walk back to the wash he asked her again what happened, reminded her again that he'd saved her life. Anna restricted her responses to grunts and nods as much as she could. It was not beyond the realm of possibility that one day Hugh's memory of those minutes would return. She was gambling that by then he'd be so in love with the story she'd told him that he'd cling to it for the rest of his days.

* * *

Enclosed in the artificial night of the shelter, the others were just beginning to stir as Anna and Pepperdine limped into camp. Outside the tent, John and Joseph Hayhurst were muttering in low voices and stamping life back into their feet.

"What the hell happened to you two?" LeFleur asked. The last vestige of heat was gone from Anna's mud pack. Not only did she look like the living dead but her wet clothes had chilled her to the point she spoke like a zombie, through clenched jaws. "Long story," she managed. "Jen's busted an ankle. You'll need a couple of guys to carry her out. Let me dump Hugh and I'll show you where she is."

Anna pulled aside the shelter flap. Paula, dutifully wearing her jacket, had nonetheless curled herself around Black Elk, sleeping cold to keep him warm.

"Everybody make it?" Anna asked as Paula woke. She laid a hand on Howard's neck. Pulse and breathing reassured her. "Not much longer now," she said, and ducked outside.

With the first rays of the sun came the welcome sound of a helicopter thumping through the still air. Common miracles but Anna felt blessed.

Joseph and John were carrying Jennifer, Anna trailing behind. They didn't even stop at the bivouac, but turned south up the trail to the heli-spot.

Two men met them. Two clean, warm, well-fed men with a stretcher and medical gear. Neither was Frederick Stanton, but Anna forgave them. "We've got a man with bad burns down in the wash. Take him and the guy with the head injury first," she said. "This woman's ankle's broken. She'll keep."

John and Joseph stepped to one side as the medics

jogged down the incline. Young and strong and handsome in their gray jumpsuits, they reminded Anna of Stephen. That life was over and it saddened her.

Up on the heli-spot the pilot was unloading coolers from a shiny Bell JetRanger. Not since Anna'd watched Cinderella's pumpkin metamorphose into a glittering carriage had she seen such a lovely equipage. The pilot, a balding overweight man in his fifties, helped Joseph and the crew boss to park Jennifer on one of the coolers. Lawrence and Neil joined the group and the pilot set about serving them with such good cheer they became heady with it. The adventure was over, they were saved. Glory hallelujah. Everybody but Jennifer drank hot cocoa and laughed too much. Jen remained shut in her own dark world. It would take more than a hot bath and a good meal to cure what ailed her.

The medics brought Hugh and Howard up to the heli-spot. Paula walked beside the stretcher, her hand resting lightly on the frame near Howard's arm. More helicopters began chopping up the segment of sky above them. "Press," the pilot said. "They've been buzzing around like flies for two days."

The medics loaded Hugh into the helicopter then slid the stretcher bearing Howard into its slot. "Paula," he said clearly. It was the first word he'd spoken in Anna couldn't remember how many hours.

"Can I go?" Paula asked simply. Gone were the sexual overtones that had once accompanied all requests.

"What do you weigh?" Helicopter pilots were the only people on earth who got an honest answer to that question. Few were willing to die for their vanity.

"A hundred and thirty-one."

"Get on board."

As Paula was buckled in, John nudged Hayhurst. "Maybe she can hang up her spurs, make an honest man of him."

"It'd save him a fortune, that's for sure," Joseph replied.

Pepperdine had been right; everyone had known but Anna.

The helicopter departed in a frenzy of wind and noise. Left again to themselves, quiet descended on the group, hilarity of relief evaporating as their losses began to sink in.

"That was some story Hugh was telling," Neil Page said. "How much of it's true?"

Anna pressed her cocoa into Jennifer's hands and poured another for herself before squeezing onto the cooler close to the other woman. Jen would need any comfort that could be offered in the next couple of minutes. Short couldn't but have noticed Stephen had not come back. Anna guessed she was afraid to ask why.

"It's true more or less," Anna answered Page.

Lawrence shook himself as if a goose walked over his grave. "They'll never find his body in that soup," he said.

Anna made no comment.

"I doubt they'll even try." LeFleur swirled the cocoa in his Styrofoam cup. "That area is too unstable, too unpredictable. I'd be damned if I'd go out there in a little rowboat and try to drag that lake. It probably goes clear down to the center of the world."

Jennifer's head was sunk between her shoulders,

her injured foot propped up in front of her. "Stephen?" she asked quietly.

"Hugh said he lost the fight and fell in that thermal lake," Page said bluntly. Anna shot him a dirty look.

"My fault," Jennifer said in a whisper so low only Anna could hear. "I should have left well enough alone."

"It wouldn't have made any difference," Anna said firmly and wondered if she was lying. She liked to think she would have figured it out anyway but there was no way of knowing.

To block everyone's pain including her own, Anna thought of home and heat and Frederick Stanton. Unconsciously, her hand went to her mud-caked hair. "How do I look?" she asked Jennifer. "I look like shit, don't I?" Jen didn't even hear. "Drink your cocoa," Anna ordered, and Short put the cup mechanically to her lips.

Neil Page rummaged through the pockets of his brush jacket and produced a rumpled pack of Harley Davidson cigarettes. Shaking one partway out of the foil, he offered it to John. LeFleur looked dumbfounded, a man seeing the Holy Grail. "You had these all along? You son of a bitch," he said, but he took the cigarette, snapped off the filter and fumbled for a light.

"There weren't enough," Neil said, unperturbed.

Anna stared at the men lighting up. All those times Neil had been sneaking off to smoke so he wouldn't have to share.

"You bummed John's last cigarette," she said, suddenly remembering.

Neil's hand, cupped around his lighter, froze for a second, then he flicked the lever and sucked in a lungful of smoke. "Forgot I had my own," he said.

Harley Davidsons. Len Nims had been smoking Harley Davidsons the morning he'd come to the medical unit tent. Page had robbed Len's corpse for smokes. Anna looked away.

The helicopter returned for a second load. Anna, Jennifer, Neil and Lawrence were loaded into the back of the Bell Jet. One of the medics stayed behind with Joseph and John to wait for the last trip.

The shriek of the engine blotted out all else and the machine lifted into the air. To the east the sun burned through in a blinding flood of life and Anna felt resurrected. Joy permeated her bones, dissolved aches, tempered cold. It was grand to be alive.

Short, crumpled in the seat next to her, her foot bare and splinted with pillows, propped on the bench opposite, experienced no such lifting of the spirits and Anna felt an overwhelming rush of pity. Grief over the death of her brother would be softened by time. Guilt over the horrible demise of Stephen Lindstrom would not. Jennifer had been to the thermal lake. There would be nightmares. As Garrison Keillor said: "Guilt is the gift that keeps on giving."

Anna looked away from the young woman's despair, stared out the window. The sky was touched with a thousand shades of peach and silver. Below, in the shadow of a distant ridge, the rising tide of light picked out a glowing spot of color.

"Want to see something pretty?" Anna shouted impulsively in Jennifer's ear.

Jennifer barely shook her head.

"Come on," Anna insisted. "It's beautiful."

"No." Jennifer mouthed the word soundlessly.

"Look, damn it." Putting a hand on the back of Jennifer's neck, Anna dragged the woman halfway across her lap, directing her eyes out the window.

For a moment Jen stared without seeing. "Look down, the far ridge," Anna yelled.

Then Jennifer saw it, a tiny speck of bright NoMex yellow working its way purposefully toward the rising sun. She shot Anna a questioning look and Anna nodded.

Jennifer laughed. "God, but that's gorgeous." She looked a moment longer then straightened up, smiling.

"I told you," Anna shouted. A moment later she leaned over and yelled: "Frederick's meeting me. How do I look?"

"Like shit."

"You're a pain in the ass, you know that?"

"I know," Jennifer shouted back. She took Anna's hand and held it till they'd landed.

Enter The World of Nevada Barr

Agatha, Macavity, and Anthony Award-winning author Nevada Barr has captivated readers with inventive mysteries and breathtaking descriptions of our national parks. Her detective, Anna Pigeon, finds trouble in the most unlikely spots—in a dusty New Mexico canyon or deep beneath Lake Superior—nature's beauty marred by man's cruelty and greed. The pages that follow exemplify Barr's striking characters and memorable scenes.

Track of the Cat

TRACK OF THE CAT is Nevada Barr's first mystery in the Anna Pigeon series. Winner of both the Agatha and Anthony Awards for best first mystery, it's a chilling tale of murder set against the backdrop of Texas's Guadalupe Mountains.

Here, while out tracking mountain lions, Anna comes across the body of a fellow ranger. She must spend the night with the corpse before help can arrive, so Anna devotes herself to finding clues to Sheila Drury's untimely death.

Anna fished two of the soggy lemon slices from her water bottle, mashed them to a pulp, and rubbed the pulp into her wet handkerchief. Tying it over her mouth and nose, she fervently hoped it would cut the stench of death down to a tolerable level.

Next she took the camera she'd been using on the lion transect and hung it around her neck. Switching on the headlamp, though it was not yet dark enough to do her much good, she waded into the saw grass.

The camera helped. It gave her distance. Through its lens she was able to see more clearly. Sheila Drury was parceled out into photographic units. As she clicked, Anna made mental notes: no scrapes, no bruises, no twisted limbs. Drury probably hadn't fallen.

Freaks of nature did happen now and then. Anna looked up at the cliff above, imagined Drury falling, dying instantly on impact: no contusions. Unlikely enough even if catclaw eight and ten feet high hadn't tangled close along the edge. Why would she fight cross-country through it in a full pack?

Anna turned her attention back to the corpse.

The skin of the face and arms was clear, smooth, the tongue unswollen. The Dog Canyon Ranger had not died of hunger, thirst, or exposure. Anna had more or less ruled those out anyway. Guadalupe Mountains National Park, though rugged and unforgiving, was barely twelve miles across. For a ranger familiar with the country to stay lost long enough to perish from the elements was highly improbable. Too, one presumed Drury had water, food—the stuff of survival—in her pack. A tent and sleeping bag were strapped on the outside.

No obvious powder burns, bullet holes, or stabbing wounds. Evidently the woman had not been waylaid by drug runners hiding in the wilderness.

Despite the tragic situation, Anna smiled. Edith, her mother-in-law, a veteran of the Bronx ("But darling, it was very middle class in the forties"), of the Great Depression, the number two train from Wall Street, and WWII, stood aghast at the concept of a woman camping alone in the wilderness. ("Anna, there's *nobody* there. *Anyone* could be there . . .")

Anna believed the truth was, alone was safe. A woman alone would live the longest. Criminals were a lazy bunch. If they weren't, they'd get their MBAs and rob with impunity. They most assuredly wouldn't walk eight hard miles to hide. They'd check into a Motel 6 on the Interstate, watch afternoon TV and hope for the best.

What did that leave, she wondered, her eye once again against the viewfinder. Suicide? A bit odd to do one's self in in full gear in a saw grass swamp. Heart attack? Stroke? Drowning? Lots of ways to die. Suddenly Anna felt fragile.

Evening was settling into the canyon's bottom. Soon she'd be wasting film. Three pictures left on the roll. Careful not to disturb anything, Anna leaned down and drew the curtain of heavy dark hair from Sheila Drury's face and throat.

There it was: another way to die. Oddly, the last and the first she had considered: lion kill. Claw marks cut up from Drury's clavicle to her chin. Puncture wounds—claws or teeth—made neat dark holes above the collarbone. Anna did not doubt that Sheila's neck had been snapped as well. It was the way the big cats made their kills.

For a long moment Anna stood, the dead woman at her feet, oblivious to the gathering darkness. Tears welling from deep inside spilled down her face and dripped from the square line of her jaw.

Now the lions would be hunted down and killed. Now every trigger-happy Texan would blast away at every tawny shadow that flickered in the brush. The government's bounty quotas on predators of domestic livestock would go up. Lions would die and die.

"Damn you, Drury," Anna whispered as ways to obscure the evidence appeared in and were discarded from her mind. "What in hell were you doing here?"

Steeling herself to accept the touch of dead flesh, Anna felt down Drury's jaw and neck, then lifted her arm. Rigor had already passed off. She'd been dead a while. Since sometime Friday afternoon or night, Anna guessed.

Her light trained on the ground, she moved past the body. Above Drury's head were two perfect paw prints. Behind them several feet were two more. Anna measured the distance with her eyes: a big lion.

Soon stars would begin to appear in the silver-gray ribbon of sky overhead. Before the shadowy tracks vanished in the growing gloom, she clicked a couple pictures of the prints and one last shot of the body.

There was no more film; no more to be done till morning. Aware of how desperately tired she was, Anna readjusted her headlamp to light her footsteps and trudged out of the saw grass. It seemed all she could do to drag one foot after the other.

The vultures did not drop down in her wake to resume their meal. Evidently the big birds did not feed at night. Anna was grateful. Notwithstanding her appreciation of the food chain, she wasn't sure she could've stood a night listening to its graphic demonstration. The sepulchral snacking would've been unsettling, to say the least.

Wearily, she wondered why the lion hadn't eaten more of its kill, eviscerated it as lions usually did. Something must have frightened it off. Perhaps a hiker unaware that less than fifteen yards away, a corpse lay in the grasses, a lion hunkered by. The canyon was closed but occasionally hikers did wander in.

Surely, in this dry season with game so scarce, the lion would return. It might be nearby, waiting. One of the forsworn gods' little jokes: to have Anna's long-coveted first lion sighting be her last sight on this earth.

Anna didn't know if she was scared or not. She supposed she was because she found herself groping through her pack to curl her fingers around the cold comfort of her .357 Smith & Wesson service revolver. It was hard to be philosophical in the night. There was something too primeval in the closeness of death.

To her surprise, she was hungry. Life reasserting its claim, insisting on its rights and privileges. There was probably food in Drury's pack but Anna wasn't that hungry. Vultures watching a lion watching her hunt for the food their food was carrying: the chain grew too tangled.

Sheila Drury, was she watching as well? Anna didn't have to believe in God to wonder where people's spirits went when they died. Wonder if hers would go there, too.

Ghost stories from childhood crept uninvited into her thoughts and she found herself afraid to look toward the saw grass, afraid she'd see, not a lion, but a floating wraith.

With a physical shake of her shoulders, Anna pushed the night's terrors from her. Since Zach had died, and every night had been a night alone, she learned to put away fear.

Those nights, she remembered, she'd prayed for a ghost—a voice, a touch, anything. There was nothing then. And nothing now. Except a hungry night and, perhaps, a hungry lion.

Darkness closed on this rattling of thoughts. Overhead, the stream of stars grew deeper. Cold air settled into the canyon, flowed around her where she sat, knees drawn up, .357 by her side, staring into the melting mirror of the pool.

At some point Anna dug out the four Ritz crackers, the last chocolate pudding, and half a handful of gorp from her backpack and ate them. At some point after moonrise, when a light unseasonal rain began to fall, she unrolled her sleeping bag and crawled into it. At some point, though she would've denied it, Anna slept.

A Superior Death

In A SUPERIOR DEATH, Nevada Barr's second book, Anna Pigeon leaves the deserts of the Southwest behind and faces danger of an entirely different type on the unforgiving surface of Lake Superior. A dead body is found floating in a turn-of-the-century shipwreck two hundred feet below the lake. The only problem is that this body is quite contemporary.

These killers of fish, she thought, will do anything. Through the streaming windscreen Anna could just make out a pale shape bobbing in two-meter waves gray as slate and as unforgiving. An acid-green blip on the radar screen confirmed the boat's unwelcome existence. A quarter of a mile to the northeast a second blip told her of yet another fool out on some fool's errand.

She fiddled irritably with the radar, as if she could clear the lake fog by focusing the screen. Her mind flashed on an old acquaintance, a wide-shouldered fellow named Lou, with whom she had argued the appeal—or lack thereof—of Hemingway. Finally in frustration Lou had delivered the ultimate thrust: "You're a woman. You can't understand Papa Hemingway."

Anna banged open her side window, felt the rain on her cheek, running under the cuff of her jacket sleeve. "We don't understand fishing, either," she shouted into the wind.

The hull of the Bertram slammed down against

the back of a retreating swell. For a moment the bow blocked the windscreen, then dropped away; a false horizon falling sickeningly toward an uncertain finish. In a crashing curtain of water, the boat found the lake once more. Anna swore on impact and thought better of further discourse with the elements. The next pounding might slam her teeth closed on her tongue.

Five weeks before, when she'd been first loosed on Superior with her boating license still crisp and new in her wallet, she'd tried to comfort herself with the engineering specs on the Bertram. It was one of the sturdiest twenty-six-foot vessels made. According to its supporters and the substantiating literature, the Bertram could withstand just about anything short of an enemy torpedo.

On a more kindly lake Anna might have found solace in that assessment. On Superior's gun-metal waves, the thought of enemy torpedoes seemed the lesser of assorted evils. Torpedoes were prone to human miscalculation. What man could send, woman could dodge. Lake Superior waited. She had plenty of time and lots of fishes to feed.

The *Belle Isle* plowed through the crest of a three-meter wave and, in the seconds of visibility allowed between the beat of water and wiper blades, Anna saw the running lights of a small vessel ahead and fifty yards to the right.

She braced herself between the dash and the butt-high pilot's bench and picked up the radio mike. "The *Low Dollar*, the *Low Dollar*, this is the *Belle Isle*. Do you read?" Through the garble of static a man's voice replied: "Yeah, yeah. Is that you over there?"

Not for the first time Anna marveled at the number of boaters who survived Superior each summer. There were no piloting requirements. Any man, woman, or child who could get his or her hands on a boat was free to drive it out amid the reefs and shoals, commercial liners and weekend fishing vessels. The Coast Guard's array of warning signs—Diver Down, Shallow Water, Buoy, No Wake—were just so many pretty wayside decorations to half the pilots on the lake. "Go to six-eight." Anna switched her radio from the hailing frequency to the working channel: "Affirmative, it's me over here. I'm going to come alongside on your port side. Repeat: port side. On your left," she threw in for good measure.

"Um . . . ten-four," came the reply.

For the next few minutes Anna put all of her concentration into feeling the boat, the force of the engines, the buck of the wind and the lift of the water. There were people on the island—Holly Bradshaw, who crewed on the dive boat the *3rd Sister*, Chief Ranger Lucas Vega, all of the old-timers from Fisherman's Home and Barnums' Island, who held commercial fishing rights from before Isle Royale had become a national park—who could dock a speedboat to a whirlwind at high tide. Anna was not among this elite.

She missed Gideon, her saddle horse in Texas. Even at his most recalcitrant she could always get him in and out of the paddock without risk of humiliation. The *Belle Isle* took considerably more conning and, she thought grumpily, wasn't nearly as good company.

The *Low Dollar* hove into sight, riding the slick gray back of a wave. Anna reached out of her side window and shoved a fender down to protect the side of the boat. The stern fender was already out. Leaving Amygdaloid Ranger Station, she'd forgotten to pull it in and it had been banging in the water the whole way.

I'll never be an old salt, Anna told herself. Sighing inwardly, she pushed right throttle, eased back on left, and sidled up behind the smaller boat. Together they sank into a trough.

The *Low Dollar* wallowed and heaved like a blowsy old woman trying to climb out of a water bed. Her gunwales lay dangerously close to waterline and Anna could see a bucket, a wooden-backed scrub brush, and an empty Heaven Hill bourbon bottle drowning in their own little sea on the flooded deck.

Two men, haggard with fear and the ice-slap of the wind, slogged through the bilge to grapple at the *Belle Isle* with bare hands and boat hooks. "Stand off, stand off, you turkeys," Anna muttered under her breath. Shouting, even if she could be heard over the wind, would be a waste of time. These men could no more keep their hands off the *Belle Isle* than a drowning man could keep his hands off the proverbial straw.

There was a creak of hull against hull as they jerked the boats together, undoing her careful maneuvering.

The man at the bow, wind-whipped in an oversized Kmart slicker, dragged out a yellow nylon cord and began lashing the two boats together as if afraid Anna would abandon them.

She shut down to an idle and climbed up the two steps from the cabin. The fisherman at the *Low Dollar*'s starboard quarter began to tie the sterns together. "Hey! Hey!" Anna shouted. "Don't you tie my boat to that—" "Piece of junk" was the logical end of the sentence, but a fairly recent lecture from Lucas Vega on the importance of positive visitor contact and maintaining a good relationship with the armies of sport fishermen that invaded the island every summer passed through her thoughts.

"Untie that," she shouted against the wind. "Untie it." The man, probably in his mid-forties but looking older in a shapeless sweatshirt and cap with earflaps, turned a blank face toward her. He stopped tying but didn't begin untying. Instead he looked to his buddy, still wrapping loops of line round and round the bow cleats.

"Hal?" he bleated plaintively, wanting corroboration from a proper authority.

Anna waited, her hands on the *Low Dollar*'s gunwale. The old tub had enough buoyancy left that a few more minutes wouldn't make much difference. And, by the sagging flesh of the man's cheeks and his dilated pupils, Anna guessed he was about half shocky with fear and cold.

Hal finished his pile of Boy Scout knots and made his way back the length of the boat. He was younger than the man white-knuckling the stern line, maybe thirty-five. Fear etched hard lines around his eyes and mouth but he looked, if not entirely reasonable, at least able to listen.

"Hi," Anna said calmly. "I'm Anna Pigeon. Hal, I take it?" He nodded dumbly. "Are you the captain of the *Low Dollar*, Hal?" Again the nod. "You've taken on a bit of water, it looks like."

The commonplace words were having their desired effect. The life-and-death look began to fade from his pale blue eyes. He wiped his mouth with his sleeve as if turning on the switch that would allow his lips to function. "Yeah," he managed. "Hit something in Little Todd. Didn't pay much attention. Time we got here we were taking on more'n we could bail. We started radioing then. I think the propeller got dinged and we're taking on water around the shaft."

Normalcy somewhat restored—given the world continued to pitch in a colorless panorama of blustering cloud and billowing wave—Anna spoke again. "Here's what's going to happen, Hal. First put on life jackets. You got any?"

He dragged two disreputable-looking orange vests out from beneath a seat and the men began buckling them on.

When Hal's hands were free again, Anna said: "You'll need to cut that bow line loose. You . . . ?" She looked at the second man, who was beginning to come to life.

"Kenny. Ken."

"Ken. You untie the stern. Hal, I'm going to hand you my towline. Make it fast to the bow. Then the both of you get aboard my boat. The *Low Dollar*'s riding too low in the water. I'd just as soon nobody was on board. Got all that?"

Kenny started unlooping his line and Hal returned to the bow to tug and jerk at the knots he'd made. The boats climbed a slick cold hill of water, teetered at its summit, then slid down on the other side. Kenny screamed out that his hand was caught between the two hulls, but he was more frightened than hurt.

The yell did a good turn, convincing Hal that slicing through a $1.59 piece of rope might be worth the time saved fumbling with his desperate knots.

In another minute both men were on board the *Belle Isle* and Anna was powering slowly away.

Ill Wind

An ILL WIND blows no one good in the third Anna Pigeon mystery. Over a thousand years ago, the Anasazi disappeared from what is now Mesa Verde National Park, leaving behind an entire city of cliff dwellings. The mystery of their sudden departure is only matched by the current events in the park. Visitors are dropping with respiratory ailments. A strange ghost wind blows on moonlit nights. And one of Anna's friends is found murdered. Is it the restless spirits of the Old Ones or something more mortal?

No graveyards; that bothered Anna. People died. Unless you ate them, burned them, or mailed them to a friend, the bodies had to go somewhere. In any event, there would at least be bones. A civilization that lived and died for six hundred years should leave a mountain of bones.

No graveyards and then no people. Inhabitants cooking, weaving, farming one day, then, the next, gone. Pots still on cold ashes, doormats rotting in doorways, tools lying beside half-finished jobs.

So: an invading army swooped down and massacred everybody. Then where were the bashed-in skulls? Chipped bone fragments? Teeth sown like corn?

A plague: the American version of the Black Death, an antiquated form of Captain Tripps, killing two out of every three people. The survivors abandoning a desolated community, carting thousands and thousands of dead bodies with them? Not bloody likely. Not in a society without benefit of the wheel.

Once people got factored into an equation all bets were off; still, there ought to be corpses. Anna couldn't think of any civilization that couldn't be counted on to leave corpses and garbage for the next generation.

A hand smacked down on the Formica and Anna started in her chair.

"Where were you?" hissed Alberta Stinson, head of Interpretation for Chapin Mesa.

"Anywhere but here, Al," Anna whispered back. She dragged a hand down her face to clear it of dreams and looked surreptitiously at her watch. The staff meeting had been dragging on for two hours. The coffee was gone and there never had been any doughnuts.

Stinson poked Anna in the ribs with a blunt forefinger. "Stay awake. The Boys are on a rampage." Al always referred to Mesa Verde's administration rather disdainfully as "The Boys." Stinson was fifteen pounds over what the glossy magazines recommended, with salt-and-pepper hair that looked as if it had been cut with pinking shears. Leading tours, giving programs, wandering the myriad ruins on the mesas, she had a face creased by the weather from forehead to chin, and the skin around her eyes was crinkled from squinting against the sun's glare. Near as Anna could tell, the woman had but two passions in life: discovering why the Old Ones had vanished and seeing to it that any despoilers of their relics did likewise.

Anna pulled Stinson's yellow pad toward her. Beneath Al's sketches of nooses, guillotines, and other means of mayhem, she scribbled: "No help here. I'm a lowly GS-7. No teeth."

Al snorted.

Thirty minutes had elapsed since Anna had mentally checked out and still the debate raged. Money had come down from Congress, scads of the stuff, allocated for the digging up and replacing of the antiquated waterline serving the homes and public buildings of Mesa Verde National Park. Since May heavy machinery and heated arguments had roared over the ancient land. Meetings had been called and called off on a weekly basis.

The resultant acrimony clogged the high desert air like dust from the ditcher. As always in small towns, toxins trickled down. When the powers that be waged war, the peasants took sides. Even the seasonals gathered in tight groups, biting assorted backs and sipping righteous indignation with beer chasers.

New to the mesa, Anna'd not been drafted into either army, but the constant dissension wore at her nerves and aggravated her hermit tendencies.

Around a table of metal and Formica—the kind usually reserved for the serving of bad chicken at awards banquets—sat the leading players: a lean and hungry-looking administrative officer with a head for figures and an eye for progress; the chief ranger, a wary whip of a man determined to drag the park out of the dark ages of plumbing and into the more impressive visitation statistics additional water would allow; Ted Greeley, the contractor hired to pull off this feat in a timely manner; and Al Stinson: historian, archaeologist, and defender of the dead. Or at least the sanctity of science's claim on the dead.

When the Anasazi had vanished from the mesa, their twelfth-century secrets had vanished with them. Stinson was determined to stop twentieth-century machinery from destroying any clue before it was studied. Since the entire landscape of Chapin

Mesa was a treasure trove of artifacts, the digging of so much as a post hole gave the archaeologist nightmares. The contractor had been brought on board to trench seventeen miles of land six feet deep.

Theodore Roosevelt Greeley of Greeley Construction had a job to do and was being paid handsomely to do it. Though Greeley had a veneer of bonhomie, he struck Anna as a hard-core capitalist. She suspected that to his modern Manifest Destiny mentality, the only good Indian was a profitable Indian.

Fingers ever-tensed on the purse strings, the chief ranger and the administrative officer leaned toward Greeley's camp.

Anna and Hills Dutton, the district ranger, were the only noncombatants present. Dutton's impressive form was slouched in a folding chair near the end of the table. He'd removed the ammunition from the magazine of his Sig Sauer nine-millimeter and appeared to be inventorying it bullet by bullet.

"Anna?"

As was his wont, the chief ranger was mumbling and it took her a second to recognize her name.

"What?"

"Any input?" The chief was just shifting the heat from himself. None of this august body gave two hoots about what she thought. She and Hills were there only because the secretary refused to go for coffee.

"Well, if all nonessential personnel were required to live out of the park the problem would be alleviated considerably." Nonessential included not only seasonal interpreters, but also archaeologists, department heads, the administrative officer, the chief ranger, and the superintendent himself. Anna's suggestion was met with annoyed silence. Satisfied she'd offended everyone at the table and it would be a good long time before they again bothered her for her "input," Anna retreated back into her own world.

When visitors left for the day and evening light replaced noon's scientific glare, she escaped the hubbub.

It soothed her to be where the people weren't. After working backcountry in wilderness parks—Guadalupe Mountains in Texas and Isle Royale in Lake Superior—Mesa Verde, with its quarter million-plus visitors each year, struck her as urban. During the day, when the ruins were open to the public, she couldn't walk far enough to escape the hum of traffic and the sullen growl of buses idling as they disgorged tour groups.

After closing time, on the pretext of a patrol, she would slip down into the new quiet of Cliff Palace, one of the largest of the Anasazi villages ever discovered. Climbing as high as was allowed, she would sit with her back to the still-warm stone of the ancient walls, around her rooms and turrets and towers, sunken chambers connected by tunnels, plazas with stone depressions for grinding.

The pueblo hung above a world that fell away for a hundred miles, mesas, buttes, and green valleys fading to the blue of the distant mountain ranges that drifted into the blue of the sky. The air was crisp and thin. Without moisture to laden it with perfumes, it carried only the sharp scent baked from piñon and ponderosa.

From her perch high in the ruin she would gaze down Cliff Canyon. Dwellings appeared singly, first one, then two, then half a dozen, like the hidden pictures in a child's puzzle.

Tiny jewel cities tucked in natural alcoves beneath the mesa stood sentinel over the twisting valleys. Nearly all faced west or southwest, catching the heat of the winters' sun, providing shade through the summers. The towns were built with fine craftsmanship, the work of practiced masons evident in the hand-chipped and fitted stones. Walls were whitewashed and painted, and decorations of stars and handprints enlivened the sandstone. Doorways were made in the shape of keyholes. Ladders, constructed of juniper and hide, reached rooms built on shelves forty and fifty feet above the slate of the alcove's floor.

These were not tents for folding and slipping away silently into the night. These were edifices, art, architecture. Homes built to last the centuries. If the builders had been driven out, surely the marauders would have taken up residence, enjoyed their spoils?

If the Old Ones had not died and they'd not left of their own volition and they'd not been driven out . . .

Then what? Anna thought.

Food for thought.

Plots for Von Daniken.